Simon Louvish is the author of eight previous novels,
including the acclaimed *Blok* trilogy, *The Silencer* and
Resurrections From the Dustbin of History. He was born
in Glasgow sometime after the Second World War, but
lived in Israel from 1949 to 1968. He has been a military
cameraman, a documentary film maker, and a lapsed
Trotskyite fellow traveller. He currently resides in London, is legally married and teaches film at the London
International Film School. His next book, an epic of the
Middle East in its perpetual crisis, will appear, he trusts,
before the Apocalypse which is prefigured and docu-
mented in the volume to hand.

SIMON LOUVISH

What's Up God?

A ROMANCE OF THE APOCALYPSE

*IN*D*I*GO

First published in Great Britain 1995
by Victor Gollancz

This Indigo edition published 1996
Indigo is an imprint of the Cassell Group
Wellington House, 125 Strand, London WC2R 0BB

A catalogue record for this book is
available from the British Library.

ISBN 0 575 40025 0

Printed and bound in Great Britain by
Guernsey Press Co. Ltd,
Guernsey, Channel Isles

96 97 98 99   10 9 8 7 6 5 4 3 2 1

For Mairi, of course.

PART 1

The Coming

1

Ia! Shub-Nigurrath! The Goat with a Thousand Young!

There I am, rattling about in the tube like a dry pea in a storm-tossed pod, reading Lovecraft's *Haunter of the Dark and Other Tales*, while all about me the midday punters of the Piccadilly Line are deep in uplift, devouring Saint Thomas Aquinas, the *Selected Political Writings*, or the *Life and Miracles of Saint Francis of Assisi*, or the Good Book itself, the Old and the New Testament, the Koran, Hadith, the Jewish Siddur or Saint Benedict's Rules for Monasteries. It's Desperation Time. The Ides of March. The Resurrection, the real thing, has been set for April 30th, two weeks after Easter, and the Day of Judgement itself, we all have been served notice, will be the 7th of May, 1999, at the crack of dawn, daylight saving.

In fact, it's set for 3:00 a.m. I know the precise time, play-mates, because I have a foot, or rather some keyboard fingers, on the inside, updating the databanks on the Recording Angels' software, Hammersmith–Fulham Branch, London, W6. It seems that the Angels, quite wisely, don't want everyone wide awake, bright eyed and bushy tailed and alert to make their defence, but will emulate old tried and true methods. Get 'em when they're groggy, gargling and sneezing, before they realize what's hitting them. Whether they'll see the last sunrise or not is a matter of organization.

Myself, I'm going to hell. I know, because, having access to the databank, I hacked into my own file deep in the main-frame to check the balance to date by the books. The spread-shit of my dissolute life. Religion: Nil. Family Values: Nil. Compassion Factor: 4.5 (must lodge an appeal there, if one could lodge an appeal, but it's all up to the Final Day). Patriotism: Nil. Obedience Factor: −12. Morality: 3.2.

Sayonara, Jerry Davis. The pit of the shaggoths looms. *Ia! Ia! Yog Sothoth!* No wonder I am reading pulp on the tube. *Their hand is at your throats, yet ye see Them not. Man rules now where They ruled once; They shall soon rule where Man rules now.* I curl my lip, darting my varnished gaze at my fellow passengers on the road to Golgotha (formerly Piccadilly) Circus. But they are too deeply immersed in their devotions. Time is ticking away. The meter is running.

The Kingdom of God was proclaimed officially on Christmas Day, December 25th, 1998, a mere three and a half months ago. How time flies when you're having fun. I was sitting at home with my lived in partner, Karen, who has, of course, since departed in a headlong rush to distance herself from my damnation. We had eaten the Marks & Spencer's Free Range Turkey (Given Freedom of Access to the Outdoors) and had settled in for the Queen's Speech, except that it was no longer the Queen's Speech, but the King's, the Celestial Ruler of the Universe, delivered by his Archangel, Gabriel. I had always been curious about what the Archangel Gabriel might look like, or how he might deal with the autocue, but I needn't have worried. He was as smooth as any extinct Tory minister telling us why the promised land of economic utopia had vanished into the dust of all our tomorrows. He was an imposing figure, without a doubt, seated before a bare desk with the globe of the earth revolving slowly behind him, demonstrably addressing us from the father ship, his face a kind of deep mahogany, with that blurred physiognomy that appeared African at one moment, then possibly Arab, then Mongolian-Chinese, then almost Nordic. A TV tariff man's nightmare, as they jig and juggle the colour balance.

'Good afternoon. I am the Archangel Gabriel. God has come. All Life be praised.'

We were told later the face spoke to every people on the globe in their own language, at the same time, with matching

10

lip movements. A miracle. But miracles are mundane by now. They barely make the six o'clock news. So a mountain moved a hundred miles in Sri Lanka to allow some tribe access to fertile fields. Ehh! What's on Cable 16? More ranting evangelists, eyes bulging, collars torn, pouring sweat, recruiting like there's no tomorrow. What's that you say? There really is no tomorrow? Well, whadaya know . . .

Once upon a time I used to be a valued member of society. A rotten society, mind you, but who can pick and choose . . .? After the hopes of the late eighties, and the Depression of the early nineties, we settled down to take things as they came. Me, I was beginning to make some progress as a funny man. What used to be called stand up. Before we all fell down. I stood in front of glazed audiences at the Comedy Shop in Leicester Square, desperately foaming at the mouth as I was introduced by a compère wearing the interior decor of the Lloyds Tower. 'Ladies and gentlemen, the funniest and filthiest man in London . . .!' And there I was, falling out of my dustbin. Occasionally it got a cackle. I tell a lie, there were good moments. And then the Channel 4 job, and the Cables. Actual dosh. Now I had to fake the torn pants and grotty raincoat, rather than just turn up as I was. Warming up the crowd:

'Suck my dick!'

Well, those days are over. Flaccidity beckons on a cosmic scale. Is There Sex After Death is no longer just a silly conceit, but a question of eternal consequence. I asked my Recording Angel, Hoppy, about it.

'What is sex?' he asked.

Sometimes these people, if they are people, are clearly disconnected from the scene. On the other hand this may have been Hoppy's peculiar sense of humour, the giggly empathy that made him take me on as his data accessor, when I sat before him after cooling my heels for three hours in the waiting room of the newly created Office of Moral Records (OfMor), Hammersmith & Fulham District. January 3, Day

11

Seventeen after the Manifestation. He clucking his tongue over a concertina print-out which turned out to be my dossier, his red hair and the rather stunted off-white wings sticking out of his white gown at the shoulder-blades giving him the air of a giant misplaced chicken.

'Oh dear, Brother Davis. This really doesn't look at all good. We have some proper catching up to do.'

'So what's the problem, Doc?' I could afford to be flippant at that point. It was all so new, so sudden, so un-real. The Manifestation. The Days of Miracles. The Fall of all the Governments. The Dispensation. The Recording. The people crowding into the anterooms, each clutching the mimeographed Summons, murmuring, complaining, resigned in silence, many praying to their respective Gods: the Lord, Jehovah, Allah, Mumu. And the click, click, click of the red-haired Recorder on the expropriated council keyboards.

'We have been a very naughty boy, haven't we, Gerald? Cursing, swearing, taking the Lord's name in vain, coveting your neighbour's house, fornication, frivolity, making graven images.'

'It's my mother who sent you, right?' Some jokes have too much frost on them. 'You forgot my neighbour's ox,' I told him, 'and his cattle, and his kine. Particularly his kine.'

He looked at me with that pained expression, and then the giggles came. His wings shook and flapped together, little flecks of feathers flying free.

'Ooh, you are naughty,' he said. 'But I like you. I'm going to make you an offer you can't refuse, hee hee. It says here you graduated in computer studies at Enfield Polytechnic, before chucking it all in to tell dirty jokes in public. Do you want a proper job? It will give you points, I can guarantee that. And boy, do you need points. Hee hee hee.' His shoulder feathers shook again.

Well, it was not my type of humour. But my type of humour was dead. Mine was one of two hundred and twenty-four categories of livelihood listed by the Board of Records as negative equity in the race to the balance. Anti-social activity, along with armaments manufacture, member of parliament, banking and financial services, managerial practice, military personnel, writers, publishers, literary agents, bailiffs, cinema and television services if not for instructional purpose, prison warders, insurance personnel, advertising, prostitution, professional crime, living off inheritance and unearned income, landlords, perjurers and the press – the list went on and on. It was not intended, the Angels proclaimed in one of their earlier interviews, to ban or stop people from practising their crafts, but was of a strictly advisory nature given that the Day of Judgement was fixed.

Naturally it was the weaker professions that cancelled, doors closing, clientele disappearing, shoes and toothbrushes thrown out in the street. The arms industry continued producing, seeing as there was no harm in it, after the Neutralization, when all the world's armies suddenly became impotent, their weapons, from handguns to interballistic missiles, ceasing to function, refusing to fire, becoming mere lumps of steel. Still, they could be used as clubs, and they were, in war zones from Bolivia to Bosnia, before the choirs of Angels came to turn the perpetrators to stone – only temporarily, but it must have been a nasty jar. Aggression stopped pretty quickly after that, barring the usual amateur psychopaths, who are never far from our thoughts.

Yes, folks, the Kingdom of Heaven! One day we're all minding our own business, getting up in the morning, scratching our groin, mourning our ravaged puss in the mirror, groaning at the drivel on the breakfast news, preparing to face another day of dolour contemplating the decline of civilization when, presto! It's the Actual Fall! A delirious newsreader – I remember the time exactly, it was 10:45 a.m. on the 18th of December, and I was dragging myself, foot by foot, hand after hand, to my toilette, in an express ambition to exit the house in the direction of the Channel 4 studio before fifteen hours GMT – this man came on in a newsflash, interrupting the Pets

Hour Phone-In ('Oh, Brian, my cat doesn't want to come out from under the bed. It's been four weeks already and he just snarls and spits . . .' How perfectly understandable) with an incoherent gabbled spiel:

'Reports are coming in from various parts of the country, and from many sources abroad, about giant spaceships which seem to be hovering over government buildings, army barracks, police headquarters, town halls, churches, cathedrals, mosques, synagogues, temples and other places of worship. This is not a hoax. I repeat, we have had several thousand sightings pouring in over the last half hour . . .'

So move over, Orson Welles. Don't these people have the merest spark of originality? I expect better for my hundred quid's TV and radio licence, not that I paid it, as I shelled out ten punt for one of those gadgets that jams the licence dodgers' van. And not that my TV was *in situ*, as it was out for repair at Old Rentals. But the wireless rapped on, making no sense whatever, babbling about the lack of blips on radar screens. They must think they'll get all the unemployed to rush out into the streets so they can be shovelled up for Gummer's Workfare Centres. Or is it another Animal Rights stunt? Since they managed to dispatch the entire Cabinet and half of Downing Street in '97 anything's possible with those clowns. Bequeathing us the führership of John Selwyn Gummer, Gummo to us hard-worked hacks. We were right down to the N team. And then we plummeted to Z. Now even that's gone, alleluia! Can you imagine, pining for that lot?

I speeded up, to arrive at Channel 4 at twelvish. A crowd was gathered in reception, glued to the screens. There they all were, big, beautiful round things, looking like gargantuan cream biscuits, looming over Big Ben, the White House, Eiffel Tower, L'Etoile, Kremlin et al. Eat your heart out, Inoshiro Honda.

'It's a fake, a *coup d'état* by Gummo!' But the voices of reason were growing weaker. The inside buzz was: It's for real. Somebody recalled an old Arthur C. Clarke story, 'Childhood's End', in which the invaders hover for fifty years before coming out to reveal their physical resemblance to the human image of the devil, complete with pointed tail and horns. But these space invaders were in a much greater hurry. Reports were coming in that all attempts to intercept the vessels had been complete failures. Missiles had been fired by several defence forces, bursting like harmless firecrackers against their impervious hulls. Then the head of the channel came bubbling up from the basement, his jug ears and youthful complexion glowing, his Jagger lips sucking at his obligatory cigar.

'The government's just announced a cut-in,' he gabbled in his ersatz cockney glottal. 'We're going over to emergency broadcast in exactly fifteen minutes. Quayle and Gummer are going to speak jointly. The Pope's also expected. Apart from that, I don't know any more than you do.'

'What about *Sesame Street*?' wailed a bedraggled scheduler. But she was hauled off and was administered a nostrum. When the fifteen minutes were up we were on tenterhooks, shifting from one leg to another like massed football fans dying to pee. On a split screen the cherub cheeks of President Quayle and the pimples of our own PM clipped into focus for a brief instant, then were as abruptly replaced by a view of a serene, floating blue and green globe: the earth from outer space, and a deep, resonant and mellifluous voice welling up on sound:

'God bless you all, my children. For though I have tarried, I have arrived. For I am alpha and omega, the beginning and the end, saith the Lord. *Yehi shem adonai mevorach le'olam va'ed. Allahu akbar, bismillah el rahim, el hanin . . .'*

2

Forget *Sesame Street*. Now come the real Muppets, it's open season for the Evangelicals, bobbing and weaving, cajoling, gloating and jacking off at the mouth on every channel. They Who Were Exiled to Channels 65 thru 70 on obscure cable nets broadcasting from a hole in the ground in Coombe Cheedle are now upfront on 1 thru 8. All the preachers, pastors, primates, celestial picadors and other spiritual plumbers. All the rabbis, mullahs and mad monks. Every sky pilot testing their new-found wings. Every sweating body who had told us so:

AND BEHOLD! I SAW AN ANGEL COME DOWN FROM HEAVEN, HAVING THE KEY OF THE BOTTOMLESS PIT AND A GREAT CHAIN IN HIS HAND . . .

For here's the rub: the Angels, as they appeared, appeared to each nation in the spirit of their own tradition and practice: quoting in accordance, in different places, from the Old, the New Testament, the Koran, Buddhist scriptures, Tantric and Vedic texts. The timing, however, on the eve of Xmas, culminating in the Archangel's speech on the Birthday, clinched the deal for our own no-soothsayers: our Truth – and all the rest is lies . . . as the preachers foam and gush, their bloated, pinched faces pocked with onanistic guilt, smoothed with cosmetic innocence, brightened by hope, speckled with doom. And the punters, flocking like a host of lemmings who had taken a detour back to dry land.

ALLELUIA!!

'I sympathize,' said Hoppy, two large tear drops rolling in perfect symmetry down his cherub cheeks. 'The death of all frivolity. It's hard to take. I like a joke myself, now and again.

16

The Archangel himself has been known to pass a cracker occasionally at General Call. We don't endorse all those people who claim to speak in Our Name. But we can hardly stop them, unless they take up arms. We have had to establish minimum benchmarks for the Dispensation.'

The End of Days. And suddenly every nut in the history of the whole damn schmeer is justified. It certainly was a subdued New Year. Ring out the old, ring in the new . . . the final chorus on kazoos. The greying doyen of the grill-masters of telly is wheeled on, old Paxman, rolling his Os around his Es, as the Archangel folds his wings around the interviewer's swivel chair. 'Weeooolll, you say you are the representative of God Almighty, the Lord, Allah, Jehovah, whoever He might call Himself, and that the Resurrection of the Dead will occur on April the thirtieth, and the actual Day of Judgement will occur one week after that, on the seventh of May, no less. Can you explain this?'

'Well, you see, Jeremy, there have been various speculations on these matters, but we thought we owed it to the public to get things straight right at the outset, so that there should be no arguments or conflicts on the basic principles of the Dispensation, and so as to minimize public alarm and distress. It is a fact that the Dead will return, physically, at the age and in the appearance each person had when at the last moment of their full vigour, that is, people should not fear that their infirm or dying loved ones will become a burden and a source of pain and suffering. Ages will vary in accordance with the age of death, but there will be no illness, no senile decay, no anguish.'

'But the world will become somewhat crowded, will it not? This seems inevitable. How far back will these, er, deceased and resurrected people go? I mean, are we going to see the dead of our century, or back into the Middle Ages, or the Roman and Pharaonic eras, or back all the way to the cavemen, or what?'

'All will return, Jeremy, in the course of the final week. There will be an adjustment in stages. But the final, uh, overcrowding, as you put it, will not last for very long.'

17

'This is because the Judgement Day will be imminent, is that what you're telling me, Archangel?'

'Yes, judgement will be universal. From dawn to dusk, all will be judged.'

'That's an awful lot of people, if I may say so, Archangel. Our own computer predictions, taking into account uncertainties concerning past generations, and factoring in the exponential growth of populations since prehistorical times, have come up with a rough figure of eighty-five trillion souls. That is, eighty-five thousand billion. Surely the earth can't take such numbers, not to speak of the, er, bureaucratic problems you'll have in processing these, er, multitudes in the course of one day . . .'

'I don't blame you for being sceptical, Jeremy. If We had come at any previous juncture in history it might have been easier to put Our point across. But I assure you that We have done Our sums, and We are confident that We can handle whatever problems might arise. We have done this sort of thing before, after all.'

'You have? May I ask where?'

'I think I'll have to take a rain check on that one, Jeremy. But I do assure you, We will do whatever We can to ensure the smoothest possible transition.'

'You're talking about the, er, destination of, er, each one of us, presumably, on that day, are you not? Are we talking about heaven and hell?'

'Yes, I'm afraid we are, Jeremy. Generally speaking, uh, yes.'

'And all our deeds throughout our life up till that point will be, er, weighed up and taken into consideration.'

'Yes.'

'Can you enlighten me on that a little, before we pass on to the, er, exact, er, nature, if one may use that word, of this, er, heaven and, er, hell . . . By what moral code are our deeds to be totted up, as it were? I mean, is this the Christian code of the Middle Ages, or the Islamic code of the Koran, or the six hundred and thirteen *mitsvot* of Jewish orthodoxy, or what? Morality has been historically very flexible, is that not the case?'

'Not at all, Jeremy. You know very well that in each generation and among each people and each religion, and even in atheistic creeds, people do know what is right and what is wrong. Details might differ, but the moral code, as you call it, has remained fairly constant throughout human history. As you may have noticed, we have put a fair amount of effort into ensuring that it is so.'

'The Ten Commandments and all that stuff?'

'Absolutely, Jeremy.'

'Well, we might get to that a bit later on. I'm still not getting, I'm afraid, a straight answer about this matter of the moral codes. The Bible, for example, the Old Testament, has a great deal to say about issues that are seen in quite a different light today. Homosexuality, for example, or masturbation – onanism – or adultery, matters of that kind which, in those days, were seen I believe as capital offences. Surely people have a right to know on what level they are going to be judged, or is it all just relative, as you seem to be suggesting. That it's all according to what we feel is a, er, sin . . . I presume we are talking about sins?'

'No, I still insist it's not relative, Jeremy. People know what's right and what's wrong.'

'But is homosexuality a sin, then, in your eyes, or in the eyes of, er, whoever might be the judges on May the seventh. Or masturbation? Or idolatry?'

'Do you think those are sins?'

'No, not at all. Not in my book, Mr, er, Gabriel.'

'Then you clearly have nothing to worry about.'

'Well, there you have it. If my guest, the Archangel Gabriel, is to be believed, we're never going to see the year two thousand, let alone two thousand and one. That's all we have time for this evening. Good night!'

Happy New Year! Some habits die hard. The ominous

chiming of the last annual twelve bongs of Big Ben. In Moscow's White Square, three hours before, it turned out, a mass drunken panic led to carnage and disaster. One thousand people trampled to death and subsequent breakdown of all law and order. Fanatics rushing with flamethrowers through the streets. The city burned by morning and the Kremlin gutted, the Pamyat government in hiding, and an Empire of the Risen Christ proclaimed. The next day a rival Christ declared in Saint Petersburg. And then all communications ceased . . .

In New York, five hours later than London, hysterical crowds also mobbed Times Square. A radical black group, Sons of Elijah, fired with automatic weapons into the crowd. By morning the National Guard had moved into ghetto areas in Brooklyn and the Bronx, and other US cities. Southern Los Angeles was an open war zone.

So many excitable people. But in Rome the entire population, swollen by millions drifting in from other areas, filled the plaza of Saint Peter's, in a great silent vigil. Waiting for the Pope, who had not been seen since December 27th. It was rumoured he had been conveyed by the Angels to the Fathership, to meet the Lord. Commentators were already commenting on the suspicious absence of the Deity in Whose Name all this New Dispensation was dispensing. But Pope Lucien, too, had not been seen. And preachers in Ulster were already muttering about Catholic plots, though they seemed a minority in the circumstances.

In the Islamic world, and other eastern nations, too, the Great Awaiting. The masses gathered, in mosques, temples, synagogues. Prayers in a thousand and one tongues. A hundred different civil wars interrupted. But no one bothering to bury the dead. They piled them up inside or outside places of worship and city morgues, packing them in ice or shrouds. Ready for the Awakening . . .

All flesh is as grass. Happy New Year! Karen, who had been teaching young women to assert themselves in Putney for the now defunct local council, was still with me at that point, joined by Marek Maus and Dave Drucker and Parveen and Aisleen and the two Martins. Drowning our confusions in the annual punchbowl with its lethal cocktail of whiskys, brandys, gins, vodkas, ouzos, slivovitz. Who fears a boozy death, with Resurrection round the corner and all the excuses building up for the end?

'I don't remember anything about that, your honour. I was completely blotto.' Will one be able to plead insanity? Temporary or permanent? Lack of responsibility for one's actions. On those grounds we might all get off . . .

But Karen was already succumbing to the spirit of the age, the month, the week:

'There is a limit, Jerry. Do you think this is all a great practical joke? One big huge April fool's prank? That on the Day the old man with the white beard will just appear on the telly and say, "That's all folks, we're going back home now", and the ships will vanish towards Alpha Centauri, leaving us all to get on with our rotten, trivial, stupid, inconsiderate lives? It's not the way it's going to be.'

What does a non-believer do when confronted with proof of the contrary? I don't feel any different. I don't feel anything inside has changed. I don't feel any wrenching of the gut, no mental electricity, no shaking of the nerve ends or the cells. Nothing but an extraordinary level of very ordinary anxiety. Kill me, flay me, hang me upside down over hot embers, burn me at the stake, I can't feel a Rebirth. But Karen, sensing the cool, firm hand of a rediscovered destiny on her brow, has a regression to her own upbringing in an obscure fundamentalist Christian sect in Warwickshire, the Shemonites, an offshoot of a rural Arizona community, Bible belters who were belted to the literal meaning of the Bible, a straitjacket turned recast womb.

'You ran away from these people when you were twelve years old, Karen-kookie.'

'But it turns out they were right all along.'

When it hits that close to home, it's serious. We lolled

21

about, in my top-floor pitch in Iffley Road, Hammersmith, listening to ersatz Scots countrydancing on downstairs' BBC1. 'Will ye no' come back again' . . . quite so. Dave Drucker was describing the apocalyptic scenes in Edgware. Orthodox Jewish families had gutted the High Street, all the way down to Burnt Oak, stockpiling pickled goods and cashews. There was not a honeyroast peanut to be found within the *eruv*, the religious sphere of influence. The property market in north London had crashed, as everyone rushed to sell in the expectation of instant transference to the Holy Land. This had happened before in history. Messianic waves. People climbed on roofs, in the seventeenth century, waiting for the clouds that were to waft them south-east . . .

'Nobody's buying airline tickets,' Dave told us. 'They see no point when it's all going to be free. But some people have booked rooms in hotels for their relatives for the Resurrection. It's only practical. Come the glut.'

'In the Asian community, everyone's making room,' said Parveen. 'You can't find an airbed anywhere, for love or money. All the women are weaving quilts.'

'In Poland, like in Russia, it doesn't matter,' quipped Marek. 'After a decade of the free market, nobody will be able to tell the quick from the dead.'

The two Martins were already blasted on my carpet, joined in unisex foreplay. What kind of sins, indeed, are on the books, now that self-assertion, male or female, has been pulverized?

'Is there anything that can be done, Hoppy,' I asked my comedy-fan Angel, back in the office, 'between now and Doomsday?'

'Just close your eyes and think of England,' he said.

3

It's amazing what you learn to take for granted. Shake rattle and roll on the Golgotha Line. Putting Lovecraft aside I unfolded the renamed *Good News Standard*:

US SPECIAL PROSECUTOR TO INVESTIGATE FAMOUS
DEAD RETURNING.
PLANS TO QUESTION JFK, OSWALD, HOOVER.
EXCITEMENT OVER LENNON, MARILYN, ELVIS.
VIGIL AT LINCOLN MEMORIAL, KING, OTHER TOMBS.

The crowd waiting at the Ayatollah Khomeini's grave has swollen to ten million. Everywhere people are camping in cemeteries: bereaved sons, daughters, husbands, wives, mothers and fathers. Swindlers are selling divining sticks to detect the first signs.

But there are six weeks to go . . .

Karen left me on the 1st of February. A freezing cold day, black clouds and frost and biting wind. Despite the Theological Revolution, as the BBC now called it, the weather was having truck with none of it. No change in the customary climatic conditions, say the weathermen. Bully for them.

'I can't live with you, Jerry. You're polluting my mind. I love you, but you're not making any effort. I'll pray for you to be saved, don't laugh at that now, Jerry. I'm going back to the community.'

Back to War-and-wick-shire, the pigs, the loaves and the fishes. Headscarves and non-synthetic legwear and no zips! It's so strange what God decreed. Will every human being who wears a zipper rather than buttons on his breeks be damned? Karen's family certainly think so. That will leave nice wide open spaces in heaven, a zillion acres for each of the

23

beatified, under their own vine and fig tree. Singing the praises. Planting the eternal seed. Perhaps my plight is not to be so feared . . .

'But what is it like?' I asked Hoppy, in a break between keying in the missing Council Tax non-payers of Hammersmith. I unfolding a tuna sandwich with homemade mayonnaise (those liars are for it), he ticking over with his odd catlike purr. One wonders . . .

'What's what like?'

'Hell, Hoppy. Inferno, Hades, Abaddon, Gehenna, Tartarus.'

'Oh, that's not my department, Gerald.'

I had been boning up, on Joyce's *Portrait of the Artist*, the school preacher's exegesis on the abode of the damned, that

> . . . dark and foul smelling prison . . . filled with fire and smoke . . . expressly designed by God to punish those who refused to be bound by His laws . . . the prisoners are heaped together in their awful prison, the walls of which are said to be four thousand miles thick: and the damned are so utterly bound and helpless that, as a blessed saint, Saint Anselm, writes in his book on similitudes, they are not even able to remove from the eye a worm that gnaws it . . .

And so on. All the filth of the world, the vast reeking sewer, the brimstone, the loathsome burning corpses, the lake of fire which is boundless, shoreless and bottomless, the blood seething and bubbling in the veins, the brains boiling in the skull, the leprous corruption and suffocating slime, the yells of the suffering sinners, and the devils, afflicting the damned with reproaches, like one's mother: you see, I told you so, but would you listen? Would you ever?

Ever. A word I'm not growing fond of. But why should a half-Jew end up in a Catholic hell? Talk to me, I'm working the bloody programme! Trying to disentangle tax evaders from corpses. Show me bugless software and I'll go down on your grandmother! Oops, and there's another notch on my stick . . .

The Jewish hell is a far vaguer thing than old Jimmie's. Mostly it seems to be an absence, a denial of the next world. More purgatory than hell. That suits me fine. I can crawl up the mountain, slowly, like Dante, hoping for escape, away from the pit . . .

GUMMER SAYS JUDGEMENT DAY NO THREAT TO LAW-
    ABIDING CITIZENS.

How the fuck would he know? But what is the point of all these lists? Hoppy says we have to register the living so they may have at least a chance to make good. To notch up enough brownie points to push the Balance on the Day a bit towards the plus. The Dead will just have to take their chances with what's been done. But there's still ten weeks for us living to D-Day!

Desperate times and desperate tithes. People are hoovering up the homeless from the streets, feeding them soup, saving Boudous from drowning, dragging old ladies across every street, leading singsongs in supermarkets, tearing off their earrings for the starving in Africa. Instead of buskers drilling our ears in the tube with 'Highway Sixty-Nine' we have afternoon preachers answering the Call between Gloucester Road and South Kensington. The competition between them is so fierce, they have to rise to new heights of repartee:

'Now is the winter of our discontent made glorious summer by this Son of God!'

Smartarse. The one telling absence in this whole affair is the Man, you know, Messiah, Christos. Not a dickie bird. Even Paxman couldn't coax an answer out of the Archangel Gabriel, who simply ducked and weaved and left the whole thing to our imagination. Which was at least a relief, seeing there was not much else left to it. Aside from the conspiracy buffs, who hooked you around the arm in the Castle Tavern and whispered in your ear:

'That whole thing last night on the news: the levitation of the White House. Virtual Reality. See it a mile away. It's all a con. NATO. Been planning it for years. Discredited governments. Pissed-off populations. Recession. Loss of power. Fascism. It's back. Wait till the so-called Resurrection. That's when the mass arrests will start.'

All the inevitable theories. It's nothing to do with God. It is, just as Arthur C. predicted, the long-awaited Invasion from Outer Space. The Spielbergian Encounter of the Third, Fourth, Fifth kind. It's not salvation but slavery. If we could scratch the skin off our Angels we'd find slimy, slithy reptile carapaces, with wriggling antennae and ten thousand eyes. Some people did attack Angels, with fists, cudgels, axes, knives. But the Angels always anticipated them, and could place a finger, just so . . . *Deus* jitsu. And weapons, of course, would not fire. But still the speculation slithered. One remembered tales by Philip K. Dick: Seduced into emigrating to star-bright utopias, the masses find themselves in faceless barracks toiling in the dark satanic mines. Not God — but the Other. Some of this was even aired on my own Channel 4. No bolts of lightning struck the building in Horseferry Road, but a devout and terrified crowd gathered outside, sinking to its collective knees in a vigil for all the damned souls inside.

Karen left me on a freezing cold day of black clouds and frost and biting wind. The claps of thunder, the lightning sheering the sky. She couldn't take my jokes any more, even the most everyday and anodyne, like sticking the dinner in the oven and crying out 'Slam in the Lamb!' They are a habit, these commercial jingles, but Karen accused me of taking the Name in vain. Now that we know there is a price to pay. She had turned into her maternal grandmother, who used to stand on soap boxes outside Lancashire pubs, during the first Depression, crying out, 'Strong drink taks thee straight to hell!' One item of sinful consumption whose sales increased dramatically over Yule, as many decided simply to waft themselves wherever upon familiar moonshine fumes.

Repent! Repent! The writing on the wall emerging on that first, neo-Wellesian day. The gathering of the Channel 4 wallahs, fingers poised over the abort button of my New Year's

Eve Special: Blast Out the Past! Six stand-ups on the cutting edge of transmissibility spewing up our midnight bile. Then there were the Seven Strumpets of the Apocalypse, an all-female gig. Down the plughole we all went, replaced with a repeat of *Kind Hearts and Coronets*. So what's wrong with *The Sound of Music*? That too, gibbered out of the vault. Alone with every meek family flick that flickered since the Flintstones cut rock. Tout le *Lassie*, *Swiss Family Robinson*, *Ma and Pa Kettle*, *Old Yeller*, *Winnie the Pooh*, not to speak of the *Woodentops*, *Basil Brush*, *Snagglepuss*, *Pinky and Perky* and *Bertie Bonkers* the baby elephant, nudging up from the morning death-slot straightaway to primetime. Christian, the inaptly named, jug-eared Channel director, was rushing into production a twenty-six-part series titled *Sins of the Century*. A massive corporate breast-beating *ultima culpa*. The last episode was to be broadcast the night before the Day of Judgement, with the Day itself to be covered by fifteen camera teams transmitting live, the management fondly hoped, from wherever they might end up, 'As It Happens'. But by the time it was clear the entire executive echelon of the company had descended into tooth-gnashing, nose-picking drivel, I showed them all a clean pair of my heels.

That's if one could show a clean pair, with every service in the country, big or small, degenerating into futility. Even in the laundromat, one is assailed by the owner, a fat beefy Venezuelan called Gonzalo, who pins one up against the driers bellowing in your face like a Prudential salesman: 'Haff you redeemed? Haff you redeemed?' His whole place a riot of coloured posters and icons of the Virgin Mary, the Saviour and every conceivable saint he could lay his hands on from Abachum to Zita. Piped hymns blasted from the front loaders, bells tolled and vaporous incense sent the crazed customers reeling into the street for air.

Escaping the underground imams I clatter up the escalator at Golgotha (née Piccadilly) station, pushing towards the Shaftesbury Avenue exit. Anything but Heaven's Gate, the renamed Eros, the central plaza where every lunatic and his familiar have set up shop to wail their wares. If there is humour left prepare to use it now . . . But it's too late, the armies of solemnity have flattened all in their path.

A man tugged at my elbow as I pressed up the exit stairs. I tried to pull my sleeve free but he persisted, dragging on until I reached the street corner, dodging with me as I slipped past the ubiquitous pamphleteers. 'God's Commands Interpreted by the Reverend Donald Pilbrewer.' A likely tale. I look into the man's face. A pinched, horse-like frontage, narrow and sallow, a stockbroker's pinstripes and short slicked grey hair. The kind of face that used to stare at us morning, noon and night from the box, dispensing economic soothsay, before that all went down the flush.

'Mr Davis. Mr Davis.'

Yer middle-class twang, Tory *sprechen*. 'I'm sorry to intrude on your time, but if I may—'

'Whadayou want? I'm busy.'

'Indeed? Busy at what?'

Touché. I couldn't answer that one without incriminating myself with some sin or other, lethargy, lycanthropy, loucheness. Lovecraft was well hidden in my sidesack. In fact I had been overtaken by an irrepressible urge to see if my favourite quick-serve Chinese restaurant, the Lido, was still serving down in Chinatown. Some things, like won tons and lotus-fried shrimps, might have survived the Dispensation. I paused by an afternoon rag poster proclaiming: QUAYLE AND LORD TO MEET? Of some things there is enough already.

'What is all this about?' I asked him, but he just stood and blinked at me sadly in the pale winter sun. The self-proclaimed messengers of glory were fulminating beyond the traffic in the plaza, and a plump little Angel was recording their words on to a portable cassette machine, for all the world like a Japanese tourist in the days before travel stopped broadening anybody's mind.

28

'I'm sorry to approach you in this way and without warning,' he said, in his plummy patois, 'but you will appreciate one has to take precautions. Let us walk among the crowd. It's safer.'

Safer than what? We manoeuvred up the road. Past the once brash theatres now proclaiming, hoarding to hoarding, *Godspell*, *Epistle Time*, *The Little Shepherd Boy*, *Joseph and His Mono-Coloured Dreamcoat*, *Amazing Grace*.

'I will not beat about the bush, Mr Davis. You are a man whose help would be invaluable in a cause we know you must support.'

'I support no causes,' I hurried to tell him, in mounting panic. 'I already gave at the door.'

'I understand your concerns totally,' he said. 'I know there is no reason for you to accept my assurances. But I would like you to come with me to a place nearby. By trusting you, we hope you will trust us.'

'Us?' This was sounding worse and worse. A single fruitcake who can avoid these days? But 'Us' is ominous beyond belief. Still, curiosity killed the cat. A dead feline spoke:

'Who is "Us"?'

'I represent the Government of the United Kingdom and Northern Ireland,' he said. 'I know it is a defunct concept. The Gummer Regime we can, of course, dismiss. A puppet government of the occupying power. We know some things about it that not many do. After all, we have had our resources ready for just such an eventuality, though the provenance of the threat took us, like everyone else, by surprise. But we have survived, underground, in bunkers, nuclear shelters, regional hubs. We need the help of every sceptic, patriot or not; the stakes are far too high. The entire planet is in danger, as you well know. You have a choice: to walk away now and to perish, or to take that slim chance for freedom.'

'I'll walk away, thank you very much.'

I walked away, up the curve of the street, towards the restaurant. But after twenty paces I looked back. He was still standing, waiting, by the Apollo Theatre, under a lighted sign for *The Apostle's Song*. Starring Richard Mayall and Sir Benjamin Elton. How have the mighty fallen. I looked at their names, high above the multitude. I looked at the small, pin-striped, dwarfed Tory, hunched and forlorn beneath the omens.

I walked back to stand, warily, before him.

'I'm a complete asshole and sucker,' I told him. 'I don't know what I'm doing.'

'Thank God,' he said. 'An uncertain man.'

4

He marched me down towards Great Windmill Street and up into Soho. The ghost town of earthly delights, where only two months before were cheerful open doorways at which pale ladies called all and sundry to enjoy the fruits of a mild transgression. The peep shows, the videostores, the rows of magazines with tiny red dots plastered over any incident of penetration to vainly placate the vice laws. Everything in the best possible taste. But it is all boarded up and shut now. The old Windmill, once Le Vie en Rose, is now the London Mormon Centre, while the magshop opposite has been taken over as a distribution depot for the *Watchtower*. Other clipjoints have been pasted over by all the usual calls to shape up in readiness to ship out. The Mormons, the Church of the Latter Day Saints (and you can't get any more latter than now) are using the old hall for video projections of *Life in Heaven for the Blessed*. A long line of quiet, anxious punters stretches round the bend into Brewer Street, shuffling, weeping and clearing their throats.

'Good to see business is finally booming,' said my Tory seducer, revealing a dim dabble of wit. We passed through the line, muttering our 'scuse I's, into the narrow bone of Lexington Street. Warehouses, print shops and a smatter of eateries. Restaurants have been doing well, too. The one sin the Angels could not care less about, it turned out, was gluttony. They took to it like ducks to pâté. Not an evening passes in which one cannot see them stuffing their gobs in the Gay Hussar, the Red Fort, Luigi's, or the Frog's Legs. The one thing they had clearly not anticipated was the narrowness of British doors: the struggle to squeeze their wings through them might have sparked a thousand and one skits and satires, only yesterday . . . Nix the thousand, if only we had the one.

But the Tory rebel was not ushering me, alas, into the nice Cypriot kebabery on the corner of Beak Street, but into a small photocopying establishment on the other side of the road, where a bespectacled balding man with a smudge of toner on his nose nodded us towards a little grey owl-like lady sorting piles of name cards at an old formica table, who pressed a buzzer, and otherwise ignored our presence. We passed into a back room full of museum-piece printing machines, which I remember my father using to churn out the leaflets of his International Socialist Workers' Movement (ISWORM) when I was but a child in rompers. As Groucho might correct, I was not brought up in Rompers, but in deepest Islington, back in the soaring seventies, the last real boom before the bust.

We were quite close, my dad and I, until I started taking the piss in a professional rather than a personal way. 'I don't care what you think of the Movement,' he used to tell me, 'as long as you don't go rabbi or Tory. Socialism is not as dead as you think it is.' The other thing he disliked was what he called 'fucking bad language'. 'Don't you fucking use fucking bad language in my fucking 'ouse.' The unkindest cut was that I used him as a model for one of my early acts. He was really Heckling Ham, the Opposites Man. Everything opposed on the spot. But he felt he was carrying through the tradition of Great-Grandpa Joseph Duvid, who was the Secretary-General of the East London Branch of the Amalgamated Schmutter Workers and Allied Trades (ASWAT) and had personally split open the skull of fifteen Mosleyites in the Battle of Cable Street of 1936. He repudiated his son, my grandfather, Vladimir V. Davis (the V stood for Vissarionovitch, poor bugger, but he changed his first names by deed poll to William and became a chartered accountant in Ipswich). But he doted on my dad, named Joseph after him, though he didn't live to see Dad become a Trotskyist. All those dead creeds. My God! I carry redundancy in my blood stream.

My mother, Sophie, was the daughter of Italian immigrants, who named her Sophia Benedicta (Dad always said she was named for the mustard). Her ma and pa returned to Italy to retire, and died there while I was still a bambino. She met Dad at a Day of Action in Hackney. She was a nurse, and was standing nearby when he was hit on the head with a brick by a supporter of the rival Socialist International Revolutionary Workers' Group (SIRWOG, later renamed Workers' Power, or WOPOs). It was love at first sight, and eighteen stitches. She had been a member of an all-women rock group called the Sufferin' Jets, but by the time I came along had put aside childish things and redefined herself as a 'crone', after reading a book by Germaine Greer. Although she was barely thirty she dyed her hair white and began gathering mushrooms in Epping Forest. Later she published a whole series of Funghi cookery sagas and thus sustained our small ménage. I am an only child. Thank God at least for that.

I found them on Boxing Day, after the Manifestation, spending the night in cardboard boxes on the Embankment, to raise consciousness in aid of the homeless. My father tossed unhappily in his old March for Jobs sleeping bag while my mother's mussed hair and bleary eyes stared at me over the flap of a Zanussi Washer-Dryer carton. On one side of them a bedraggled Labour MP, who was obviously regretting the generous impulse, blinked unhappily. On the other side, the Bishop of London, Eddie 'the Mouth' Edwards, siphoned up lentil soup from a paper cup.

'Mum, Dad, howy'doin'? Whadyouthink of what's going on?'

'People are hungry, Jerry, that's what's going on,' said my mother primly. 'Hungry for bread and butter, meat and potatoes. None of this Tory God crap, begging your pardon, Bishop.'

'Don't worry about me, Sophie,' said the Bishop. 'I have a few bones to pick with God myself. I'm really looking forward to the opportunity.'

'It's all the same old con,' said my dad. 'Wait a couple o' days, they'll find all these Angel bastards are from some crazy cult in Texas. The world's going to buggery and this is all they can think of. Come and join us, son. There a spare box 'ere. The Liberal Democrat's buggered off.'

'No thanks, Dad, I have to get back to Karen.' I didn't mention the turkey in the oven. But now Karen's gone and the only turkey is me and I'm hobnobbing with the vilest class enemy . . .

The generic whiff of printer's ink faded as the Tory Rebel opened a side door with two keys. We found ourselves in a tiny enclosed storeroom full of broken machines, empty crates, used toner cartridges and other spare parts.

'What now, brown cow?' I asked, veering to the conclusion that I had fallen prey to yet another of the city's proliferating paranoiacs.

'It's down the rabbit hole for us,' he said dryly, looking not unsatisfied at my confusion. Perhaps if I brained him with one of the empty cartridges and crashed through the door back into real life I might yet make good an escape. But to what? I hesitated long enough to hear the hum of something moving behind the blank peeling wall in front of us. And then the whole caboodle slid aside. My Carrollian interlocutor motioned me forward on to the floor of a sturdy-looking lift, all gleaming corporate grey walls, but no control panels or floors numbers that one could notice.

The door slid shut behind us and my seducer spoke to the ceiling in a loud and clear voice.

'Roast mutton,' he said.

I saw no sign of it. But the lift moved and began to descend.

'Voiceprint identification,' explained the Tory. 'I have not introduced myself. You may call me the Dodo. We have adopted Alice names in this facility. It's the human touch. Keeps us alive. Not that Alice is, as yet, with us.'

I wished he wouldn't use that name. But I barely had time to think, before the lift stopped and the opposite wall slid open. We stepped out into a barren steel corridor with pipes running along its top and a blank wall which consisted almost entirely of a thick-looking bomb shelter door. It was emblazoned with a nuclear shelter symbol and the legend: AUTHORIZED PERSONNEL ON ULTIMATE DUTY ONLY. We paused, while a buzzing, clicking noise emanated from a concealed source.

'We have to wait before entering the Caucus,' the Tory Dodo said politely. 'Ultimate Security is a morass of precautions. If I had not been voiceprint identified above we would have been gassed and incapacitated for inspection. Equally, if we don't pass muster here . . .' He stopped, giving me a mischievous look.

'They turn us into pumpkins,' I suggested.

'Pumpkin stew, more like,' he said, breezily. 'No chances down below. The shredding pellets. It's shoot first and don't bother with the questions.'

'I'm so glad the government trusts the people,' I told him. It seemed clearer now that he was on the level. Though what level was yet to be discovered.

'Foresight,' he said, obviously passing the time while we waited for the passage or the pellets. 'You never know when a thing comes in useful. We voted to abandon all this, you know, back in ninety-two. End of the cold war. No more nuclear panic. Stuff civil defence. The people hated the idea. Politicians scurry down the boltholes leaving the general populace to shrivel and burn. Not a great vote-catching wheeze. Sealed up a couple of regional caucuses in Sheffield, Hull. Labour fiefs. The nuclear-free zones. But the only nuclear-free zone is here. Cheated on our promises as usual. Good thing we did. Comes an unexpected event like this, thank our lucky stars. Foresight. I think they've decided we're friendlies. Jolly good.'

The great door swung open from inside. Three thugs in sky-blue overalls stood within, guns at ease. A huge Alsatian dog sprang forward, sniffing at both our crotches, arses, thighs, rising up to shove its massive schnozzle in our armpits. Then it barked three times and scurried off.

'They love us, they love us not,' said the Dodo. 'But we have as clean a bill of health as you can get in this burgh. Come, let's go to the Mad Hatter's Tea Party.' He ushered me into a waiting golf-buggy and we drove off, just the two of us, leaving the blue goons by the door.

'Or is it you,' he said, 'that's Alice?' Looking at me sharply as he noticed that something made me wince at that name.

'Struck a raw nerve? Special jitters? Something we ought to know?'

'Personal.'

'Dear boy, the personal is over. Isn't that what this is all about?'

5

Jerry loves Alice. If we had been six years old we would have carved it on a tree. But as we were both nineteen we chiselled it on the back of the bed at the hostel in the Via di Croce just off the Spanish Steps in Rome. It was Luna time. We met just like that, halfway between Perugia and Assisi where she and her two travelling companions, Annemarie and Anthea, had broken down in their Fiat Uno. I was tooling down alone in the souped up Trabant, a vehicle no one could believe was on the road, which I'd been lent by my only surviving sane relative, Adolfo, who was a restorer of lost-hope cars in Terni. Mum and Dad used to take me to visit her family in Milan, when I was knee-high to a musk-rat, and the bi-annual Italian holidays continued, much to my delight, after her parents' demise, as my mother loved to smell the air of her native Umbria, although she had been born in Hounslow. She too was an only child. The family legend was that my maternal grandfather had come from a line of ducal castoffs from Urbino, while Nonna had come from a tiny Umbrian village which hid from man, for good reason, as its name was Bastardo.

There was no one in Bastardo who remembered our name, or who wanted to be known to the outside world, but we did track down Adolfo and his old mother in the bustling town of Terni. They were twelfth cousins thrice removed, or something. But I returned, for the first time alone, in '89, to the rolling countryside, the hilltop towns, and the three damosels . . .

I peeled Alice off the other two with a consummate ease which belied my natural state as clubfoot-and-mouth. Some-

37

how I disentangled my vowels, straightened my carriage and stopped dribbling into the antipasti. She was a dark-haired somewhat wispy presence from the folds of Wiltzhire, oh yes the honey hills of Bath-Avon. We were still a crowd of four in Assisi, as we clip-clopped through the winding saintly streets past the souvenir shops with their thousand tiny plastic monks, but the two of us managed to lose Annemarie and Anthea in the Basilica, and climbed the mountain at dusk. It's amazing how corny the real thing turns out to be. But we headed south, after arranging a liaison between the superfluous duo and two very workmanlike Italian garage attendants, who, unlike Saint Francis, had no interest in the birds and the bees. We last saw the quartet heading north in a Lamborghini which had been left in their care. I took Alice through Bastardo but we did not stop till Orvieto, where we climbed to the castle and parked for the night. And then it was down Numero Uno to Roma, the Spanish Steps, the Collosseo San Pietro. They had unveiled the restored Michelangelos in the Sistine Chapel, that primary riot of reds, greens, oranges and blues. But the dour masterpiece of the *Last Judgement* was still hidden by canvas. The Pope had to decide whether the restorers would be permitted to take the knickers off the nude figures which had been covered up by the great artist's enemies immediately after his death. We speculated on the effect of the restored mural, given the other panels; the intense burst of unfaded genius. But I never saw it, as I never returned to Italy.

Alice died. We returned, on separate flights, to Blighty determined to set up shop forever in a remote cottage in Freedonia, and live off love, nectar and pine kernels. As it happens I researched a one-bed flat in Notting Hill. She worked for a conglomerate travel agent, and enjoyed a whole raft of freebies. They gave her an assignment to spot holiday chalets in Portugal. The plane went down over northern Spain. *Finis* Alice.

We never got, you see, to the usual stage: the morning

muss, the drab discovery of nauseating habits, the hair in the comb, the blanket stealing, the night belches, the hiding of one's sneakers, the incompatibility of in-laws, the clash of tastes in food, art, music. We were just stuck in Rumpelstilt-skin and Rapunzel. Abelard and Louise. Heckel and Jeckel.

Her parents collected what was left of the body and buried it in Bath. What's past is the past. What's gone is gone. The dead are dead. Or are they?

I had watched with the blood draining from my face as the Archangel Gabriel told Paxman:

'All will return, at the age, and in the appearance each person had when at the last moment of their full vigour. There will be no decay, no illness, no anguish.'

The age-old saw. If only . . . We've read enough novels, seen enough special effects shimmering on the big or small screen . . . Boy, we ain't seen nuthin' yet . . .

The personal is over, says the Dodo.

But what if it's only just beginning?

First love. What a barrel of onions. The Dodo was looking at me shrewdly.

'The Spanish Steps,' I said.

'I never learnt them,' he remarked. 'The twist, the cha-cha and the foxtrot. I went to tango classes once. But that lambada – forget it.'

I couldn't answer that. The golf-buggy rolled on down the steel corridor. Networks of pipes and cables crisscrossing above. Narrow catwalks on either side. A bit like the Channel Tunnel. But no fresh croissants, I'll bet, on the other side.

'Beautiful, was she?' He gave me that shrewd look again. Taking his eyes off the road, not that there was anything there to see. 'Blonde, waving hair in the sunlight? Peaches and cream?'

I shook my head, not ready to articulate.

'That's the whole problem, you see,' he chattered. '*Requiescat in pace*. Rest in peace. What's the point of raking over old coals? Opening every bloody old wound we thought was properly healed. Consider the financial ballyhoo. Parents demanding back their inheritance. Mortgages rejigged. Insurance claims. Personal and public equity will collapse overnight. Forget the governments, nobody misses us. But without the markets ticking over . . . I know you chaps think we should be sharing and sharing alike but you need something to share to start with. And think of all the poor old and even not so old dead people who we thought had found their peace. What of their shock? Will they welcome it? It's not British. It's not right. How can they be fed, cared for, housed? What about employment? Social security? What if the Day of Judgement is delayed? Can you trust these Angel people? Who are they? Where have they come from? That's what we've been trying to find out. That's where you come in, Gerald.'

Me? Hang about, mate! But the buggy has come to a stop, coming round the bend into an open arena of rows of men and women tending monitor screens. A cornucopia of shimmering images, radar blips and strobing lines. Above the whole a radial projection of the world which looked as if it had been lifted from the set of *Doctor Strangelove*. But no multiple Peter Sellerses. Tiny lights blinked all over the map, from little England to the vastness of Russia, China, the United States and everywhere else.

Ici Londres. *Ici Londres*. 'This is the Caucus Room,' said the Dodo, nudging me into one screen-strewn corner. 'And these are my fellows, Duck, Lory, Mouse and Eaglet. Magpie and Canary are over there. Crab across that pile – ' he waved to an appropriately hunched figure with what looked like barnacles on his bare skull, and a pinkish claw waved back. 'We'll need a working name for you. How about Rabbit? Brown, White's out on patrol.'

Very droll. Four eager young men and two earnest young women gave me the eye, out of crisp white airline uniforms. Piloting the ship of state through the fog. Or the *Titanic*, reborn in Disneyworld.

'Jerry Davis,' I named myself, keeping demonstrably out of this Wonderland.

'Where's the Mad Hatter?' the Dodo asked the Eaglet, who was a pert wee blonde with a pony tail.

'He's in the croquet court with the Queen,' said the Eaglet. 'They're trying to wake up the Dormouse.'

'Well, we'll just have to wait our turn,' said the Dodo, throwing me an apologetic glance. 'We get a bit carried away with our similes, I'm afraid. Keeps our spirits up. This corner of a foreign field and so on. Although we're actually directly under Wandsworth. It's amazing what goes on under people's noses. You see, we try to keep tabs on as much as possible. Dealing with a unique challenge. Not having the foggiest idea of whether any of our secrets are secret. Enemies of God. It used to be a criminal offence in Iran. Very serious. But so far we're still ticking over.'

'I'm not so sure I understand this,' I said, reluctantly entering into some kind of intercourse with this phantasm. 'If you're the government, what's the position of the, er, people up above in Whitehall? The puppet PM and all the other Pinocchios?'

'Indeed, the little wooden men who dance without strings. Well put. At the end of the day, it depends what you have faith in, your country or a pig in the poke.'

'So this is not God at all we're dealing with? You think there'll be no resurrections?' My heart gave a little flop and thump of dread, or relief?

'We're not saying that. We've closed no options. We're keeping an open mind. We know the enemy has the capability. There have been tryouts, in the Punjab and Kazakhstan. We've monitored remote villages in which the population appeared to have spontaneously expanded. A rash of old people suddenly crowding the villages, but after that the story's blurred. Streets emptied, everyone staying indoors. Then all surveillance failed. A blanket blindness. As if they know when we're watching, and we can be turned on or off.'

'Surely,' I said, spotting another flaw, 'if there's a government, whatever it is, in Downing Street, they would have access to this place. Or have you locked them off?'

'We've had the option since the Massacre of ninety-seven. One can't entrust politics to politicians, especially if they get themselves blown up, don't you think? Those in the public eye are too vulnerable to be in control of ultimate options. We activated the Committee. The White Queen's Court. It's a broad church. Very catholic. We have Labour members, Lib-Democrats, Jocks, Taffys. The Mock Turtle is a Paddy. Defence of the realm. No shilly-shallying. We saw off the Eurofudge of the early nineties. If the PM wants to sell us out now to some external, bureaucratic sky jockeys he can think again. We got rid of divine rights long ago. The PM knows we're here. But he hasn't been given the keys. If his new masters want to fight their way in we'll give them a bloody raw welcome.'

'And if it's all true? The Resurrection, the Last Judgement?'

'Then I for one will stand up like a man and say, "I fought for Queen and Country and I'm proud of it. Do your worst." Just take it on the chin and no snivelling.'

'Stiff upper lip in the face of eternal damnation.'

'I can promise you nothing but blood, toil, tears and sweat.'

6

I like a man who makes realistic promises.

So here I am, deposited back at ground level, in a disused toilet at Clapham Junction. Having just been recruited by my ancestral enemies to rebel against God and all his cohorts. Pushing my way with a special key out on to the platforms, the SouthEasCo trains rushing back and forth, emitting and engorging glazed-eyed commuters shuffling through the last days of normality. Work, coffee break, lunch, office banter, a touch of sexual harassment, tea break, home, dinner, TV, bedtime. Sex *sans* rubber or chemical prophylactic, the only theologically secure fuck.

What have I done? Job was sent batches of emissaries, blight, plague of the unborn, withering relatives, locusts, stricken kine, boils, warts, weevils – the works – and still would not deny the Almighty. I was given a kook's tour behind the Tory looking-glass, a tuna sandwich and a bag of peanuts and hey ho, I am a mole for Lucifer. *I Was a Communist for the FBI* had nothing on me. I can see myself exchanged across the Pearly Gate Checkpoint for some bedraggled Angel caged in Whooping Common, six thousand years in the future, when tempers have cooled. The celestial glasnost. Or is this going to be, indeed, the Last, Last Hurrah, and all will then be silence, or the eternal scream?

Not even to be able to remove from the eye a worm that gnaws it. But it is only railway grit, thrown up from the track. The ticket collector catches me at the exit and is not satisfied by last week's expired Travelcard. He takes my name and address, and my Quikitspaid Number. I should be thankful the arresting officer is absent, or I might be booked for an

InstiCourt trial. Three hundred pounds fine or three months in the hoosegow. Didn't I know this was Customer Awareness Week?

'Haven't you heard?' I told him. 'It's the Last Trump coming. Not a single train will be running, except the cattle trucks taking us all to oblivion.'

'Everybady's makin' the same axcuse, man,' he said, 'but Jah alone know you gotta pay yah ticket, even on the chariot toa glory.'

I walked away, but he shouted after me: 'Rendah unto Caesar what is Caesar's. Glory toa tha Lard Gad of Hasts!'

They want it coming and going. They think it will all be the same, only more so. Like the Orthodox Jews, who have been transferring their assets to Israel, expecting the Messiah but not a severe break in the fortunes of the righteous. Again and again you hear it from people. It's the other guy, the wrong-doer, who will be done in the apocalypse. The earth will simply be a sweeter, more spacious, prosperous place for the faithful. The doctrine of revenge. Heaven is the removal of your enemy, your obnoxious neighbour, your landlord, the council tax officers, the man who trod on your foot in the queue.

'This is what we require of you,' said the Dodo, as we flicked the luncheon crumbs off our laps. 'We know you have rare access to the computers at your local Fulham Recording Office. The Angels have been conducting an update and verification of their population lists. We have been able to hack into their data only up to a point. Then we're blocked. It's all fuzzy. They're aware of our efforts, but so far our eyes and ears are still functioning. We have become aware that there are mainframe databanks dealing with the Angels them-selves. Their actual tasks, their taskload, perhaps their sources, perhaps their objectives, destinations. We know that, bingo, on the eighteenth of December, nineteen ninety-eight, seven-teen thousand eight hundred and fifty-three vessels, skyborne and gravity defying, appeared in their locations. But neither we, nor the Yanks, nor the Russkies, nor the Chinks, nor the Nips, as far as we can make out, know where they came from. Attempts to abduct an Angel or capture a vessel to examine their chemical or biological substance have all failed. We have analysed particles shed from their wings. They are real feathers, akin to eagles, or condors. That tells us nothing, they may be attached artificially. They use no artefacts, no rods or staffs of power. Energy materializes telekinetically, without traceable sources. The philosopher's stone, power from nothing. Or it may be, even in our advanced state, we have no instruments capable of detecting their power. Various top-secret projects trawling for extraterrestrial evidence have turned up hints of unsourced emissions. Quarks appearing from nowhere, radio calls from the furthest reaches of the cosmos that have a pattern, but no sense. Probably the *Jimmy Young Show* of Optima Centauri. Or is it a case of parallel worlds? The Yanks built a thingamabob in Kansas, deeper underground than any other installation, to examine things like the hollow earth theory and other crackpot and semi-occult notions. But not a dickiebird, as far as we know. Of course, they may have been holding out on us. Everybody may be holding out on us. We're just the whipping boy of every new chap and his dog.'

Jerry Davis, the long arm of the Last Chance British Revival. Bulldog Gubbins. The Spy With the Cold Nose. Why me? I was not the only non-Angelic keyboard operator, as far as I knew. I was the only one at Fulham, but I spoke on the phone with a man at Ilford, and a woman in East Cheam. Leastways, I am sure they were a man and a woman, they lacked the unctuous resonance of the Angels, as if someone was forcing human speech un-naturally.

God the Alien. So what else is new? He made Adam in His image, but not in His substance, apparently. We are the clay, He the spirit, or pneuma. Leastways, that's what I read in a dog-eared paperback called *The Nature of God*, which Karen brought back to the house from Skoob Books a few days before she decided to drop this particular loam:

45

> And strange to tell, among that Earthen lot,
> Some could articulate, while others not:
> And suddenly one more impatient cried:
> 'Who is the Potter, pray, and who the Pot?'

My old friend, Omar Khayyam, the mystic boozer. But no room for Sufi sophistry now. It's back to the real fundamentals . . .

'We have to understand how minuscule and unimportant we are,' Karen told me, 'before His glory. Our individual soul is just a loan. We give it back at death. And now it's requital time. The final balance. All the loans are being called in.'

The Divine Bank. That really got my goat. I suggested to her that somebody up there must have made a dud investment in Consolidated Sin, or Ineffables, something to the tune of fifty quintillion astral zlotys poured down the celestial plughole. So the poor shmucks at the sharp end with their measly few billion current accounts have to be zapped.

'Where is Mephistopheles now that I need him?' I cried out. But it only drove her further from me. She sat up all night in the kitchen reading the Bible.

At least she never mentioned Alice. We came apart before we could unwind that skein. I think that, though she believed, she never quite related it to concrete life, a real event. I think she thought it would all happen while we, or at any rate, the Awakened, were in a state of heightened, suprahuman bliss. It would not be our world transformed. It would be the true spirit emerging from that clay, the potter's peat.

I remember when we staggered into the Sistine Chapel, Alice and I, after that long push with the crowds threading the Vatican maze like a crazed centipede, rushing past chapels of stupendous Raphaels as if they were bathroom graffiti, bursting in to that tall, gloomy chamber, crammed like the lounge of some immense ocean liner, with all the punters craning to gaze at the masterpieces on the ceiling, while a sad murmuring voice intoned amid the click of a thousand and one cameras, in twenty-three languages:

'Ladies and gentlemen. Please keep silent and refrain from all photography. *Signore et signori* . . .'

And up above, imploding in its riot of mauves, crimsons and blues, those immortal panels of that angry God casting forth the sun and the moon and the planets, the male musculature of the outrageous nude 'athletes', the expulsion of Adam and Eve from Paradise, Noah and the Flood, and that most famous of all icons, God stretching out his finger to Adam's. Not the angry deity but that powerful elder reaching out to a younger lover. The image stared at and misunderstood for four hundred years. Join the club.

And, at the side, the great scaffolding concealing the last of Michelangelo's sootened wonders: the *Last Judgement*. The hidden mural represented by a huge copy. The saved and the damned. The angels, floating above, had no wings, but the limbs and torsos of Swedish stevedores. The central figure of Jesus, an older but sadder Adam, turning away with a gesture of despair and even boredom from the whole hullabaloo. His mother Mary curled up at his back, and both covered over with the ugly swirl of the semi-transparent garments air-brushed on them by a generation of prudes.

Heaven, purgatory and hell. But we saw only art, through the adrenalin rush of our own mooching. Nothing holy, just two bodies clinging to each other, rubbernecking with the rest of them while dying to get into each other's pants . . . I have always associated Michelangelo since then with the most outrageous boner. The old reprobate might well have been pleased.

But here I am, far from any Renaissance, staggering towards an actual medieval nightmare down the Battersea Bridge Road. Facing the toy-like conceits of Chelsea Wharf with its trinket marts and guppie cafés. The looming bulk of the largest Sainsbury's in the world, now emblazoned with the gargantuan message: HE IS COME. STOCK UP FOR THE DAY!

a marvellous image of the city's summonsed masses queuing with chock-full supermarket trolleys in the slow march into Moloch's maw. Shitake mushrooms, organically grown courgettes, new age potatoes, frozen peas, Birds Eye fishfingers, lo-cal yoghurts and ready-to-eat chicken korma. Economy packs of Sainsbury's vegiburgers and tinned spaghetti hoops to last for all eternity. You never know what the nosh might be like in hell. Doner kebab and chips, forever. The long line yaws and twitters, aware that no one will return to the checkout to collect their coin deposit on the trolleys.

You're never alone with schizophrenia. My father used to love that old sixties' saw. Perhaps this has all been in my mind, an acute solipsistic hallucination from which I will jerk out at any moment to be booted on to the stage of the Comedy Shop, making with the mouth and drivelling all my old catchphrases:

'Well, how much lower can you get?'

The sneering mush, the filthy raincoat, the unwashed shock of hair, the two cigarettes dribbling from either side of the mouth, the noose hanging from the neck, the axe in the head and the stiletto stuck in the back. Well, it got me on television. Though Dad never liked any part of it:

'There's no wit any more, just verbal vomit. No class consciousness. No understanding. You look at society and all you see is a can of wriggling worms. But that's all inside your own 'ead, son.

Too true. The worm gnawing at the eye, the ear, the tongue. And will they in truth return from that putrescence? Will the suppurating mass of jelly and dried bones, gnawed in the grave, actually push through the well-tamped earth, the careful lawns, the stone, the muted inscription:

1970–1989
ALICE PATRICIA HOWARD
FOREVER IN OUR HEARTS

And should remain there? Or push on up, the thigh bone connecting to the hip bone, the hip bone connecting to the backbone, the backbone connecting to the neck bone, now hear de word of de Lawd . . .

To walk, just as she was before? The unblotched flesh, the rounded arms, the taut abdomen and firm small breasts, the dimple in the chin, the slight ever-amused curl of the lips, the button nose, the laughing eyes. The very breath of that person snuffed out on impact with the Cantabrian Mountains and reduced to a mound of dreadful, proto-biological glop . . . the borrowed soul, the floating pneuma, the temporary loan from the Divine Bank of Jehovah, Allah and Associates, now back on short term offer.

It cannot be!!

I am in sudden, horrible, malevolent empathy with my new Tory ally. It can't be right! It's not British! It's not, in the widest possible sense, human. The whole thing is an abomination, a mutation to be rejected wholesale. Standing on the bridge, between gentrified Battersea and petrified Chelsea, the ersatz wharves, the cold muddy seepage of the Thames crawling down to the Dockland ghost cities of Thatcho-Majorism, between the devil and the deep blue sea, the fishless reaches of this sinking island, I, Gerald the Herald Davis declare: 'They shall not pass! The tide must roll back! I, Canute, hereby echo the old Dodo call: we shall fight them on the beaches! We shall fight them in the streets! We shall fight them in the New Age cafés and in the Sushi bars and in Ed's Diner and in the Conceptual Galleries and Tai-Chi studios and Fitness Clubs and Council offices! We shall never surrender!'

And yet, as I stumble onwards towards my mission to betray Hoppy and all the winged, flightless Armies of the Lord, the Supreme Being, Creator of Heaven and Earth, the Judge, Our Father, Alpha and Omega, I feel the small, low gurgle of my stomach acids curdling my insides. Couldn't you take on someone your own size, Gerald? Like, for instance, a dying, geriatric dog, or a helpless cripple with a paper cup?

Talk about lost causes.

And yet the earth still stands, the sky has not yet fallen.

So I stride on, with a tear in my eye and a spring in my step. But the fear rising in my intestines . . .

PART 2

The Rising

7

Forty-eight hours to go before the Return. Everything has become very private. Commerce has stopped. Art is dead. No one goes to the ballet or the opera. Cinemas, theatres are closed. Football games are played to empty grandstands, with three players a side. Licensed premises have gone dry. People are staying at home nursing their locked desires and terrors.

Everyone, except me, is watching TV. The medium that anticipates everything but prepares us for nothing, the talisman that provides no protection. Regurgitations of cause and effect, beginnings and ends, predestinations, chastisements. The Paxmans have gone the way of all sceptics and now it's wall-to-wall gospel choirs, cantors, hare krishnas, all singing for their last supper. The endless curates brooding on the cosmic egg. Even my own Channel 4 has buckled under the pressure and is playing safe with wildlife repeats: king penguins waddle over the ice, balancing their wives' eggs on their toes. Bats deposit mountains of guano in caves. Giraffes gyrate. And even these programmes have been bowdlerized, shorn of all hints of lust and procreation, the new-old taboos of the age . . .

What's happening in the maternity wards? What of the bairns? Orthodoxy has it all wrapped up. Those who are without sin go to the good place, at the very top of the queue. Hosannaing and clashing cymbals. But what's the cutoff point? Confirmation? Bar Mitzvah? What is the knife-edge between heaven and hell? Is there a moment between jam yesterday and jam tomorrow? What's your last word, Archangel?

But the Archangel's been silent, since his drubbing by Paxman, letting his myrmidons hustle and bustle about the emptying streets in their egg-like bubblecars, punching out names on their little palmtops, matching bodies to available spaces, requisitioning halls and reception centres, stuffing every doorway with their terse little leaflets:

And thank you for flying Jehovah. We are sorry we can't offer you any services in the future, but we hope you have enjoyed the journey so far . . .

And when he had opened the seventh seal, there was silence in heaven about the space of half an hour . . . Just the slot for a one-off comedy act, ads included.

I told a white lie, for reasons of dramatic effect. The buses are still moving, occasionally; the subways still undulating through their tunnels; my milk is still delivered, if not Long Life; and grocers are still selling last week's bread. And the Kinema: some theatres are nevertheless open, some obsessions defying the saints. Marek Maus, co-couch potato and proprietor of the two-hundred seat Fulham Roxy, down on the Broadway, has kept his projectors running for the small trickle of devotees who can't get by without their celluloid fix. We concocted the Last Programme together, over the dregs of my last flask of Drambuie (having neglected to stock up on anything better before the Dry Act suddenly shut all the pubs), out of what we could still salvage from retiring distributors. The Festival of the Afterlife: *Heaven Can Wait, That's the Spirit, It's a Wonderful Life, Field of Dreams, Diane Keaton's Heaven*, and my own favourite, *Between Two Worlds*, in which Paul Henreid and Eleanor Parker find themselves on board a ship sailing nowhere in the mist with a cargo of fading character actors who slowly discover that they have died, but not at the box office, which, it appears, was quite decent in 1944. John Garfield played my role, the tough-talking, card-sharping journalist who figures it out and realizes that there are no angles. Sara Allgood is the society dame who wants a decent room and bath at the other end, and Sydney Greenstreet is the judge who turns up at journey's end to dispatch the passengers up or down. There is a great deal of atmospheric silence and much play with a faint sound of tinkling glass, which refers to the window which breaks to rescue the suiciding couples. Edmund Gwenn, a suicide himself, as the steward who has to remain on ship, cruising forever, bore an unsettling resemblance to Hoppy, my own Angel. But I tried to put that aside . . .

By the time we projected the picture there was no audience. Marek and I watched it alone in the theatre, leaving the large 16mm reel to run unattended in the projection booth. The film broke, before the lovers could be rescued by the obligatory happy ending. Even coincidence was against us. After splicing the break, out of habit, we locked the hall and sashayed out into the Broadway, with its shuttered shops and abandoned Thai restaurants. The spattering of April showers. A brace of Angels approached from Jerdan Place and scanned us with their portable list stick. Satisfied that we were not Unregistered they ambled on, clucking softly.

'Did you ever think it would look like this?' I asked Marek. 'The End of the World: a dull drizzle, the usual squashed crates all over the pavement, everyone sitting at home watching television and funny people with wings tickling your groin.'

'Yes, it does seem appropriate,' said Marek. 'We appear to get the apocalypse that we deserve.'

'The crime fits the punishment.'

And Sydney Greenstreet is the appropriate executioner. I had told Marek nothing above my involvement with the underground Caucus. The plot against God. If he'd believed me he'd have wanted to join, and that's one soul too many to have on my conscience. Now is the time to hedge your bets. Too late for me. My dad, Joseph, and Mum, Sophie, ironically, tried to rope me into their own dissent, in the shape of a permanent demonstration, utilizing the cardboard boxes of the Yuletide Poverty Protest to set up camp in Whitehall, at the mouth of Downing Street, with placards announcing: DIVINE LIES TRIP – DEMOCRACY NOT THEOCRACY – PROPHETS = PROFITS – JOBS NOT BLOBS – 'GOD' GO HOME.

'It's the last gasp of Tory trickery, Jerry,' said my dad, poking his bedraggled head out of his box. 'Twenty years in power and this is all they can think of. It's pathetic, innit? The "Kingdom of God!" You can imagine all them Tory ladies in Basildon stitching wings on all those fat party gits. Well, there's some people what ain't falling for it.'

'You have to stand up for what you believe,' added my mother, who was lying down on an old mattress under a red parasol with 'WAGES NOT SAGES' painted all over it.

'They've done everything they could,' said my father Joseph. 'They massacred our basic industries, they closed the pits, they shut down all the steelworks, they sold the whole country to the Germans and the Japanese capitalists and now they've nothing more to sell they're shutting up shop completely. They're telling everybody: Oi, this wasn't our fault, this was the Divine Plan, no less. You don't 'ave to worry about being unemployed and wiped out with no future, because there ain't no future to be 'ad! It's all the End of Days! The Resurrection! Dictatorship is what it is. The British people won't stand for it. They just need somebody that says No. Somebody that says, We ain't 'aving it. Sod your Angels and bollocks to your "Last Judgement!" This is Custer's Last Stand, old son.'

How I longed to tell him I had heard exactly the same sentiments from his arch-enemies, the Tory liars hiding in their underground bunkers. But then, he'd never have believed me. It would only have been the last betrayal, the most odious piss-take of them all.

'I just hope you're right, Dad,' I told him, lamely, as the tiny group of thirty ageing stalwarts waved their banners and jeered at a passing bubblecar. The two policemen guarding the gates of Downing Street just looked fatigued and bored.

'Listen to me, son,' he said to me. 'When this Resurrection Day comes and nothing 'appens, and the dead stay in the graves where they belong, then the people will want answers to a lot of questions. On that day, we will no longer be alone.'

'I certainly hope so, Dad. I'll see you.'

Marek and I walked on up Dawes Road. I cradling my secret. Marek, I suppose, cradling his own. These are the times in which we all are thinking about those things even the gabbiest would not confess to. Those thoughts or deeds that even the wildest horses couldn't drag from the most pious Catholic at the most tempting confessional in the world. The deepest ur sins of Yom Kippur. All those shameful little infamies, from the day you stole your best friend's Ninja Turtle in kindergarten to the location of your stash of hard-core videos. Masturbating in Miss Chatterjee's purloined panties. Attempted homosexual transgressions in Old Brompton Cemetery. And that's just mentioning the material in my poor dead act! Forbidden thoughts, like the slithering beasts of Lovecraft's Cthulthu Mythos, will all those too be carried forward on the last spreadsheet of all?

Ia! Yog-Sothoth! And what about high treason? My futile efforts to carry out my assignment for the Dodo. Queen and country. Give me a break. Late nights at the Recording Office, alone, racked by sneezing caused by Hoppy's moulting feathers scattered like dandruff all over the keyboard. Ah, the terror! the terror! PASSWORD: HOLY HOPE. Options: Database. PowerLink. HomeFiles. I had tried to sneak in to the last two before, while Hoppy's back was turned, or he was grooming his wings, or scratching whatever was underneath his robe, but no breakthroughs. It was always ACCESS DENIED. My hacking days were in the distant past, but nevertheless I had a proper go. It occurred to me the internal passwords might be in another character set, or hidden language. I curled my way round the system files and eventually nudged up against the mainframe. One hundred and thirty-seven gigabytes in hidden files! I drooled on the keys. It occurred to me that the kind of system I was stroking here would not ignore my entry, and any moment I could expect bands of seraphim armed with cudgels or blue-black tentacles to burst through the ceiling or floor, sucking out my tongue, my lungs, my eyes. I had seen too many horror movies, too many Freddies, Zombies, Living Dead. I could not expect the real thing to be any different.

But I could not break in. No alarms bell rang, and no celestial goons came through the walls. Hoppy found me in the morning, exhausted, on the couch he used to take his frequent naps and siestas. He revived me with a wet towel. Fortunately I had logged off the system as usual. He seemed oblivious of everything, just his normal, gormless, cheery, grating self. I told him I couldn't sleep because of noisy neighbours, hosannaing to the Lord all night long. He sighed and made his habitual exasperating tut-tutting sound, like an old nanny. 'People have to learn to calm down,' he said. 'The softest thoughts are the clearest heard.' So what about my loud, shrieking impulses? The scarlet flame of my heretical treachery?

'He either knows it all and it's not even a pin prick, or they're not as omnipotent as they seem,' I told the Dodo. We had met, as prearranged at our first encounter, at the Burger King in Lower Regent Street, halfway to the Mall, a place still frequented by wayward youth gathering at 'Golgotha'. Uniformed soldiers of the Armed Guard of Jesus spent their lunch hour *in situ*, festooned with badges from a bygone age. SAVE THE WHALE. SMASH THE POLL TAX. KILL THE BILL. COAL NOT DOLE. KISS ME, I'M SWEDISH. SOLIDARNOSC. YOU ARE NOW ENTERING FREE DERRY. MACHO SLUTS. NO MORE NUKES. (What are 'whales'? Only kidding.) Some of these insignia ran up and down their trouser legs and festooned their black berets. They had taken to marching all over what used to be the West End singing hymns and ancient Cliff Richard numbers. But at these hallowed tables one was only subjected to the stolid munching sounds of bad teeth on meat patties. (And what of the animals? Have they indeed no souls? Will they or won't they be called at the Final Hour? The Angels always fudged this issue. Will one be waiting in line with a nervous hippopotamus, or a neurotic aardvark worrying about the ghosts of dead ants?) Sometimes one's mind really feels it is giving way . . .

'We might assume they're not omnipotent or they would have crushed us long ago,' said the Dodo, surveying a Big Whopper. 'Or, as you say, it's all grist to the mill. But as they've gone to so much trouble to register everyone, you might think they would try and rummage our way. There is, as you have found out, an inconsistency. We are not the only ones outside their net. There are untouched vagrants and, at the other end of the scale, VIPs who have evaded their snares. Men and women of industry, or royal blood, circling the globe in private ships or aircraft. People of power who are making their own plans to escape what seems in store . . . There are more things in heaven and earth, Horatio, than are dreamt of in your theology. And apropos of that, something interesting . . .'

He leant forward, so that his words would be swallowed by the rustle of milkshakes. 'Our boffins have discovered something. They've been trying to peek into the mother ships. They keep shifting position, but at any one time there are one thousand and twelve of them in global orbit. They have some sci-fi kind of shield that muffles our probes, but we have detected a massive moving energy source in one of the larger ships lying directly over Ecuador. Calculating from bounce effects and all sorts of mumbo-jumbo that I or you couldn't make head nor tail of, they concluded that something akin to a black hole, a collapsed energy of incalculable dimensions, is actually inside the vessel. The Mad Hatter said it was at the frontiers of Hawkian Theory. What do you think of that?'

'God, in hibernation?'

'So what happens when He wakes up and comes out, eh, sonny boy? Whatever it is, it's contained, so far. But we'll all know soon, eh? If it's the real thing, or a bluff.' His cheek muscles twitched in a pained rictus. 'My ex-wife would be due back, for a start. Not to speak of . . .' The flabby face collapsed like a spent balloon. 'Think of all those whose undiscovered crimes will be found out. Think of all the soldiers, the cannon fodder of all the wars, calling to redeem their sacrifice. People we've really loved . . . I know there's someone you . . . well, nuff said.'

Nuff indeed. Marek and I dragging Dawes Road, up into the crossing of Munster Road and the vigil by the Fulham Cross Cemetery. Despite the leaflets and the TV and radio announcements and the stickers and posters everywhere, people have gathered at the graveyards. Sitting by the gates, camped by the graves, a silent mass, mainly older men and women, squatting in blankets like Albanian refugees, swaying to and fro softly, a low murmur throbbing through the rain. The Angels were nowhere to be seen, and the melancholy air of a suppressed panic drove us further up Lillie Road. At the corner of Fulham Palace Road and the green triangle of the Recreation Ground we stopped short at an eerie sight: There were the Angels, quite a large group of them, perhaps thirty or forty, trying out their wings in the drizzle. They would take short runs, of a dozen feet or so, then hop on one leg for another dozen, flapping their soggy white appendages, then soar, for a brief moment, like the Wright Brothers' first abortive experiments, about ten or twelve feet high in the air, before coming down in the mud-scoured lawn, tumbling over on their bellies and knees. Then they would get up, brush the mud off their soiled robes, take another run, and try again. They looked for all the world like a flock of chickens trying to recapture a lost genetic arcadia. We stood, Marek and I, for about ten minutes, at the tree-lined gate to the tiny park, watching, unseen or ignored. We could hear the very human 'ooomph' as yet another clumsy body hit the turf, the flap of the wings, the splash of the heavy feet. Very far from Signor Dante's bright beacons easing the blessed up to paradise. I thought of the 'black hole' oozing far above Ecuador. And, again, the terror took hold of my soul.

8

Marek Maus spent the night on my couch. Neither of us slept. We were kept awake by the loud keening of my neighbours on the starboard side. They were a family of Trinidadians who were devout Seventh Day Adventists. I know they believe in the Second Coming and the literal Resurrection, without the need for leaflets thrust through their door. The righteous dead will come forth immortalized. I know their doctrine because they bent my ear one day when I called to convey my congratulations on their daughter's wedding.

They do not believe in an eternal punishment but in a heaven on earth restored by Christ. Why then are they crying all night as if their heart was shattered to smithereens? It's a complete mystery. Marek stayed over because he couldn't bear the solitude of his basement flat in Fairholme Road, crushed in among the last hedonists of West Kensington; people who took the end of days as an excuse to play their sound systems at an even louder level than before, if such a thing were possible. Complaints were answered with a brusque 'We're all gonna be dead in a week, so fuck off.' But I had not bargained for my weeping neighbours. We sat up late and finished all the herbal teas. Rosehip, hibiscus lemon, Mandarin orange spice, celestial seasoning, natural and exotic. The first company in America to use only oxygen bleached tea bags, says the packet: 'We believe in nurturing people's bodies and uplifting their souls. We believe in caring for and preserving the environment. Our boxes are 100 per cent recycled paperboard.' And who will care and nurture any more?

Everything trite and everyday seems to take on a new meaning when judged against the coming doom. The kitchen was in dire need of an upgrade even before Karen left the fold. She despised every form of housework, despite, or probably because of, her puritanical upbringing, but could not abide grime and dirt. Every three weekends we used to don our overalls and asbestos suits and hose the place down. But you can't teach an old dog new tricks and you can't make a set of cracked, creaking seventies cabinets into the Ideal Home of 1998. In trashing the herb teas I came across cans and jars which she had brought with her when she moved in. Two Heinz baked beans, two doppel-concentrato tomato purée, one evil-looking Tabasco, ditto Lea and Perrins special soy sauce, and a strange mustard jar with an even stranger mould round its rim.

What will happen to it after we're gone? When the Last Trump sounds, and we all traipse to the Centres, and are all dispatched, whichever way that is, climbing in, perhaps, to the great mother ships which will land to whisk us up or down . . . And will a great silence fall upon the earth, for much more than the space of half an hour, and a cold wind, or maybe a cleansing sirocco, blow across the empty streets and pavements filled with the last rubbish, the detritus of all of vanished humanity, torn shoes, orange peels, burger cartons, Kentucky bones, tattered newspapers with nothing left to report, and blowing in through the broken windows to abandoned kitchens, scattering the unused bottles of Mazola oil, Knorr soups and drying out mixed cashew nuts, rotting onions and potatoes sprouting strange protuberances for no purpose that can ever meet an eye . . . Unmade beds that will never be slept in again, condoms and diaphragms that will never more be used, dusty sofas which will grow ever dustier and crumpled pillows that will never be smoothed, carpets that will never have those specks of tandoori sauce removed, bookshelves that will never be dusted and books that will never again be read, cupboards cluttered forever with the obscure debris of mislaid bits and bobs, little wind-up toys which will never be wound, frozen in their plastic desire, refrigerators which will shut down and darken as the switches of power stations lie untouched, and food passing well beyond sell-by dates by a margin of a few million years.

Or will there only be that slight pause, and another horde of unknown beasts, out of another waiting fleet of giant ships, beyond our ken, come forth, slouching towards Hammersmith to be born, to replace our failed, cancelled species . . .? The race of Angels, sexless and hopeless, given enough rope to test out their wings . . .

'Whadoyou think, Marek, is it all a great galactic con?'

'Whatever it is, we certainly fell for the bugger.' The carrying on beyond the wall. In the kitchen it was not as audible. We sat at my little table cradling our mugs of celestial seasoning. There were still the signs of the telephone numbers I used to scribble on it before Karen stopped me. She tried to scrub my soul clean too, a double failure. Is she happy now, alert with her tribe? Singing songs of praise in deepest Norwich. Or are they also staying up all night, shivering, shedding inexplicable tears?

'I'm just glad all my dead ones are far away, in Poland,' said Marek. 'Not to speak of the live ones. Poor bastards.' Marek's parents, his sister and two brothers had returned to live in Warsaw after the ousting of Walesa. But they had deserted their apartment, and Marek assumed they were now mere dots somewhere in the crowd at the Shrine of the Holy Virgin of Czestochowa, where the entire population had gathered, waiting for the past three weeks for the Pope, who had not returned from a date with the Archangels, or someone senior, in the regional mothership over Hamburg. 'It's easier for me, but not for you, *kochanyi*.'

'Alice is buried in Bath, or what's left of her,' I told him. 'I wonder what her dad and mum would do if she turned up. There'll be a zillion cups of tea on the boil. A trillion kettles, whistling like banshees.'

'It's so bizarre, the cultural heritage,' said Marek. 'How easily they've taken control. How easily they slipped through all the defences of state and citizens, paupers and princes. They found the oldest exposed nerve everywhere and just squeezed. Who doesn't want to get the chance to go to heaven? Taking their chances with the other place. You'd think there would have been more resistance: armies underground, special forces, mass protests, union days of action, civil disobedience. But at the end of the day we found out the fragility and shallowness of all our social structures. A fistful of miracles, some missile bases made impotent, weapons disfunctioned, OK. But where's the spirit of rebellion? I'm not talking of those usual rentacrowd people, excusing your old folks, Jerry, down in Whitehall. Angels, Angels, Angels. Out, Out, Out! It's a poor joke, my friend.'

'I don't expect she'll be able to travel to London,' I mused. 'Not from Bath, not down the M4 at the best of times. But with a hundred billion new oldies . . .' I gazed at myself in the grimy cabinet mirror. 'What would she want with me now anyway? She left a happy young man of nineteen. Not James Dean but at least breathing regularly.' A dreadful, sagging, moribund puss stared at me like Bob in *Twin Peaks*. The mongrel face of dashed experience. Twenty-four o'clock shadow and bags of coal under eyes that looked like dried up fried eggs. What would an even more ragged corpus feel, a poor old sod of eighty who lost his wife at twenty-three, for instance. Or an old widow waiting for a toy boy? This is indeed a poor joke to play on mankind.

'Jews, Christians, Moslems, we've all been taken,' Marek was still trudging down his own track. 'What will be the face of the Jewish Messiah? Will he be an old rabbi, or a young man in uniform? What will the Prophet look like to the Moslems? What of all the mutually contradicting prophecies? Every religion was promised the world for its own on the Final Day. What of the Revelations? War and thunder and smoke and ashes. The Four Horsemen, bringing plague and disease.'

'You wait for ages for a horseman of the apocalypse,' I quipped, 'and then four turn up together.' It was the best I could do under the circumstances. For a long time now I haven't been able to dredge up a single proper joke from this predicament. When one's whole life has become a lampoon, how do you lampoon the lampoon? 'Better to leave her in Bath, with her parents. I wonder what an awayday fare would be like, with all one's gathered ancestors? Remember those ads: The Whole Family for the Price of Two . . .'

'Where have all the governments gone?' Marek mused on, dreamily. 'Isn't it time to wonder where they've disappeared? Has this all been an almighty plot? Pardon the inadvertent pun, my dear. But what about all the dead politicians? Ronald Reagan and Stalin and Bierut and Bogdan Chmielnitski and God knows who else? Remember the last *Panorama*, before they sacked Paxman? The entire Nazi leadership returning to Berlin. My God, Jerry, what is lying in store for us?'

I wanted so much to confess my own grotty secret.

'Marek . . .' I began.

'Yes, Gerald?' he turned to me.

'Marek, my friend . . .' The burden of collusion.

'Yes, again, Gerald?'

The Adventists were still weeping, though a little more softly, on the other side of the wall.

'Never mind. Just empty brain waves.'

So do I believe? Is it true?

9

The newspapers, bless their stone hearts, are still publishing. As I amble down Iffley Road towards the shopping mall, past the big chains, Smugs, Safeways, Currys, Comet are all closed, but Nazim's Newsagent's is still open:

TWENTY-FOUR HOURS TO LAST TRUMP (*Guardian*)

PRESIDENT QUAYLE CLAIMS ALMIGHTY SUMMIT SUCCESSFUL. DEMOCRATS ALLEGE FRAUD (*Independent & Courier*)

THE WORLD WAITS FOR FINAL DAYS (*The Times*)

QUEEN PREPARES PALACE FOR PREDECESSORS (*Daily Telegraph*)

MARKETS SUSPEND JUDGEMENT FOR END OF DAYS (*Financial Times*)

WAIT FOR YOUR DEAD! (*Star*, and *Today*)

DEAD ON TIME! (*People*)

TIME'S UP! (*Sun*)

'Quiet day, Nazim. Is it worth the trouble?'

'There are still mouths to feed, Mr Jerry.'

'I suppose so, Nazim . . .'

I didn't take any of those rags but bought the last issue of *Personal Computer World*. These people never give up. It's beyond me. At the brink of the abyss they're still offering redundant 686's at knock-down prices. 'The Best Deals Money Can Buy!' 'Anything Less than a XXXX Is Obsolete!' 'Get off to a Flying Start with ZZZZ!' 'Allow 28 days for delivery!!' It warms the cockles of the heart, or freezes the blood, delete the inapplicable. *Vogue*, too, is soldiering on: 'The Bucharest Look'. 'Estonian Elegance'. 'The Steaming World of Hot Pants. Hotter than we can handle, very soon, my darlings.' 'Jody Foster: Growing Old Grace-fully.'

Perhaps, after all, by force of the will . . . Where are you, Nietzsche, now that we need you? God is dead – Nietzsche. Nietzsche is dead – God. Who would I most like to converse with, of old? Marek and I and Aisleen and the two Martins played this parlour game several times. Marek opted for Erich von Stroheim, but I think he needs his head examined. I think I would opt, every time, for Mark Twain, the sanest mind in the universe: 'If I had my time to live again – I'd blow the gaff on the whole human race.' Exactly. But how much time will there be? Now there's an advocate to have at that final moment. But it's all been thrashed out. There will be no advocates. No prosecution, no defence. No ritzy lawyers. Just judge and defendant. And who will the judge be? No comment.

'Give me a break, Hoppy,' I asked the Angel, more than once. 'You've bent one rule, just bend a couple more. Tell me what to expect. How should I behave? How should I dress? Should it be the full three-piece Moss Bros special or the old schmutter, sandals and staff? Should I exude confidence, contrition or concurrence? Should I smile, cry, or be completely po-faced? Should I be concerned, nonchalant or hysterical? Should I de-emphasize the negative or accentuate the positive?'

'Just be yourself, Gerald. It's up to you.'

What was it Philip Roth wrote in *Portnoy's Complaint*? 'Everyone in the outside world seemed to be an emanation of my mother.' Why does one never see a properly female Angel? No one has yet been able to answer the 'hermaphroditic question', to peek behind the robe. I know there is a Y-front, or a jockstrap of some sort, since I brushed against it once when he leant over to correct some keying that had gone astray. A fleshy arm, but none of that male odour, the sweaty grease or soaped up pores. The Angels had no smell at all. No divine spice, no myrrh or roses, no reek of sulphur or brimstone or any other celestial halitosis. Just a nullity. An android race? One hasn't read forty novels by Philip K. Dick for nothing. It's always, of course, a possibility, though they could have dosed them with *eau des hommes* or whatever as they leapt out of those mother ships. And they might have been made to fly better.

So who, or what, are the puppet-masters? The face behind the face. The old occult problem. Alchemical or masonic symbols. The shifting hole over Ecuador. Wheels within wheels. Mantras within mantras. Weeping in the dark, perhaps that's the right thing. Those who are closest to faith may be the first ones to know when they're beat. Perhaps they too have come to realize that heaven isn't what we want at all . . .

Thought for the day. This morning's speaker is Gerald Davis, redundant stand-up comic and all round schlemiel. His subject will be Why I would like everything to be as it was before. Roll back the world, says Mr Fotheringay, the man who can no longer work miracles. Once upon a time I was happy and carefree, snug as a bug and rolling in clover. I got up every day with a song on my face and a smile on my hips, filed my teeth, brushed my nails and sped off to work with my snickersnee, cutting through life's dreck and doldrums. Audiences loved my sparkling wit and repartee, throwing rolled up bags of coins at my feet, if not at my head. Some even obliged me with fresh vegetables, to augment my natural diet. I appeared on the *Harry Enfield Show*, the *Mayall Clinic*, *Mel and Griff's Christmas Special*, and endless runs of *The Grunge*. Within a year I was going to have my own show on Channel 4. Big Chief Terrence was a personal fan. I was going to show Karen I too could assert myself, I too could be a personality, not just a used Hoover bag.

A Face in the Crowd: Andy Griffith, Patricia Neal, Kim Novak. My favourite movie; Marek would run it for me twice a year. The rise and fall of a cracker-barrel singing star. You never know what you got till it's over . . . Kim Novak, now there's an Immortal to conjure with . . .

So farewell then Jerry Davis,
What a way to earn a living —
that was your catchphrase.
Keith's mum says you stole it
from Morecambe and Wise.
Those were the days.
Whose catchphrase was that?

E. J. Davidovitch, 97¾

The streets of Hammersmith were very quiet. I walked down towards the river. The muddy stretch of the Thames. Planks and plastic bottles floating east. East, where the lost Garden of Eden languishes somewhere in the marshes of Iraq. The dead dictator, Saddam Hussein, drained the marshes to get at his enemies hiding armed in the reeds. And how are they waiting, in Baghdad now, for the Rising of all the hundreds of thousands of his victims, and their oppressor? And in Tehran, for the deified Imam? And in Beijing, for the disgraced Chairman Mao? The legions of the legions of the legions of those gone before. Fulham–Hammersmith should be a doddle.

Nothing moves on the river except a few stolid ducks. No putt-putt of boats or jogging lovers. The benches and tables outside the riverside pubs are deserted, the taverns locked. Who wants to sit sipping orange juice? Anyone who has a stash of booze keeps it quietly by the bed, to go blotto in blissful privacy before the grand glut of conviviality. Do not go gentle into that long night. And death shall have no dominion. A man needs to be drunk to throw out such a challenge. But there has been so little time to prepare . . .

Last night's rain cleared the air and a breeze is scudding the usual grey clouds across the sky with blips of blue. Life is after all a precious commodity, no kidding. Who would have known it. Perhaps, after all, this is just a massive testing ground: like God's testing of Abraham over Isaac. *And he said, Behold, here I am. Take now thy son, thine only son, Isaac, whom*

70

thou lovest, and get thee into the Land of Moriah, and offer him there for a burnt offering . . . But who is binding whom to the stake? Or are the Angels only unwitting tools, in whose hands? We're back to the black hole again.

Around and around. The Hammersmith Roundabout. It took them ten years to build this site with its tatty malls and round-the-clock jingle bells, now deserted, echoing silence. The world headquarters of Coca-Cola. Give us a break. Or at least a Kit-Kat. Around and around. Everything that was familiar and reviled and taken for granted. For what?

Will we know, at the end? Will a great hand roll back the great veil and a great voice call forth with great force: this is why it has been so and so?

Back home. Calling Marek Maus. No answer. He must have decided to spend the last day with majestic Anjeska, his on and off bedmate, in St John's Wood. Every man to his sorrows. I have a choice of comestibles: spaghetti cheese, tuna in the can, or with rice and mushrooms, Captain Birds Eye's Yummy Fish Cutlets. What a choice for a last supper. What would one pick? The *Michelin Guide* to final repasts. Memories of gourmet events. Mutton hot pot at Chez Paul near the Place d'Italie. The Empire Szechuan Gourmet on Columbus Avenue. The Phoenicia Lebanese in South Ken. The Red Fort. The What-sitsname in Roma. There's a scene I hadn't thought of for a long time. Just a little ristorante we chose because the customers looked as if they were having such a good time eating there. *Mangiare* with no *parlare*. I ordered scampi and was stunned to get the whole damn beasts, all ratchety claws and eyes. Alice's guffaws at my confusion. Two idiots abroad. Teenage Dumbos. You can believe an elephant flies.

Snatches of grace that cannot be resnatched. In the ordinary familiarity of my hideaway flat, after the ordinary familiarity of the neighbourhood streets, empty as an ordinary bank holiday, I can't believe it any more. It's all a con. There are no mother ships. There are just papier mâché things on quantel graphics. Ordinary morphing, just like a genie in a bottle turns

71

into a household iron, they do those things all the time. Hoppy is no Angel, just a bad hamateur from Leatherhead. Tory clones. No wonder they can't fly. In the morning we'll all switch on the radio to find everything's turned back. And It Was All A Dream. God, how I hate stories or movies that end like that. I once threw a shoe at the screen at an MGM Murdoch at a Madonna film which had holed itself that way. But reality, now that's another matter . . .

I spent the afternoon mooning about the flat, browsing through my long-neglected library. Volumes stockpiled before a wafer-thin paperback cost forty-five ecus. My Philip K. Dicks: *Ubik. Solar Lottery. The Simulacra. Galactic Pot Healer. A Scanner Darkly.* A cornucopia of clues, or just a trail of false leads? George Orwell, the *Essays*. Sanity, sanity. Mark Twain: *A Connecticut Yankee at King Arthur's Court, An Innocent Abroad, Roughing It.* Salman Rushdie: *The Great Escape.* Flann O'Brien. Joyce. Beckett. Louvish. All the stuff I'd been intending to devour the moment I had six months to spare. *Gonzo Journals*, Volumes I thru VIII. What can one take with one to eternity??? One piece of cabin baggage per person, personal nail file, toothbrush, shaver, rubber duck. Have you packed this bag yourself, sir?

There might be enough material here for a reasonable skit on a wet Sunday afternoon in Penge. Not something to try at the Hackney Palace. Or the Brixton Ritzy. Joys of yesteryear. One book to take with you to your infernal island, apart from the Bible, Shakespeare or *Das Kapital*? – *W. C. Fields, His Follies and his Fortunes*. The defence rests. Guilty as charged.

Opted for the spaghetti cheese. The quick option. Thoughts of moseying down to Downing Street to join the folks. A last private night of nostalgia. All we are saying is, give life a chance . . . a chance to hear another rendition of the Great Poll Tax Demo of '89. 'You can still see the scar here, Jerry, where that damn copper split me 'ead open. If your mum 'adn't kicked 'im in the crotch . . .' 'He was only doing his job, Dad.' 'That's right, son. Side with the lackeys of the bourgeoisie.' If only I could, Dad, if only I could. But I could never dress right, look right or smell right. I had to laugh the bastards out of my guts.

Stayed in instead and worked the phone lines. The twilight fading out in the street. That smattering of passers-by avoiding your gaze. What could one say? 'Happen the dead are all coomin' back tomorrer like.' 'Happen.' Not much to bite on there. Caught Marek in with Anjeska. They were having a candlelit dinner en suite, goulash and piroshkis. And I thought he went there for sex. Poor deluded I. Spoke to Martin. Martin II was out, on the Last Cruise. Pre-Resurrection Night at Heaven's Gate, down on the Strand. Going out in style. The clone carmagnole. They were planning a mass assfucking on the Embankment, to welcome absent friends who might or might not turn up in the turgid gloom of the morn. The sin of pride. 'Who has the energy?' I commiserated with Martin, who was inconsolable: 'He'll come back at five a.m., covered with cherry lube, and asked to be licked off. Can you believe it?' 'It really sounds like the pits,' I agreed.

I spoke to Aisleen, and Dina, and Ronald the Rat. Babbling brooks, running into the ground. I thought of phoning strangers across the globe. Who gives a fuck for the bill? I dialled, at random, a fifteen digit number. A tired male voice answered in a far eastern language. 'Can I speak to Mr Bugs Bunny?' I asked. 'Mr Bunny not in,' he replied.

So much for trying to be a complete nerd. I nixed the phone and turned on the TV. All normal transmissions had ceased. All seventy channels were showing the same Public Service Broadcast. Instructions for Receiving your Returnees. The same spiel over and over again: They will not want to eat, drink or sleep. They will be disoriented. Do not overwhelm them with emotional extremes. Be natural. Do not pretend nothing has happened. They will be aware of their death. They will not be able to provide details of the afterlife, which can only take effect after the Last Judgement. Make a balance sheet of all your significant deeds. Be prepared for the second and third waves. Clear all cluttered corners. Follow the instructions of the Recorders. Keep calm and Do Not Panic. And the same, in a hundred and umpty languages throughout the globe . . .

The phone rang, jerking me out of my seat. It was Karen — at least some wishes are answered. But she seemed to be speaking through some strange gabbled wail.

'Are you all right, Jerry? Are you on your own?'

'No, it's all right, Karenkins, the whole gang's here.'

'I don't want you to be afraid, love. I still love you, you know that. It's just that love is not enough. Do you understand that, Jerry?'

'Not really.'

'I'm talking about her, Jerry. About Alice. I know you. I know what's going through your head.'

'What's going through my head sounds like a buzz saw, Karen. Are you torturing the cat out there?'

'It's Aunt Ada. She's talking in tongues. Everyone is getting prepared.'

'I'm glad to hear that, Karen.'

'We're all praying for you.'

'I'm over the moon.'

'Don't get angry, love. It's too late for anger. I don't want to argue with you, Jerry. I just wanted to say, leave Alice alone. She'll be with her family, they'll have to prepare together. She'll have come back, but she won't be the same.'

'I know.' I shall scream in one moment. Who has the hot line to the top, her or me?

'It's all for the best, Jerry. It had to happen. It was ordained from the beginning of time. It's so wonderful that it's happening to us.'

'Don't worry, Karen. I'm totally consumed with wonderment.'

'Don't be bitter, Jerry, I know you'll pull through.'

'I have seen the promised land, Karen. And I don't have a visa.'

'Everybody has a visa, my love.'

The wailing had become louder, threatening to bore through my ear. Then it stopped abruptly.

'I have to go now, Jerry. Aunt's had a fit.'

She could never leave well enough alone. If only I could get drunk or stoned! The cry going up in five billion households. I sank back in my tattered old sofa and opened *W. C. Fields*, by Robert Lewis Taylor, at random:

> The support was led by W. C. Fields as Sherlock Baffles, a mystery, who reminded one considerably of 'Nervy Nat,' whose antics grace the pages of a well-known humorous weekly. Mr Fields did some clever juggling when he wasn't otherwise engaged. Frederick K. Bowers sang a number of songs in energetic manner and did his share towards assisting the stars in their fun-making. David Torrence did an 'Earl of Pawtucket' part and tried to imitate, with some success, the mannerisms of Lawrence O'Dorsay. Belle Gold as Desdemona, a colored maid, danced well and sang with enthusiasm . . . The others, including the chorus, worked hard and pleased, both individually and collectively.

I wonder what the notices will be, for the Human Follies, when the show's closed, in *Divine Variety* . . . It seems a far far better thing that I do, than I have ever done . . . I closed the evening with an old video of my hero. A double bill of *The Man on the Flying Trapeze* and *Never Give a Sucker an Even Break*. Falling asleep to the nasal cry of the Clown. How else to round off the history of homo sapiens. Godfrey Daniels!! Crawled into bed, activated the answerphone. Who knows what messages might emanate, in the gloaming . . .

Tossing and turning. Dreams? I should not be surprised. The Dodo visited me with the Mad Hatter, who resembled an ice cream cone capped with a condom. They were babbling about something they called 'the divine sperm', which was about to be sprayed all over the cosmos. 'Put it on! Put it on!' they cried at me. I tried, but it snapped like a balloon. They edged away from me. 'Protect the soul,' they intoned. 'Protect the soul. Don't let them lick the cherries.'

I woke up in a sweat, but it seemed, for the moment, just a common homophobic anxiety. I thought about all those people dressed in leotards, leather straps and dildos wandering about Trafalgar Square. No wonder Nelson needed a patch on his eye. There was a faint light from the curtained window. I looked at my watch. It was six-fifteen.

Daybreak. At dawn it should have started. By the first glimmers of light, They shall emerge . . .

Whose is the Authorized Version?

And I looked, and lo, a Lamb stood on the mount Sion, and with him an hundred forty and four thousand, having his Father's name written in their foreheads . . .

'What should I do, on the day, if the day . . .?' I had asked the Dodo, at the Burger King.

'Just watch, and listen, and keep your wits about you,' he said, softly, wiping sesame seeds off his lap. 'We'll try and keep a contact. Don't call us, we'll call you.'

I lay in bed and listened. Iffley Road is a quiet street, even on noisy days. Suburban leafiness in a central location. Monday's garbage day. Alternate Saturdays the used computers man revs his jalopy. The trilling birds, yes, they're on target. At half-past seven, the Adventist kiddies would normally be off to school, though not for the past two weeks. The pitter patter of tiny feet. My neighbours downstairs, a retired Rear-Admiral and his front, old Mrs Diefenback, have been living in sin, but in blissful quiet, for nigh on thirty years. They didn't believe in the institution of marriage. Even the events of the past five months failed to shift their routine of shops, bingo clubs and pottering in the garden. Are they already doomed? Might they be expecting . . .?

The birds. The grunting dog at number twenty-five. No traffic. No surprise there. My dripping kitchen tap, to which I've grown accustomed. A toilet flush, somewhere to the left.

It's all a con. Just papier mâché. Computer graphics. It's all done with mirrors. No one can bend forks with his mind, or bring the dead to life, or conquer the universe. None can create and destroy, endow and withdraw, at will.

But all the bells are ringing at all the front doors.

10

The bell at the front door rang, rang, rang, echoed up and down the street. I tugged on my pants with trembling hands. My forehead felt cold, my scalp was burning. My throat was dry and my eyes soaking. I ripped the sleeve of my shirt. Goddamn! And all the rest in the laundry bag. Imagine the queue at the laundrette from now on.

As I staggered down the stairs of my flat I could hear the shuffle of the Rear-Admiral and Mrs Diefenback downstairs. The sliding back of their unlocked door. The fumbling with the front door bolt, and the quavering voice of the ex-seaman:

'Who is it?'

There was a faint scratching at the door but it might have been just the drawing of the bolt. Mrs Diefenback lunged forward and put her hand over his arthritic fist.

'Don't open it, Johnny.'

Johnny pulled the bolt and opened the door. For a moment I could just see his white, damp hair, and her frail bulk pulling the tail of his pyjama shirt. Then I saw her on the stoop. A small, solemn-faced child, about five years old, with raven black hair tossed over a plain white one-piece robe.

The old couple froze, as if touched by some magic wand. A cold fear flowed from their hunched bodies towards me.

'Lucy?'

The child seemed to look right through them, moving her lips, but without making a sound. The old man unfroze, breathing heavily, pulling the door wide open.

'Why don't you come in?'

They stood aside as the girl stepped forward, past the sliding door, into the ground-floor flat. The old couple still stood in the small hallway, gripping each other's gaze.

'It is Lucy,' the old man said in a weak voice. 'Go in, Gertrude. Make her a cup of tea.'

They looked at me with eyes full of a combination of awe, terror and a hope that could hardly begin to be conceived. The Rear-Admiral's mouth worked to produce words. 'We lost her, in nineteen sixty-nine,' he said. Then he lunged into his flat with a twist of desperation. Gertrude shook her head wildly and followed, round the curve of their living room.

I stepped out into the street. They were everywhere. A figure at practically every second door. They were all dressed in that one-piece Angel robe, mostly older men and women but younger ones too, and a smattering of children, poised on front porches, for all the world like a sudden glut of leafleting cultists come to bring Jesus Christ into your life. Except this was not Saturday morning, and the Saviour, whoever he was, seemed redundant. Down the road, from the direction of Hammersmith, a slow line of further figures was being disgorged by several Angelic bubblecars which had drawn up by the Godolphin School. They moved forward with a tentative but determined gait. I looked up.

The sky was full of ships.

Gee, I've always wanted to say that. But one likes one's harbingers of doom in fiction not fact. (It is Orson Welles behind all this, isn't it?) Flying versions of the Angels' bubblecars, of varying sizes, they floated silently across the crisp blue spring sky like white barrage balloons in a hurry. I could not begin to count. There were dozens of them, perhaps sixty or seventy at one time. Endless streams, moving at different heights, in all directions, south-north, east-west, diagonal. The crick in my neck, as I looked up and tried to encompass the whole field, reminded me of that rubbernecking in the Sistine Chapel, gawping at Michelangelo's glories. The creation, the vivid opening, and now the closing down sale. The beginning and the end. I ran back inside the house again, shutting the front door. Back in my familiar hallway. The old wooden hatstand, the mirror freshly cleaned by Gertrude Diefenback, the little table with the two baskets for letters. Still the propped-up circular from the Abbey National Building Society to a Mr Ricardo G. Goldberg, who does not live and has never lived at this address. Mrs Diefenback and I play this game of footsie for three weeks or so to see who weakens first and returns these to sender. Perhaps it contains one of those ubiquitous offers of fixed mortgage rates to 2009. All those zillions of unredeemed loans!! It's a long time since you had windows anywhere in corporate buildings you could jump out of. Who could guess the future would be in the past.

My mind is babbling, making every effort not to concentrate on the impossible present. The sliding door to my poor neighbours' flat being open, I can't avoid the impulse to look in. Not able to see into the front living room from the narrow hallway, I knocked on the door. No answer. 'Are you all right, Mrs Diefenback?' I called. There was a scrabble of movement and her face appeared in the living room doorway. It was wet with tears. 'Come in, Jerry,' she said. I stepped into the front room.

The Rear-Admiral was sitting flopped in the dingy old settee one of them must have brought over from Yehupetz, or at least the Shepherd's Bush flea market, his head lolling back, his eyes semi-closed, as if exhausted by the sheer magnitude of the event. The child was moving very slowly around the room, softly touching the TV, its quaint internal aerial, the rack of newspapers and magazines, the exercise bicycle (now I know why he always looked so exhausted), the mantelpiece and the set of framed photographs I had seen briefly but never questioned. A nest of tables had been opened up and a tray of tea, untouched cups and biscuits was set up by the settee's matching chair.

'You better have a cup of tea, Jerry,' said Mrs Diefenback.

'She won't touch it. There are some ginger snaps and gypsy creams.'

'Thanks,' I said. 'Maybe I will.' I sat down warily on a hard-backed chair and took the cup which the old lady passed me with a trembling hand. The curtains were closed and I could not hear anything from the street outside. The mute apocalypse. Mrs Diefenback sat in the dingy chair.

'I had Lucy when both Johnny and I were married to other people,' she told me. 'It was complicated. She was our love child. I was thirty-nine. We left our partners and came to live here together. People thought she was my grandchild. She was diagnosed with leukaemia when she was two. She spent months on end in the hospital. We buried her at Hammersmith Cemetery. I suppose she hasn't had very far to come.'

'It's the first wave,' I said, inanely. Anything to plaster over this obscene scene. The little girl took no notice of our conversation. It was as if she were trying to comprehend every object anew. 'I worked with the Recording Angel at the council. They had their own computer programme. Trying to access every person in the borough. Locations, balance sheets, prognoses . . .' I realized I shouldn't go any further. But the old lady wasn't listening anyhow.

'She won't eat or drink,' she said. 'We don't know what's wrong with her.'

'She's dead, Mrs Diefenback,' I said. 'She's still dead. The Angels never could tell quite how they'd behave. I suppose we all blocked out what they did tell us. We didn't believe them. We thought it was some kind of deception. An invasion from outer space, or some devious plot by our own government. Anything was possible.'

'I don't think she knows us,' said Mrs Diefenback, pouring herself half a cup of her own brew. 'Why should she? We're thirty years older. I was forty-four. Fit as a fiddle. Johnny was forty-six. A fine figure of a man. He was never at sea, you understand. Accounting.'

'I was forty-five,' said Johnny, lowering his head and opening his eyes. 'She knows it's us. She needs time to adjust. It's the shock. The long darkness. Like when you wake up from a very deep dream. You can't be yourself immediately. You need time. Don't rush her, Gertrude.' His face trembled with a repressed rictus. He shook his head as if throwing off water. 'I told you you shouldn't have thrown out the toys.'

'I didn't throw them out, I gave them to the hospital. You were with me, Johnny. Don't start that up now. What was gone was gone. That's what we all thought. That was life, wasn't it?' She turned to me, as an arbiter of that question.

'It, uh, certainly seemed that way,' I said. I couldn't take this one second longer. I gulped my tea and put down the cup. 'Listen,' I said. 'I'll look in on you later.' I got up hastily, banging the un-nested tables, skipping past the reunited family to the door. 'Don't worry if she doesn't eat,' I called back. 'It's normal. She doesn't need to. It's OK as it is.' Doctor Hackenbush's failed rescue. I beat a swift retreat upstairs.

The unmade bed, last night's dishes. The congealed left-overs of cheesy spag in the bin. Scattered piles of unread books. Unviewed videos. The old 586, with the dregs of the novel I thought I'd try my hand at way back when. Seduced and sidetracked by Lemmings Fifteen. I pulled up the rickety blind and peeked outside.

Goddamn you, Orson! Give up already! The ships were still sailing through the sky. You weren't lying to me, Hoppy, you fat faker! God, I wish I could wring that ugly duckling's pudgy neck. Where are you, Dodo? What price rebellion, and the Tory Restoration now? The roundheads and the dick-heads. And that's another fine mess you've gotten me into. Well, you only have yourself to blame.

The whited-robed figures were still trickling up the street, but the first wavers appeared to have vanished into the houses. Curtains drawn and blinds unpulled. How many action replays of the horror show I had just witnessed beneath? And the alarm clock tick-tocking to tell me it was still only seven-ten a.m. The day has hardly begun.

There were no messages on the answerphone. I looked at the phone. The phone looked back at me. The hell with it. I know I have that number somewhere. The Howards, Alice's mum and dad in Batheaston. Patricia and Jim. I know I kept those old address books. Or was it in the old Sharp Organizer? No, I let those batteries run out the memory years ago.

A hard copy. There must be a hard copy. Paper. A document. A living record. The phone book! London area only. Directory Enquiries! Automatic life can't have stopped. The line is still live. Dial 192. Busy. Busy. Of course, I suppose it must be: the dead phoning home. Would they get their fifty pees or BT phonecards pressed into their clammy hands as they emerge? Somebody's missed a surefire market opportunity if not. Updating guides – that's another one: *What's Happened on the Earth Since You've Been Gone*. Not that, if Lucy is anything to go by, they would care. They look a pretty morose lot . . .

Turning the whole place over. Since Karen left I can't find anything. I was always a martyr to the W. C. Fields filing system, all in apparent chaos but actually at my fingertips. No more. She took with her my sense of balance, and now I am awash in the swell. Larboard! Starboard! Helm a lee! Keep her to the wind, Mr UnChristian!! Pretty soon I am surrounded by wreckage. All the drawers, cardboard boxes, plastic holders and in- and out-trays of flotsam upended on the floor. Two old address books found but no Howards. I have the number of the Hotel San Rival, corner of Liosion and Paleologu, in Athens, but not a jot on Batheaston. An old yellowing fortune cookie slip: 'What you think might happen, might not.' Now they tell me. And who the hell is E. A. Zaghloul? My life refuses to pass before me in a flash. After an hour I lie exhausted in the debris, with old Access slips stuffed up my nose. The light streaming through the window, dappled by the shadows flitting over the sun. The sudden ringing of the phone.

'Gerald Davis, still alive!' I shouted into the receiver. It was my dad.

'That's good to hear, Jerry. Get yourself down here. You can't believe what's been happening.'

'I know what's been happening, Dad. It's been happening here too. I expect it's happening all over. It's the real McCoy, the genuine article.'

'Stop babbling, son, and get over 'ere. I'm at a coffee shop called Eco's Pizza. It's on the corner of Victoria Embankment and Bridge Street, just before Westminster Bridge. Sophie and me will be waiting for you. Get down 'ere as soon as you can.'

'I'm in Hammersmith, Dad! Do you think the District Line is still running regardless? All bets are off, Dad. Everything's different!'

'I'm asking something simple, you give me ideology! There's always a scientific explanation . . . I ain't got time now, there's someone you have to meet. Don't argue with me, Jerry, for once in your life. Trust me. This is important. Didn't you 'ave that old Nissan jalopy?'

'Karen took it to the Alleluias. Listen Dad, I have to wait for a phone call. You don't understand—'

'We'll wait for one hour. No, OK, make that one and a quarter. Seventy-five minutes. If we're not in the shop when you get here wait outside, someone will collect you. We should be together at this time, whatever's happening. Your mother needs you. And so do I.'

The man has never gone soft on me in his life. We all seem to have been changed in an instant. I looked at the cradled phone. What should I expect? She's not going to phone me. I saw the little girl. They have a different agenda, the Returning Dead. They're not into appointments, let alone dates. Dad's right, I can't sit here in this sty.

I took my bus pass and staggered out, passing by the old couple's now closed door. No sound from within. My Adventist neighbours were on the pavement, kneeling together, eyes tightly shut: father, mother, the five children, aged six to nineteen. The family that prays together frays together. The ships were still passing overhead. But the rest of the street appeared deserted. Perhaps it was all going to wind down? A trial run? Another impish test?

Those hopes were dashed when I reached the King Street Shopping Mall. It was like Christmas Eve, in ancient Bethlehem. Hordes of them, advancing up from the roundabout, still coming from the Hammersmith Cemetery. They milled about, mostly wispy elders, but with that straight, determined stride. A group of about a dozen Angels were checking them against their ubiquitous palmtops, corralling them into four large bubblecars resting on the site of the market, at the south of Hammersmith Grove. They all had that detached, rather puzzled stare, their brows furrowed, as if trying to remember. Many were moving their lips, some actually mumbling. An old, majestic woman with a shock of white hair, her sagging limbs apparent beneath the white robe, stopped me with a gesture. 'Laurel Road, Barnes?' The words came a little muffled but coherently. 'Laurel Road, Barnes?'

'I don't know,' I told her. 'You have to ask one of the Angels.' I pointed her towards the group but she just marched on, down King Street. This was not as efficient as it appeared at first. I began to imagine the scope for cock-ups, for massive errors, despite all the databanks. The circumstances were just too overwhelming, even for the Infallible . . . I pushed my way through the throng, towards the tube station.

The station was closed, of course. The gates locked, obviously unmanned since the morning. Even if one owned the joint, who would turn up? A neatly dressed, suited and tied elderly gent with a briefcase and a raincoat over his arm fumed and waved at me.

'Any excuse!' he cried. 'Any excuse!'

'It's the Resurrection!' I said to him, redundantly.

'Any excuse!' he repeated. 'Any excuse!'

Amazingly, astoundingly, we both spotted a taxi, edging

through the crowd, For Hire sign blazing. We almost collided as we sprang to hail it.

'Let's share,' I said. 'Where are you trying to go?'

'Victoria Station!' he called to the driver, putting his head through the cab window.

'There's no trains running, mate,' said the driver, a sharp-eyed, clearly relentless cabby. 'Streets are clogged. People, not traffic. All these Returnees. Don't give a monkey's, do they?' As a brace of them collided with his bonnet and veered off on either side.

'I'll take my chances,' said the elderly gent reaching for the handle, which I'd already grabbed.

'I want to get to Westminster Bridge,' I said. 'I know it's crazy, but what the hell. You can drop off this gentleman on the way.'

'Suit yourself,' said the cabbie. 'Meter charges.'

The gentleman glared at me but I had the handle. We both piled in, sliding to opposite sides of the seat. I clanged the door shut and we set off, warily, weaving through the advancing multitude.

11

The cabbie was a garrulous old pro. 'I'll 'ave to go dahn 'igh Street Ken,' he explained to us. 'The zombies are all over the Talgarth Road. I'll 'ave to go to 'yde Park Corner. No private cars arahnd, only them bubbles. Angels takin' the zombies 'ome. Me grandad drove a cab in the Blitz. Never missed a day's work, 'e said. Me dad was a cabbie too. Runs in the family. The wife wanted me to wait for Dad an' Grandad an' 'er own folks. But I told 'er, you can 'andle 'em. She 'as the two girls with 'er. Piece o' cake. They don't eat, the zombies. Jus' sit 'em dahn in front of the telly, that'll keep Dad 'appy. And Grandad, well, 'e'll just be tickled pink to see the kids grown up an' all.'

I did my best to clog my ears with mantras. Old Enfield and W. C. Fields routines. Clichéd catchphrases. 'You donwanna do it like thaat . . .' 'I 'ad that Jesus Christ in the back of the cab once . . .'

And what if she phones? Keep your nerve, Gerald. Messages from the Dead, on answer machines . . . what would I say? No, these are not the Loved Ones returning. This is another thing. The zombies. The living dead. Why couldn't they remain in our dreams? The taxi ride was shorter than I feared. The cabbie took the back streets avoiding the apparently endless streams of tottering robes and rushing bubble-cars. The sky was as cluttered as ever. Were these the same couple of hundred vessels circulating, or the thousands they seemed? Abandon logic all ye who enter here. Just go with the flow.

We dropped the old gent off at a deserted Victoria Station. No trains, no buses, no passengers, not even Returnees. An eerie emptiness, as if this once great junction of a live society was being deliberately made void. The man stood, waving his briefcase in the wilderness, shorn of his fifty ecu share of the fare. Some bubblecars curled round the roundabouts, keeping to the one-way systems. A last pathetic tick against the shrinking option of it all being an Olde Englishe lie. But hopes faded down Victoria Street as the robed marchers reappeared, trudging up from the direction of the river. Parliament Square was crammed with bubblecars. They looked like a mass of giant ostrich eggs below the old battlements of Parliament, Westminster Abbey, the clock tower with its time stopped at half-past four since 1997. Before he could back out, the cabbie was stalled in a mêlée of the white bubbles, which, in the absence of any traffic control, seemed to have got into an old-fashioned jam. My driver pressed his hooter in vain, the cry of despair of a doomed order already booked into the boneyard of history.

'Fuckin' 'ell. Who the 'ell's in charge 'ere?' Wouldn't we all want to know. I gave him my fifty ecu note and left him still stalled like a black rooster surrounded by eggs. Slipping through the jam in the square towards Westminster Bridge, looking for a way across. The traffic lights still working automatically, but here no one was taking notice. I found a chink and crossed over to the point by the Embankment where the pleasure boats used to dock. Visitor's Point.

They were coming out of the water. Naked, grey of flesh and countenance, dripping with weeds and rotting bits of rope and netting, with mud and flotsam in their hair. Steadily climbing out of the river on a string of folding ladders unfurled by the Angels over the river bank. A steady stream of them were climbing ladders up the side of the single docked river cruiser, *The Pride of Southwark*, helped over the railings by the waiting Angels who slipped a robe around each Returnee. Men and women, mostly young, many children, firm bodied, free of the bloated and distended look of the drowned. Old Father Thames relinquishing his victims. I could see them on both sides of the river, stretching right down to the Huntingdon Bridge. Heads bobbing, torsos emerging, hands reaching for the rungs. The slip slap of their wet feet as the Angels directed them up the steps, on to the Embankment, towards the bubblecars. I never saw this in Hoppy's databanks . . . What else had the bastard been holding out on me?

I steeled myself and pushed in among them, to cross the road towards the cafés by the closed entrances to Westminster station. My fingers brushed against them but they took no notice. Their flesh was clammy but not totally cold. 'Excuse me, pardon me, 'scuse I, beg your pardon.' Several Angels glanced at me with a certain compassion, or pity, but made no effort to interfere. We were all the same now, the quick and the slow. It was only a matter of organization. But I couldn't think, at this moment, of the next stage . . .

I found Eco's Pizza, and entered into an oasis of the world as it used to be. Steam from the kitchen, three young waiters in funny hats, the clink of plates and cups, plastic tables, and about a dozen people, live people, like shipwrecked sailors marooned in a hurricane. A couple of elderly tourists, holding hands across their table, three kids with parked rucksacks and bedraggled faces, two clerkish gents who seemed, like my taxi-sharer, to have defied the end of the world for no purpose, and a flustered woman who was trying to keep two small kids quiet with a Napoletana.

Dad and Mum were at a table in a corner, together with a fat, red-cheeked man with a shock of grey-white hair and a nose that must have graced a thousand pubs. He was dressed in ill-fitting dungarees and had the air of someone who had slept in the open air one night too many. Dad saw me and waved me over.

'What kept yer?'

Not a question that required an answer. I leant over to give Mum a peck. She still had her placard by their table. 'JOBS, NOT BLOBS.' Hope's slings eternal . . .

'This is Ben, Jerry,' Dad said. 'Ben, this is my son, Gerald.'

'An honour sir.' The fat man's speech was slurred, and he looked at me with eyes that were not properly focused, and a gaze that made me feel quite queasy.

'You won't believe what happened, Jerry,' said my father, a *non sequitur* if ever I heard one. 'Listen to this: we're pitched as usual outside Downing Street, when, suddenly, just before dawn, we see an 'ell of a lot of movement of vans and blacked-out cars. Not the little bubbles, but what looked like your old-fashioned badly disguised police vehicles. They park in a row just outside the Commons beside the bubblecars, who don't interfere. So we decide to move our pitch, to lobby the bastards, as they're the first sign of a civilian government we 'ave seen down 'ere for some time. But as we move down in the first light we see the first of these drowned geezers coming up from the river. It gave us quite a turn, I can tell you. But then things really got interesting.'

He paused for dramatic effect, taking out and lighting a small roll-up from the stash in his left jacket pocket. He took a toke and passed it to Mum, who declined. He passed it on to me.

'Westminster Abbey, eh, you get my drift? All those dead kings, toffs, prime ministers. They ain't gonna miss out on the action. It suddenly dawned on us when these naked geezers come out of the main gate of the Abbey. Creepy sight. Couldn't tell 'em from the rest, could you, in the flesh? The Angels come towards them with their white robes, but then these thugs come jumping out of those civilian vehicles, throwing blankets round these geezers and piling 'em into their vans. It all 'appens in a split second. The geezers from the Abbey are whisked away from under the Angels' noses. Doors slamming, vans and cars rushing off, across the bridge, with a fleet of bubblecars in 'ot pursuit.'

'Think of it, Jerry,' said my mother softly. 'I once took you to the Abbey when you were small, remember? So you should know the enemy. Henry the Seventh and Edward the Confessor and Elizabeth the First, all buried there, with Neville

Chamberlain and William Gladstone. And the poets: Chaucer, Browning, Tennyson, and the old Imperialist, Kipling. I'm sure I saw her, Jerry. Queen Elizabeth. A small, dumpy lady with short cropped hair. Very white face. I would know her anywhere from the paintings.'

'Angels of God,' said my father. 'Do me a favour. Can't see further than their noses. Right after the hoo-hah and the car chase, this guy turns up, hiding in the middle of our group. Whipped some spare clothes on 'im right away. Not a great fit, but it seems to fool the bastards. Talks, too, not like the other ones. And 'e's scoffed an éclair and two bottles of Peroni already. Owner seems to have a stash.'

'There is little to be gained in returning from the grave to a dry palate,' said the fat man. I understood that unfocused stare now, and why it made my stomach lurch.

'You know this man, Jerry,' my Dad said proudly, as if showing off his first edition of Trotsky's *Stalin Falsifies History*. 'We went to see 'is play together at the Royal Court, remember, on your fifteenth birthday? *Every Man in 'is Humour*. Puts Shakespeare in 'is place, I've always said it. 'Ere's a man who writes about real, spitting, ornery people, not about poncy kings and dooks. Buried in the Abbey with the nobs. What a joke, eh? Asked to be buried standing up, too, it's in all the guide books. Man after me own 'eart. Shake the man's 'and, Jerry: my friend, Ben Jonson, the greatest dramatist of his or any other age.'

12

Back in my flat at Iffley Road. From desperate isolation to Wembley Stadium. At any rate, a gang of four. Three live corpses, Dad, Mum and Jerry, and one dead live wire, Ben.

It had occurred to my parents that their own progenitors, mainly my grandfather, William, the black sheep accountant, grandma Edna, and great-grandpa, Joseph Duvid, and his anarchist spouse, Esther Saportchik, might be winging their way towards their home in Islington at this very moment, courtesy of God's own moujiks. Accompanied, possibly, by a phalanx of rabbis, rogues and Polish shopkeepers stretching God knows how far back. Or would they all be granted their ethnic vision, to be wafted direct to the Holy Land? The Jewish dead, I remembered, were supposed to gather in the Valley of Jehosaphat, under the walls of Jerusalem's Old City. And what of the Muslim Returnees? On second thoughts Jehosaphat could be writing another chapter in an age-old dispute, not incarnating a divine harmony.

But speculation is one thing, reality another. At any rate, my parents had decided to temper their scepticism with caution. They dragged Ben Jonson away from his Peroni and Eco's Pizza to their van, parked off Victoria Street since the breakup of the demo against God. The Angels in Parliament Square were still busy trying to channel the flow of the drowned. They had organized their bubblecars in four straight lines now, and were directing the traffic like well-trained policemen, ushering the queues along with the flap of their wings. They paid no attention to the living or to our guest in his 'human' attire. I would have thought they would be able to sniff out his post-mortem state. But there was clearly something different about him. Was it the fact that he had been buried standing up, the blood not congealing in the dead brain? At any rate, he seemed to become more alive by the minute, huffing and puffing as he strove to keep up with us, and becoming quite red in the face. It made me think, if there's one, what about others? How many deviations from the norm? Is there a norm? And if Ben Jonson, what about . . .?

Alice . . .?

'We have to analyse this thing as objectively as possible,' said my father, rummaging in my kitchen and expropriating my last jar of dry-roast peanuts. 'There's not been one day in my life in which I've believed in God or any other super-natural being. I can accept that there are phenomena that science can't explain, but mostly I've always believed it's what people think and do that counts. People 'ave imagined and constructed all kinds of cultures and belief systems. We've passed the days when we 'ad rigid categories between rational and irrational thought. We lived through the beginning and end of a system which claimed to be 'olly rational but was in the end a failed religion, nothing more. That still doesn't validate God, the church, the priests, mullahs, rabbis. While we were waiting in that pizza place one of those evangelicals turned up, with a personal sandwichboard. "Beware the Wrath" and all that jazz. 'E was completely shattered. Wanted to give us 'is sandwich board, gratis. Now that what 'e foretold 'ad 'appened 'e 'ad nowhere to go. Signor Eco gave 'im a free coffee but 'e didn't touch it, and soon staggered out. What's going on out there is nothing to do with religion, son. It's something else. A chemical imbal-ance. The ozone layer collapsing. Two centuries of pollution. We fucked the planet, and it's fucking us back. All this business with God and the Angels, it's a cover up, a front, a mask. The powers that be 'ave seen this coming and they prepared this elaborate deception, to get themselves off the 'ook.'

I'd heard this all before. I had to tell him, it made no difference now. 'The "powers that be" are as flummoxed as you are, Dad. I know, I was contacted by them. The Tory Party in exile. They've gone underground, Dad. They're living like a bunch of troglodytes in bunkers under our feet. I've seen 'em there. The Dodo and the Lory and the Eaglet and the Mad Hatter.'

'Now don't you start, son. Just because everybody's losing their marbles doesn't mean you 'ave to lose your cool. Stay calm, Jerry, we 'ave to think this through.'

'I think we should phone the house,' said Sophie. My mother had taken the opportunity of her visit to check out my poor excuse for a shower, but kept mercifully silent about the gunged up plughole. Now she was lying on my sagging sofa in a bath towel, a sight for poor Ben Jonson's sore eyes. He was swivelling his peepers between her and the video of the Great Fields in *It's a Gift*, which I had stuck in to keep him quietly awed. 'I know it sounds crazy,' said my mother, 'but what if they get there, and there's no one there to, you know . . .'

'To what?' asked my father. 'To bring Dad 'is slippers? To listen to Grandpa's spiel about Cable Street? What will a seventy-eight-year-old dead Stalinist 'ave to say about being brought back again? What will 'e say to see us all being chivvied about by an 'orde of bleeding ponces with wings? And *bubeh* with 'er fucking potato soup. I have to think it out. We can't just barge into this. There must be something we can do.'

'There's nothing we can do, Dad. It just is. It's happening.'

'It's 'appening! Listen to 'im, Sophie. The lost generation. Telling dumb jokes and poncing abaht on television like clown jesters. The kings used to keep their clowns to 'ave somebody abaht who could speak without fear. A safety valve to make sure they didn't miss out on the gossip behind their backs. Just a bleeding tool for the oppressor. Well, the working class ain't totally dead yet.'

'Everybody's going to be totally dead soon, Dad. In exactly two weeks. If this stage happened on schedule, we can be pretty sure the next will take place.'

'The Last Judgement!' Dad nearly choked on a sharp nut. 'Do me a favour, Jerry! Just don't swallow everything. There was six billion people on this planet before this Rising thing, and now 'ow many? If everybody came back? They did the sums on the telly, before it all was shut off with penguins. Three 'undred and something billion billions. At least. And they're all going to line up in one day at little booths that will say: this way to 'eaven, this way to 'ell. Every single one will be judged. That should take at least a million years. It's illogical, Jerry. You're not using your 'ead. The whole thing is completely fishy.'

'What about him then?' Sophie pointed to Ben Jonson, who was staring goggle-eyed as Fields tried desperately to prevent the blind old Mr Muckle from shattering his shop window while finding kumquats for a customer.

'I don't know,' said Dad, sitting down in my hard chair. 'I don't know what to think now. Maybe I was carried away. Just because a naked man runs out of Westminster Abbey and answers to the name . . .' He raised his hands in despair and shook his head. 'Look at 'im, he's perfectly at home at the end of the twentieth century . . . As 'omey a couch potato as anyone.'

The couch potato looked round at us. 'God's lid, this is a fair device. I have seen Master Dee conjure his visions in a crystal ball, but it hath the composition of a pig's bladder to compare. And grandmaster Roger Bacon caused a ferret to vanish into thin air inside of a metal vas. But this device doth piss on both of them.'

'QED,' said Dad, rising to look out of my window. He drew the curtain aside and stood there for a moment.

'Jerry, come over 'ere and take a look,' he said quietly. I went over and peeped into the street.

It was one p.m., and we had been in the flat for about half

95

an hour. We seemed to have been in this new world for ever, but hardly half the day had passed. The sun shone out of a clear blue sky. A bubblecar had drawn up by the next house. The other houses, up and down the street, kept their secrets shut away. Not a cat moved. When we had come in, clattering up the stairs, downstairs had remained locked and silent. It was like a Sunday on which nobody wanted to wash the car.

The bubble disgorged two old men and three old women, all black, in the standard white robes, with quiet and dignified postures. The bubble didn't wait to see if there were any greeters. It sped off in its tedious routine. The old people stood, gazing at the building. They looked around with an acute perplexity, beyond the bewilderment we had already come to recognize in the Returnees. Then they began to chant, a low African dirge which grew and rose in folds of heartache and pain. We heard the fumbling tread of the next door neighbours down their stairs, and the pulling of their front door bolt. Then the Adventists were at the old folks' feet, weeping, kissing their toes and their ankles. The man, Rodney, lifted his face to the sky, but no words came out.

And the sky was again full of ships.

13

'The second wave,' I looked at Dad. 'And they didn't come from Hammersmith.'

He turned away from me, pursing his lips.

'What are we going to do, Joe?' my mother looked suddenly very tired, very subdued. That occasional Italian melancholy that peeked through when the committed mask slipped.

'I'm not going to go without a fight,' said my father. 'There must be a resistance somewhere. And don't talk to me about Tory undergrounds.' He raised his hand to stop me speaking. Sitting down and nodding at Ben Jonson. 'This man, this man 'as the key. He's been there. He's been a part of it. What is it like, Ben? How did you come awake? Was it a sudden jerk or was there a process? Did you see anybody while you were dead? Do you 'ave any idea who's really done this?'

'This staccato speech, it doth offend the eardrum,' quoth the dramatist, turning his head reluctantly from W. C. Fields. ''I faith, I remember very little. For the greater part of't, whatever the duration, I recall composing a new play, in my cerebrum. It would contrive to build upon my little fancies of *Volpone* and *The Alchemist*, and in't would personages such as Roger Bacon, John Dee, Raymond Lully, Paracelsus and Claudius de Domenico strut the celestial stage. 'Twould follow in inverse direction the *Divina Commedia* of Dante Alighieri, commencing in a decline from Paradiso, via the Purgatorio, towards Inferno, where Satan himself is charteled to a duel by maestro Bacon. But I had only reached Act Four, Scene Three when, suddenly, the light burst round me and I found my corpus lifted from out the tomb . . .'

'Four hundred years is a long time to think of a play.' Dad

was becoming increasingly irrational in his search for rationality.

'Marry, 'twas quicker when I was young,' said the playwright, 'but death doth slow the humours.' There was a roguish glint in his eye. Dad leant forward, unwilling to give up, but then the phone rang. My heart leapt like an electrocuted dolphin, but it was only Marek Maus, from St John's Wood.

'Have they brought out your dead?' his voice echoed with desperation. Usually Marek is Mr Phlegmatic. But who can be surprised. 'Dad and Mum are here,' I told him. 'They don't want to go home, in case the old folks are really waiting.'

'They'll have to face the music sooner or later,' he said. 'Anjeska has got the guest room and the living room chock-a-block. We have Jerzy and Andrzej, and Marta, and Jasek, and Zbig, and Tadeusz, and Krystyna. Did you ever see that movie by Andrzej Munk, set in a Second World War prisoners camp? The prisoners are all living off the glory of the captain, who escaped from the Germans. Only he's not really escaped, he's being hidden in an attic inside the prison. That's what it feels like here. They somehow found a stash of Stolichnaya on the way and now they are singing the "Warszawien", a capella. Grandpapa Stach, who flew a Spitfire and was lost over Hamburg, got here a half an hour ago. You can just imagine what's happening back home.'

Where did they get the booze? This was all my mind could latch on to. 'Are you there, Jerry?' he insisted, breaking my silence. 'So far this is a pretty pathetic apocalypse. Isn't this what we deserve? It's like running *Metropolis* backwards, the proles coming out of Moloch's mouth. Did I say proles or Poles, Jerry? Each species gets the end it deserves. I knew it when I first saw those sexless puffy Angels. Faceless clerks of a bureaucratic Jehovah. No brass gongs, no trumpets, no Renaissance visions of luscious transmutations, transfigurations, annunciations. Everything seems to have been coolly calculated, except the individual response. The story of our time, eh, Jerry? Listen, why don't you come over? I know you're not Polish, but you're family to me. Come here, we'll have a two week party. We'll see the world out with a bang.'

'You're pissed, Marek, and I envy you,' I told him, 'but I can't come. Maybe I'll look in later.' I put the phone down and cut off the sounds of Slavic revelry. I shook my head at Dad's quizzical glance.

'Let's try the telly again,' said my mother. I turned, cutting Ben cruelly off from his Fields, to the channels, but they were all, as they had been when we came into the flat, blanked with identical cards:

DUE TO THE RESURRECTION NORMAL SERVICE WILL NOT BE RESUMED. DIRECTIONS AS TO THE FINAL DISPOSITION WILL BE BROADCAST AS APPROPRIATE.

I hate yellow on a blue background, but beggars cannot be choosers.

'If TV's been cancelled,' I said, 'it shows this is really serious.'

'Can we return to the jester's masque, sirrah?'

I acceded to Ben Jonson's peeved request. The screen flicked back to my hero trying to grab a kip on the porch through the interruptions of a myriad vicious objects, and an insurance salesman looking for a Carl LaFong – 'capital C, small a, small r, small l, capital L, small a, capital F, small o, small n, small g, LaFong, Carl LaFong.'

'I'm not going to stay in this madhouse,' said my father. 'I'm going back to the 'ouse, dead men or no dead men. We'll phone around, Sophie, we'll call a meeting. Rejig the Ad-Hoc Committee. Organize, Educate, Mobilize.'

'What about Ben?' asked my mother, pulling the towel off her head and heading back to the bathroom to change. 'We can't turn him in and we can't just abandon him. We're responsible, Jerry. We took charge of him.'

'Are you suggesting we spoiled something?' Dad was combative. 'What did we do, foul up 'is life? He ain't got one. Where were they taking 'im anyway? Where are they taking all those billions of dead people from previous centuries? They can't be all traced from Jamaica to 'ammersmith. They must 'ave camps somewhere. Massive gulags. Huge internment centres where they sort 'em all out. See who can work and who can't. No, that can't be right. There wouldn't be any point in killing 'em now, would there? They're already dead. They must be taking 'em to other planets. Colonization. That's the story. Whole solar systems of slave labour. It'll all come full circle. People will fight it. Even if they're dead, or 'alf dead. The whole cycle will return again. Exploitation, struggle, rebellion. You're wrong, Sophie, it's far from over. It's only just beginning. There's a job for us. There's work for people who keep their wits abaht them in this mess. Keep our eyes and ears open. Keep our minds alert. All those centuries of effort, they're not wasted. The Levellers, the Chartists, Captain Swing, the French Revolution, the Tolpuddle Martyrs, all the bloody struggles of socialism, all the efforts of ordinary people to better themselves, to break free, to clean up the planet, to de-nuclearize. It doesn't just end in a religious apotheosis. God or no God. Life continues. Even after this so-called "last judgement". And if there's life, there's struggle. And if there's struggle, like it or not, there's dissent, and even revolution.'

'I'll vouchsafe that, sir,' said Ben Jonson, turning warmly from the video. 'Those are true words and bold, sirrah. I count myself of that company. King or no king. Enough is enough. How did Will put it: "We happy few, we band of brothers . . ." Not that he did not suck cock in his time . . .'

'Where there's life, there's hope,' said Dad, decisively. 'Let's go, Jerry. Go pack a bag. The bare essentials. We won't be coming back 'ere. We 'ave to stick together now. It's family. And if old Joseph Duvid's up, he'll not be taking this lying down . . . What are you waiting for, Jerry?'

I'm waiting for the wake-up call. I'm waiting for the dig in the ribs and the light to go on and the cry to go up of 'Candid camera!'

I'm waiting for the telephone to ring. Then I remembered that Dad kept an old address book that was crammed with every number he had known since the Miners' Strike in 1984.

'Dad, do you have the Howards' number in Bath?'

'Oh no, Jerry. Please forget about that. I knew you'd think of it. I knew you'd brood. One of the reasons why I called you out to White'all. Don't think about it. What's the point, son? Look at them all, they're not what they used to be . . . they can't remember.'

'He can remember: Ben Jonson. He eats, he drinks, he makes bad jokes. He quotes Shakespeare. He's still writing plays in his head. Marek Maus has a whole World War Two squad of Polish oiks singing songs and boozing at his girl-friend's.'

'Flukes, Jerry. Nothing good can come of it.'

'Give him the number, Joe,' said my mother, coming out of the bathroom loaded for bear, in her dungarees and red head-band.

'It's not a good idea, Sophie.'

'He has to set his mind at rest. Do it.'

Dad, shaking his head, produced the big dog-eared volume from his side bag and riffled reluctantly through it.

'Here it is.'

I dialled the number. Bath 0225 X X X X . . .

The phone rang and rang.

Then a weary voice answered.

'Mr Howard?' I said. 'It's been a long time. It's me, Jerry, Jerry Davis. I'm calling from London. I'm here and . . . I know this is difficult. It's difficult for all of us. But maybe you understand. Is . . .?'

'I understand you, Jerry,' he said. 'We've been expecting your call. We didn't have your current number. You want to speak to her?'

'Yes.'

There was a pause. He had cradled the phone. I heard him call out. 'Alice! It's Jerry.'

There was another pause and the earth stood still. I motioned to Dad, who turned down the video sound. Beyond the wall, I could still hear the cacophonous combination of Christian hymns and African keening in the apartment next door.

There was a fumble at the other end of the line.

'Jerry . . .?'

14

Among Michelangelo's Sistine Chapel frescoes there is one that caught my special fancy. In it God, the archetypal angry old man with a beard, flings his arms out towards an orange disc of the sun and a purple moon. Behind him two chubby startled cherubs look out, and two other figures, with shawls, cower behind the folds of his robe. To the left of the sun two angelic figures are flying off, looking back in alarm. The outermost has his robe fallen round his thighs, revealing the cleft of the arse. It was difficult to make out details from that distance, even with the restoration, as we ants craned up. I remember pointing it out to Alice:

'We're all caught running away with our pants down.'

Am I running away or towards? The road to Bath runs along the M4 motorway, which springs out direct from Hammersmith in its concrete web. I am travelling in Dad's ancient Volkswagen van, emblazoned with his old defunct newspaper's logo: *THE NEW SOCIALIST* – NEVERTHELESS FOR A CHANGE. Sophie insisted, and Dad reluctantly agreed, that I should take the vehicle. At the end of the day your parents still harbour some soft and sentimental feelings towards you. Love? And where does that stand in this topsy-turvy world?

Imagining Rome, or Florence, or Siena, or Assisi, at this insane moment: Michelangelo, Leonardo da Vinci, Raphael, Botticelli, Bellini, Giotto, Piero della Francesca, turning up, ready to resume where they left off. In Amsterdam, Rembrandt, Van Eyck, or Bosch. And is there a Turner or a Constable milling about among these white-robed hordes upon this wretched isle? Shakespeare staggering about in

Stratford, bemused by all the memorial mugs. Or was he, too, grabbed by some Ultimate Rescue Force of the State, like Queen Liz and the Abbey mob, and spirited away to an unknown debriefing? One can imagine the scene, in one of the Carrollian bunkers, the Mad Hatter and the Magian Tudors. Confess, Edward, ya big palooka! Now Mr Chamberlain, I have this piece of paper . . . Gimme a break. And are there similar rescue squads around the globe poised to snatch George Washington, Vlad the Impaler, Attila the Hun, Ivan the Terrible, Adolf and Benito, Julius Caesar et al from the clutches of the egalitarian Angels, to some special or even more sinister fate? Is there a power struggle I am not aware of, beyond the Dodo and his deep Caucus? Was there a God Patrol, a Divine Early Warning System, in a secret state beyond the secret state?

So much has been foreseen by science fiction that nothing has been foreseen. We thought we knew it all and knew sod all. As the oldest SF of all grabbed hold of us . . . Genesis and Revelations.

Everyone who ever lived, that's a tall order. Dad is right, something's got to give . . .

There is no traffic on the motorway, not even bubblecars, although the flying eggs are still skimming overhead. A little thinned out, towards the mid-afternoon, 3:00 p.m., possibly siesta time. There had certainly seemed to be no lunch break. I stopped right at the crest of the first motorway junction, Junction One, and left the car to cross the barrier and look over the edge of the inbound lanes, remembering the cemetery at the foot of Gunnersbury Park. Curious to see the manifestation at its source. But it was not at all what I expected. The cemetery looked tranquil and abandoned, no trace of disturbed graves, uprooted tombstones, or gibbering mud-caked zombies pushing their way up through wet earth. There were only the traces of trampled lawns left by the vigilant relatives, who had now gone. It was as if nothing had happened at all.

I drove on down the M4, feeling like the last man on earth. Going to rendezvous with the last woman. The new Adam and Eve, alone and poised to breed the new race – homo less a sap perhaps than he turned out before. But this dream, too, was not to last.

First, I discovered that I was not alone on the road. A small, nondescript red car, either a Nissan or Mitsu, was following me, about two hundred yards behind. Between Junctions Two and Three I tried to slow and speed up, but it kept its distance. I thought of stopping, but I decided to postpone the surprise, whatever it was, and see how far we two were destined to be conjoined. Then at Junction Four, the turnoff to Heathrow Airport, I hit the obstacle. A huge knot of bubblecars of various sizes, blocking the road ahead and winding down the approach roads to the great complex of terminals, warehouses and the stationary aircraft, frozen as if by a magic wand in an eerie, ear-splitting silence. Away down the tarmac I could see, as I crested the blocked crossover, the vast shapes of three of the Angels' motherships, each thrice the width of the 797s parked immobile on the apron. I had never seen them this close before, and the glare bouncing off their pure white hulls made it difficult to avoid looking away. A stream of bubblecars was converging from the ships towards the junction. Presumably reinforcements in preparation for the Big Day of Truth to come.

I slowed down, of course, and stopped before the barrier. There were Angels trudging across the lanes. It had always struck me as strange, even after the scenes in the Fulham Leisure Ground, that the Angels appeared to display none of the grace and ease associated with their image. Rather they lumbered along stolidly, sometimes like nothing so much as the Three Zillion Stooges, even when they did not try to fly. Though these phalanxes did in fact take off over the edge of the motorway, making a short Wilbur Wright spin down to the hedges of the southern end of West Drayton. They took no notice of me, at first, as I gingerly crossed the lanes with them, after glancing behind me to see my tail stop about a hundred yards back. No one got out of the car. I followed the Angels up to the crash barrier as, one by one, they took a short trot and swept down. I stopped, transfixed.

The hills were alive with the mounds of Sioux sick. No, that was an old gag from . . . was it a Sid Caesar show? But the ground was covered, as far as the eye could see, with walking bodies, naked, I suppose one has to say now, as the day they were dead. They were walking, I could see from those closest to the road, in a fairly natural manner as if out for a morning stroll, except that all were walking at the same pace, though not quite fully synchronized. They seemed like a million human sheep, grazing over the meadows, striding unfazed through brambles and hedgerows, turning to avoid poles or trees. They were, literally, spread to the horizon, west to Slough and north to Uxbridge and Hayes. All converging on Junction Four. It was as if the entire world had been given the same check-in time for ten thousand flights, and had been instructed to bring no items of baggage. Not even one cabin bag per person! The mind, boggled enough, slid off the edge.

There was, I could see now, a small cemetery beyond the first perimeter road. But it, too, seemed as unscathed and undug as the one I had passed before. I tried to focus my shimmying eyes on the approaching faces but there were far too many. There was something different about these people. It seemed insane, but they did not appear local. Despite this they were obviously fresh arrivals, as I could now see the Angels below the motorway swarming forward, clothing the hordes with their ubiquitous white robes as they climbed up the verges. The first of them were being directed on to the incoming approach road, towards the cars. The faces were a little clearer now, but even more unsettling, for they did not seem completely human . . . Their chins were just that little bit heavier, their foreheads narrower, their noses wider, yet their skin was pale and European. They seemed to be coming from far, far away, not in geographical space, but in time . . .

Everyone that ever lived.

'It's a sight to see,' a familiar voice agreed just at my shoulder. 'We should thank our lucky stars the electoral rolls are closed. Would they have voted us in or out, I wonder?'

The Dodo was standing beside me, pinch-faced as ever, stockbroker stripes, ghastly mauve tie and all, hands folded in front of him and lips pursed like an estate agent wondering if he has underestimated demand. His small red Mitsu was parked just behind my Dad's old crock.

'Not much hope for the revolution, is there?' I said to him, miffed at his being able to creep up on me unawares although we were the only two live people, it appeared, in a fifteen mile range.

'Oh, I wouldn't say that,' he said, with Bertie Woosterish sang-froid. 'As the pressure increases, the cooker cooks harder and harder. Eventually something blows. It really isn't my concern any more.'

'Indeed?' I said into the ambience. 'What happened to the stiff upper lip? Fighting 'em on the beaches and in the betting shops, in Marks & Spencer's, Lewis's and Harrods?'

'They don't give a toss,' he jerked his head towards the Angels, who were ministering to the mass of Returnees regardless of our presence. 'They knew about it all the time. We weren't immune. The Caucus was invaded. Dead relatives came down the tunnels and the chutes. We weren't at our home addresses, you see, so the Wingos brought them to us where we were. The Mad Hatter's old man and old lady turned him into a leaning tower of blancmange. He was a brigadier under Churchill and she was the Dowager Lady Whatnot sired by Simon Legree off the Graf Spee. Lory's dead young hubby. Eaglet's mum and dad, aunts and grand-aunts and what have you. Not a whiff of security clearance. Guards all got the treatment too. Russkie plot, we would have said in the old days. Comic cuts. Whole place in a complete uproar. Like having the whole thing happen in a submarine. Chock-a-block. Standing room only. Definitely not cricket. Saw a film

107

like it once. Russian movie: *Solaris*. People on a space station; had fantasy characters come to live with them in their cabins. Dead wives, lovers. Made them very upset. Long-winded picture. Very mystical. This whole bloody thing, have you noticed, there doesn't seem to be that much religion in it. Once you get over all the outer trappings, God, Archangels, rising Dead – where's the moral issue? The big questions: right and wrong, good and evil, body and soul? What is the soul if it's all bodies, endless bodies, marching on to glory? What's the bloody point? What are they judging us for? And who's to judge? Don't tell me, I've given up.'

'I suppose it's all at the most basic level,' I said. 'I hacked as far as I could into the databanks. Heaven or hell. Except that Hoppy did tell me that it isn't the end of the world.'

'You could have fooled me.'

We stood there, on Junction Four, watching the Angels process the hordes of Dead into the bubblecars, which took off for sites unknown. The larger transports filling as many as two hundred at a time and shooting down towards the airport and the colossal motherships.

'Relatives in Outer Mongolia, I shouldn't wonder,' said the Dodo. 'They all look a bit Chinese to me. Neanderthal man? I was never much good at anthropology. The study of Man. We just assumed everybody and his dog were after the same thing really: a secure roof, a good guzzle and a shag with the right person at the right time. Some needed more than others. Picked out the greedy ones. Heigh ho, the "information" game. *The Prisoner*, remember that series? "What do you want? Information!" "You won't get it!" "By hook or by crook, we will!" "I am not a number, I am a free man!" Ha ha ha ha ha! Burst of lightning and that thingie ball coming on up out of the ocean. Amazing what those chaps could think of. But they couldn't think of this. Much older show. Iron copyright. You're heading west, young man?'

I nodded. I was going to ask him how he had picked me out this day, even though nothing seemed absurd amid this madness, this monstrous place in which all balance had been wrecked. But he guessed my question.

'Came out of the Caucus with nothing but my mufti,' he said, looking down at himself disarmingly. 'No one was paying attention to the work. Weeping, wailing, caressing. Eaglet lost a kid to cot death. Rolled in on an Angel's arms. Couldn't take any more. My father and mother died in an automobile accident in Australia. Twenty years ago. Knew they would turn up. Saw myself as a drooling zombie like the rest of them, losing any thread of thought. Melt-down of the personality. No more free choice or free will. Scarpered sharpish, exiting Soho. Wall to wall. Crawling mass. Pushed my way through Baker Street, where it thinned out a bit. Hot rodded this car. Should have taken a BMW or a Rolls, but remembered all those Mitsu ads. You know, go round the world on a tankful? Thought I'd be inconspicuous, didn't realize I'd be practically alone on the road. Staked out your house. Apologies and so forth, but I thought . . . God knows what I thought . . .'

I looked at him with new insight. He was fidgeting, sniffing the air like a dog, shuffling his feet. He didn't meet my gaze but looked out on to the saints who were still marching on.

'Did you have a son, Dodo?' I asked him.

'Pathetic, isn't it?' he said. 'We think we have depths but we're like bloody glass. Stupid cliché. White ragga. That's what they called it. White kids who went with black bands. Played his gigs. Did drugs. The crack scene, early ninety-four. Somebody machine-gunned a dance hall. Hackney Palace. Can you believe it? Just kids having a good time. I loved that boy. The crazier he acted to annoy me the more I loved him. The more bizarre he looked the handsomer he seemed. We were slaving in the pit so he could play the fool whichever way he wanted. As long as he was full of life and . . . alive. I didn't mind. We tried to learn from the past. Let it be. Beatles, wasn't it? My wife went crazy. Blamed me for not caring, as if I could have played the Iron Hand. Left on my own with the tinkling tunes of old England. The incredible shrinking England. A dumb idea for even dumber times.

'Still,' he said, giving me again that shrewd old glance, ' "it's an ill wind that blows no good." I've been having all these old sayings rattling through my head the past few weeks. Like life reduced to just a set of very simple notions. "What can't be cured must be endured." "Blood's thicker than water." "The proof of the pudding's in the eating." "A man's a man for all that." '

'Why didn't you wait for your son?' I asked him. 'Didn't they bring him to you underground?'

'He didn't turn up,' he said, simply. 'They told us in all their leaflets, didn't they? Returnees would be consulted where they wished to go? God knows, I suppose,' he laughed. 'God knows literally where he asked to go. Probably to Trinidad, where his idol, Shagga Hugga, came from. He was gay, my son, homosexual. Had a crush on the big black boy. No racial slur intended. Part of our life, or was. All those funny fears we had. Gone with the wind. Alyson blamed me for that too. Insufficiently macho fathering. Guilty as bloody charged.'

As more and more of the prehistorical (?) Englishmen and women marched on to the motorway we retreated towards the cars. I could not now bear to see those vacant faces up too close. One of the motherships rose, suddenly, without the trace of a noise, into the sky. It hovered for a brief moment and was gone in a twinkling. A great rush of wind whooshed over us to fill the wedge of displaced air. Some Angels tumbled over their wings, but picked themselves up and went on with their task.

'Should have had that lot in the National Health,' said the Dodo. 'Would have cured understaffing at a stroke. What a farce. Listen, Gerald. If you want me to fuck off I'll fuck off. But I'm an old idiot with nowhere to go and I expect I know where you're headed. The girlfriend. Alice Not Liddell. If you can bear the company for a while. We can back off from this traffic jam and find a way round to link up with the A4. I'll drive behind you and you can just shoot off if it suits you. When we get to Bath I can take the fucking waters. Drown myself like a good old-fashioned Roman senator. Won't do me any good, will it? Just come back like a Crazy Zombie from Hell. Maybe then I could make 'em take me to my son. Good thinking, Batman.'

'Forget it, you silly old bastard,' I told him. 'Why don't you just dump your little buggy and join me in the van? It's my Dad's cross-country special. There are a dozen full jerrycans in the back, and all the gear. Three spare tyres. She'll reach Land's End. We living people ought to stick together.'

'It's amazing, isn't it,' he said. 'When there's a crisis, there's always a reason to co-operate. I think you have just articulated a whole new category of ethnicity. Or specificity, if you will. Fuck Mitsubishi.'

'*Sayonara.*' We saluted the abandoned saloon and, backing off from the glut of transports, beetled back down the M4.

15

Through Cranford and Feltham we turned to the Staines Road and the A30, which was clear, though this meant we had to head towards Egham and Basingstoke, daunting prospects at the best of times gone by. The Dodo, who had cheered up a little, gave me a quick run-down on events around the world, as recorded by the monitors in the Caucus, before other priorities diverted them from their duties.

'TV crews staunchly rolled up on the White House lawn,' he recounted, 'hoping to catch Jack Kennedy and forty-four other presidents. But the only one who turned up was Grover Cleveland, and no one recognized him until he'd gone in. Nobody saw JFK, or Roosevelt, or Lincoln. They must have all returned in other locations. The biggest thing over the pond, just as expected, was Elvis. Two million people waited at, what's it called, Graceland. When he stepped out of the bubblecar it was pandemonium. Transmission stopped almost at once. And we were left with just fuzz and a loud, crackling mush. Not that I could ever tell the difference . . .'

'What about the rest of the world? China, Russia, the Middle East? What about the Return of Muhammad? And Jesus? Wasn't that what we were all supposed to be waiting for?'

'Great Expectations. What a let down. We had the same disruptions from all those key areas. As if our guardians were minimizing the impact. We saw glimpses of Mecca and Jerusalem, both completely swamped with Returnees. Then cut-out. From Japan we monitored coastal collapses. Hordes of the blighters climbing out of the sea. In Berlin a crowd waited for Hitler at the shopping mall that covers the old bunker. Unless they were just stocking up. Wobbly scenes of the Angels disabling weapons. One eyewitness claimed the Führer and Eva Braun and about a dozen others were seen being loaded together into a bubblecar, destination unknown. After all, he had his folks, hadn't he, in some German-Austrian border town? Everybody has at least a mother. Naked they came into the world and naked they're coming back in again. The rich and the poor, the good, the bad and the ugly. We had our own flap, down at the Abbey. Disentombment of a whole bunch of mackamucks.'

'I know,' I said. 'My dad and mum were there. Somebody snatched them before the Angels could move in.'

'Special Royal Defence Squad. Very hush-hush. Certain Royals had occult anxieties. Amazing what comes in useful. Preserving the heritage. Took 'em all off to Sandringham. Imagine them sitting there with Elizabeth the First and all the Henrys, glowering at each other over the dunkin' donuts. A nightmare for the succession, eh? Not that it matters now. All grass is as flesh. Who gives a flying fuck?'

Who, indeed? 'There was one that got away.' I felt I could safely tell him. 'Ben Jonson. The playwright. My parents picked him up. He turned out to be a more lively corpse than most of the living.'

'You don't say? I saw one of his plays, once. *Volpone*. Sharp stuff. Oh yes. They're all back, aren't they? Shakespeare and Marlowe and Proust and Cervantes and Dickens and Shaw and Oscar Wilde – oh, there's a man who'd have some words for all this!'

'Mishandling a first coming is a misfortune. Mishandling the second sounds like carelessness.'

'*Touché, mon brave.*'

As we barrelled on down past Bagshot and Frogmore, Hartfordbridge and Phoenix Green. The last day of an April spring, fading towards May. A handful of cars on the road, with people huddled inside, one couldn't tell whether living or dead. The landscape surprisingly barren, though the bubbles were still flying overhead, as much a fixture now as the Jumbo jets in a previous age thundering in and out of Heathrow. The Dodo beside me looking more than ever like a retired stockbroker heading home for the weekend. I, watching myself in a detached manner as my hands steered Dad's van towards a rendezvous with the dead love of my misspent youth. A modern Tristan riding towards his Isolde. Or wasn't it the other way around? He took the poison, and she keened . . .

No point in mythology when it's all happening before your eyes. Or did I drink the poison potion, somehow? In the morning I'll wake up and laugh it all off as I confront my bleary puss in the bathroom mirror. Yes, It Was All a Dream. What a sucker. Show him a few pale faces in bedsheets and he'll believe the moon is made of green cheese. Just pull yourself together, man. Switch on the PC and think of a few good jokes for the autumn comedy season:

Muhammad, Jesus and Buddha meet at the Pearly Gates . . . Aw, forget it. Where is Hoppy now that I need him? Six days to go, and then – 'What will you tell them at your trial, Dodo?' I asked him. 'Is it still stiff upper lip and whistling Bogey? Do you think there'll be a counsel for the defence?'

'I doubt it,' said the Dodo. 'It sounds like the army game. "Sergeant, read out the charge." "How do you plead, soldier?" "Two weeks confined to barracks. Dismissed!" Everything on the double. No chance of a plea bargain. No jury, neither. Diplock rules. I could challenge the court's jurisdiction. Didn't do much good for the Irish, though.'

The shadows lengthened as we entered Basingstoke. An empty town, in contrast to the massed Junction. Even the dead won't be seen alive here. And not a feather of an Angel. Just one poor lost soul, in his winding sheet, flagging us down. An old gent with silvery hair and that familiar glazed look. I stopped and poked my head out the van window.

'Are you all right, mate?'

What a ludicrous question. He bent down towards me, his mouth working without words. 'Poor sod,' said the Dodo. 'The Angels must have mislaid him, or delivered him to the wrong place. Where do you need to go, sir?' The old man could not emit words. I snatched the pad with attached pen that Dad always kept on the dashboard and handed it to him. He looked at it as if trying to remember and then scrawled an address:

58 NASTURTIUM AVENUE

I slid open the door and the man climbed in the back seat. 'You'll have to direct me,' I told him wearily. So we set off, into the suburbs of Basingstoke, guided by a bodily ghost who had been perfectly happy to be a pile of mouldering bones only last night. I had to shake my head to remind myself that all this had begun barely thirteen or fourteen hours ago. When homo sap still held sway ... What are we but poor imitations of something that doesn't want to be poorly imitated any more?

How far back is it going to go? Are the Neanderthals of Junction Four the end, or the beginning? Are we going to meet the Missing Link, in his zillions, straggling over Salisbury Plain? And what then? Will all the monkeys awake? The gibbering of primal desire ...

The dead man mercifully knew Basingstoke. It was still light when we arrived at a small street of identical houses with identical white gates leading to identical neat little porches. We dropped him off at number fifty-eight and waited as he slipped the gate latch and walked up to the front door, which opened to show a stooped old woman in the doorway. He turned to wave to us and stepped in nonchalantly, as if he had just returned from a normal office day, and the door closed behind him.

'The English,' said the Dodo. 'Isn't it a marvel?'

Nothing is a marvel when the normal has ceased. We pressed on to join the A4 at Newbury. More clusters of the Dead, staggering up from a large cemetery left of the road. Once again no sign of disturbed turf or uprooted graves. A traffic Angel waving us past. Now the light was really failing and the Dead were picked out in the headlights of the van like moths fluttering too close to a candle. Like kangaroos in the Australian Outback mesmerized by the beams. I had to slow and manoeuvre through them with ultimate care as the night fell. Who knows what might happen if you knock down a Returnee? They look anything but indestructible. Ben Jonson apart, they did not look as if they might outlast the seven day deadline even if it were abolished – or extended? Forlorn hopes. Everything so far was going according to the plan hatched by that 'black hole' over Ecuador . . . 'And is it still there?' I asked the Dodo. 'At the last accounting, yes, I suppose so,' he said, becoming less and less sure by the minute. How I missed Ben Jonson already, the man who had stood on his own two feet in the underworld . . . And was there a way out of Eternity? Should I have stayed with Dad and Mum to plot and carry out the ultimate dissent and rebellion?

Night proper, and the dead drifting all over Wiltshire. This has always been a spooky county: corn circles appearing in the small hours, girls with head-bands muttering over magic crystals and cod-Druidic blood rites, with, occasionally, the sacrifice of a free-range chicken. How mundane it all seems now, with the dead picking their way through the hedgerows, waiting patiently by the verge for their transport. The Angel cars giving off a luminous glow, like perfect fireflies flitting who knows where. It all had a kind of austere beauty, but was a total hazard for the motorist. Quite literally, because there was only one. I gave the wheel over to the Dodo, realizing I was becoming incapable of distinguishing between the road and hallucinations.

Batheaston. This is where it gets personal. Moment of truth. The lights of the houses glittering on either side of the main road into the town. Bubblecars once again filling the sky. It must be the Resurrection rush hour. That old, recognizable turn to the toll road, and the quaint old bridge which charges cars ten pence a crossing, carthorses five pence, stagecoaches three ha'pence per passenger, sheep a ha'poth the head. Right at the top, the old red-roofed house with the annexe built by Alice's father with his own two hands and two drunken builders, sloping at a familiar crazy angle. We slept there, with the old folks shifting and sighing on the other side of the bathroom. Young blood. And now I am the one who feels dry and desiccated, like the mad scientist in that old movie *Doctor X*, with his musky croak of 'Synthetic flesh!'

It is I who am returning from the dead. And she, in the reconstructed bloom of youth, reborn from the shards of burnt offerings to the gods of mass transit. A second chance, an unimagined possibility, that could last at most for six days before the Reckoning . . .

I parked the van. The Dodo and I climbed out from its opposite sides, bent as crabs. The fireflies of the apocalypse flitting above us. Or is that static sliver the moon? 'Time, stand still,' cries Mr Fotheringay. If the earth stopped, we would all fly off, into oblivion. But oblivion is now a fixed object.

'Afraid, Gerald?' said the Dodo, standing at my shoulder. That English reticence, with only pseudopoda touching.

'Fucking terrified,' I told him. My knees were practically knocking. My teeth chattering in the warm air. I was poised at the declining pathway to the porch, that cracked step at which I had always stumbled, and her hand poised to support me.

'Watch it, Jerry.'

'Do you want me to wait in the van? I can curl up in the back and heigh ho.' That English discretion. Defunct manners. So many generations, centuries and millennia of convention and habit down the drain. Should one dress to the right or to the left? 'Wife Divorces Husband, Ate Peas With Knife.' All those thousands of books on good etiquette. *The Scarsdale Diet. How to Succeed at Cost Accounting. DIY Scuba-Diving. Breed Your Own Rabbits.* Everything that made life – life. The whole damn messy schmeer.

And now it's dreamtime.

'Don't be an ass, Dodo. Come hold my hand.'

He walked a couple of steps behind me down the path. I stood on the porch with memories flooding back to me. The old walks further down, towards the canal. The river walk along the Avon to Bath. The bridges and the majestic Georgian houses. The Pizza Hut where we spread out our maps and guide books and planned our return to Italy. We were going to do Florence, Siena and the rest of Chiantishire. We were going to commune with Michelangelo and Botticelli and Fra Angelico and Piero della Francesca. We were going to construct our own Renaissance. Our Return to Eden, God notwithstanding. I reached the front door. A warm light glowing within.

Knock knock.

'Who's there?'

16

I sat, with a cream scone balanced on my knee, staring at her. The air in the living room was almost suffocating. The Howards seemed to have insisted on keeping the windows closed, perhaps in case unauthorized Dead clambered through. They had good reason – they were not alone.

I might have known it. There were twelve other dead people in the room to whom I had to be introduced in turn. Jim Howard's parents, Evelyn and Evelyn, Patricia's parents, Greta and Matt, three aunts and two uncles, I was not sure whose, and three grandparents, Joss, Ermintrude and Adoniah. There were about fifty untouched cups of tea scattered on every surface, and enough uneaten currant cake for a salvation army.

The Howards were perched on their sofa, red-eyed, with Brian, their eldest son, her brother, looking at me as if I were the intruder from hell. They looked more dazed than the Dead, the eldest of whom, Ermintrude, was busy knitting in a corner. She had a garish mauve sleeve already half finished. I did not want to think who it was intended for. One of the uncles was lacklustrely scanning the *Batheaston Echo*. Others were absentmindedly playing with their teaspoons or feeling up their own fingers. The Dodo squatted on the floor among them, Arab fashion, having accepted a tall Bell's from our host.

What do you say to the girl who was your first love, at nineteen? The fresh breeze of the oldest cliché? The peck of her lips on my cheek reviving me at the doorway. They were surprisingly warm, the breath a little musty.

'Hi, Jerry.'

Her voice as resonant as it had been earlier in the day, on the phone. 'Are you coming over, Jerry? Dad and Mum are a bit upset, but I'm OK.'

Rooted to the spot, my imitation of a pot plant.

'Alice.'

But I'm the one through the looking-glass. The touch of her hand, a little moist, but not cold. The soft blonde hair, the green eyes, the almost baby soft skin. They had dressed her in an old T-shirt and jeans. The other Dead, in a profusion of old sweaters, peering at me, round her back, with apathetic compassion. The family dog, Buster, nuzzling her crotch and whining breathlessly for us both. Amazing that he was still alive, after ten years, that geriatric Labrador, with hair like a lawn-mowered carpet.

'Alice.'

The Dodo's firm hand on my shoulder, and his stout whisper. 'Steady on, Geronimo.'

And the tremble of her voice. 'I'm OK, Jerry. Come in and say hello to the folks.'

The Dead are nothing if not polite, and apparently docile . . . the legacy of that long immobility. But what appeared in the mass a resigned uniformity breaks down at closer quarters. As we the still living sit there, trying to cut swathes in the currant cake, troublesome looks shoot out between the Returned generations. The grandparents clearly less than enamoured to see their offspring older than themselves. The children unnerved at their younger parents. Once they all recover their ability to speak, I wonder what might be in store. There might be a stern logic in the Angels only allowing a week between this cataclysmic day and the next . . . But a week is a long time in ontology . . .

'Alice.' I am reduced to puerile repetition. If I say it three times, is it true? The futile attempt at private glances in the midst of this reunion of epochs. And who might yet knock at the door in the next wave?

There appeared to be no room for small talk. My teacup

clinked like a battleship. Grandma's knitting needles were like machine-gun fire.

Mrs Howard's mouth opened wordlessly. She seemed to have been struck as dumb as her guests. What can she have had to say to her daughter: 'What are your plans?'

'You should go to bed, Mum.' Brian, the Good Son holds her arm. He used to be an army engineer. He was ready to build bridges across war torn battlefields. Later on he became a surveyor for the Bradford and Bingley Building Society. 'Alice should be in your room tonight. She's had a hard day.'

Not an argument that could be refuted, despite its ulterior motive. He never liked me, the neo-fascist martinet. 'We should all take stock of this situation and sleep on it. Talk it through in the morning.' I loved the intimation of options. 'I'll look after the guests. Jerry, I think you'll have to rough it. The old folks are in the spare room and the annexe. But the shed is clean and I've got some sleeping bags.'

He never rose above lieutenant-colonel. But somebody has to take command in a crisis, and it certainly wasn't going to be me. I sat dumbly with my teacup in one hand and a crumbling cream scone in the other, as Alice followed her parents quietly out the room.

'Goodnight, Jerry.'

'Goodnight, Alice. See you in the morning.'

We bedded down in the garden shed, the Dodo and I, in Brian's old Ordnance Corps sleeping bags. The Dead did not sleep, remaining in the living room, coughing and mumbling between themselves. Perhaps, after all, they knew something we didn't. Brian had set out some packs of cards and an old Scrabble board that wrenched my memory, but there seemed to be no takers. We saw him through the kitchen window, bustling to make more and more cups of useless tea and pig-headedly extracting from the cupboard more packets of digestive biscuits.

There was no way I could sleep, with or without a sleeping bag. My head, between two spades, was leaning against a rusty, broken, tyreless bicycle. I remembered it well. She used to ride it into Bath and back, up and down the Wiltshire hills. Pumping those lithe and strong leg muscles . . .

'Dodo.'

'Yes.'

'Are you asleep?'

'Working on it, *ya habibi*.'

'What's your real name?'

'Norman Leonard Armstead. Of the Nottingham Armsteads, not the Chingford's. They were streamlined loansharks. Our lot were Action Men. Brawn not brain. The sort of people who gave you Passchendaele, Suez, and the Falklands. It seemed a good idea at the time.'

'What am I going to do, Dodo?'

'I don't know, Gerald. It's a sticky one, isn't it. Looks like grounds for an elopement.'

'Does she see me as what I was or what I might have been? Is it really her? I don't remember the freckles. And that spot under the chin. I can't be sure about anything any more.'

'Rose-tinted recall. I remember my son as a toddler. All blue wool and soft bootees. Those chubby cheeks. Before the safety pins and studs and the dreadlocks. He had a tattoo of Haile Selassie, the Lion of Jah, done on his right arm. Or was it the left?'

'I don't think I can cope with this, Dodo. It just takes me back to the first weeks after she died. That feeling as though I had been plastered against a brick wall. Everything stopped, except the agony. Time had no way to move. It had just stuck, so nothing could heal. And Jim and Pat, and the funeral. And then you realize that you just have to walk away. You just have to turn your back. You have to betray the memory. After all, it was just an overgrown kid's dream. It was never real. It never came down from the clouds. I never saw the spot under the chin. I should never have come. I should have stayed in Hammersmith.'

'We should never have done anything that we did. "Vanity of vanities," saith the preacher. "What profit has a man of his labour which he took under the sun?" Not a bloody sausage.'

'Would you have lived differently, Dodo?'

'I would have stayed in Barbados. They offered me the station. Keeping an eye on the Yanks and their bloody missile projects. Could have sent the bastards in Curzon Street blueprints of vacuum cleaners, like Alec Guinness, *Our Man in Havana*. Settled down with a local dusky maiden. Bouncing coffee-coloured babies. Ragga rags. Show the white world a clean pair of heels. Become a character in a Conrad novel. Drink myself into the next world.'

'Why didn't you take it?'

'Ambition. Brain damage. Hubris. The rat race and the cheese in the mousetrap. Married an air-vice-marshal's daughter. Didn't realize exactly what vice. In which we serve. Yes, minister. Remember Maggie Thatcher? A bit before your time. Her husband made money out of garbage companies in Florida. And what was it all for?'

'You tell me, Dodo.'

'Sweet FA, boy, sweet FA.'

A familiar doctrine of despair. So what do we do? Commit suicide? Now there's a purely temporary solution . . .

I couldn't sleep but I fell asleep anyway. Either that or it was a crossed line of miracles. I dreamt that I was being taken up into the sky in one of the Angels' motherships. They had me spread out naked on my stomach on a billiard table, with a catheter up my arse. It was the old aliens-from-outer-space-rectal-probe plot. Alice was there, imprisoned inside a plastic dome. The Angels had attached a tube to her private parts and were pumping in their ripening seedlings. Before my eyes I could see her stomach inflate and grow into a bloated pregnancy. Strange, inchoate forms moved inside her. I wanted to cry out but my mouth was stuffed with feathers. A gnarled old Angel, who looked like Dorian Gray after the transformation, was pushing his elbows into my groin. They were hard and bony as an ancient washerwoman's. I woke up in a sweat to find the Dodo rolling in his sleeping bag over my legs, muttering. I pushed him off and he lapsed into a discordant snore.

This couldn't be endured much longer. I felt as if I were entombed in the shed, with every other tomb in the cosmos emptied. Somehow I disengaged myself from the sleeping bag and pushed open the creaking wooden door.

The garden was full of dead people. They were squatting all over the squashed shrubbery, the ornamental plants, the green lawn. They were all naked, men, women and children. All pensive and silent. Had the Angels run out of robes? I had a vision of the celestial weavers standing around a broken loom. Or an industrial stoppage against unpaid overtime. There must have been a couple of hundred of them. Waiting, perhaps, for instructions? I tried to avoid their gaze, fearful that if I gave any sign they might all rise and follow me like the Pied Piper of Hamelin. Thank God I hadn't brought my flute.

'Jerry!'

I turned my head towards the fierce whisper. She was standing by the back door of the annexe. A svelte ghost in her yellow T-shirt and old denims, her white face and the blonde cascade of her hair strobing in the luminous flicker of the bubblecars in the sky.

I walked through the Dead towards her, brushing faces, knees, limbs. None of them tried to stop me, or even ask for spare cash. I reached Alice and we embraced as if it was the simplest thing in the world.

'Let's go, Jerry,' she said. 'I don't want to stay here. I know what's coming. I love Mum and Dad but I don't want to spend eternity with them. I want to spend it with you.'

What can one say to such an offer? Leaping over the dead shards of expectations, political correctness and dreams . .

'I'm not going to heaven,' I told her. 'I looked it up in my file. Hoppy, my Angel, showed me. I'm down for the other place.'

'I don't care,' she said. 'I know I lost you once. I know I died. It's no big deal. It just takes time to recover. I want to go with you now.'

I didn't hesitate a second time. But I still had a problem.

'I can't abandon the Dodo,' I whispered. 'It's a buddy, buddy thing. A man's gotta do. It's probably a good idea to have him along anyhow. He can drive part of the way and he knows secret places.' Her driving licence must have lapsed on death, I convinced myself. My brain was whirling incoherently.

'It's OK,' she said. 'I don't mind. But don't wake up the living.'

We walked back through the apathetic Dead, down the garden. The Dodo was still tossing and turning, mewling like a buggered sheep. I shook his arm.

'Wake up, Norman Leonard Armstead,' I told him. 'We're taking your advice. We're eloping. Snore three times if you want to stay.'

'I'm up,' he said immediately. 'I'm moving. Get me out of this thing.'

We bounced him out, like a nocturnal sack race. Threading our way to the peripheral pathway. Skirting the house on tiptoe and heading up towards the main road. Before we got there we were ambushed by the geriatric dog, Buster, who wheezed up between our legs.

'Go home, good doggie,' Alice urged him. But he was having none of it, and followed us to the van. The Dodo slid the side door open as quietly as possible. We clambered in, pushing the dog in the back.

'I'll drive,' said the Dodo. 'At least I can keep my eyes on the road.'

Alice and I got in beside him. He gunned the motor. But before we could move off a figure appeared at the passenger side window. It was Ermintrude, Pat or Jim Howard's dead grandmother, carrying a small blue holdall.

'Let me in,' she said. 'I want to get out of here.'

We shook our heads, but she rattled the handle. 'I'll holler and wake everybody up,' she said determinedly.

'OK,' I said. 'Get in the back.'

She climbed in spryly, joining the dog, which embraced her.

'This is a fine kettle of fish,' mumbled the Dodo. 'Where do y'all want to go?'

'Where do you want to go?' I asked Alice.

'I don't care,' she said, pressing her arms around me.

'North, to Alaska,' I told the Dodo. 'Settle for Inverkeithing.'

He released the handbrake, and we shot off, executing an illegal U-turn, back up the A4, towards the motorway.

17

Ermintrude was demolishing every stereotype I had built up of the fatalism of the Dead. She was, it appeared, Patricia Howard's great-grandmother, not her grandmother, and had been born in 1871, in the year, she reminded us, of the Paris Commune. She had become a pioneer of women's suffrage and had served a term of three months' penal servitude for pelting Prime Minister Gladstone with an egg. In 1901 she had had an affair with Bertrand Russell, who was then working on his massive collaborative tome *Principia Mathematica*.

She had a great deal to say about 'Dirty Bertie', who, she said, had his knickers washed only once a month. Her next lover was a crazed Polish poet, Wladislaw Polonek, who wished to establish a free love commune in Essex. Had he waited ninety odd years he would have not caused a single dislocated eyebrow, but at the time he was drummed out of the shire. Ermintrude lived with him in deep squalor in Paris until he blew his brains out with his service revolver. He does not seem to have served anywhere, but everyone had, she assured us, a service revolver in those days.

In the First World War she was an ambulance driver and was almost executed for pacifist agitation. But before then she had already managed to marry Patricia's great-grandfather, a penniless student, who fathered a son on her and then escaped to Zanzibar. The son was brought up by Claire nuns in Bournemouth, and later in life became a landscape gardener. Ermintrude was obsessed, she revealed, throughout the nineteen-twenties, with a desire to assassinate Bertrand Russell for hypocrisy and grotesque dereliction of hygiene. But in the forties she settled down with a third husband, Cole

Frobisher, of Frobisher and De Wytte, Glazing Consultants. He had the largest prick in the Midlands, she told us. But she refused to have any more children. Before she died, in 1953, she left instructions to be buried next to this paragon, but something went wrong, because she was in the wrong cemetery when she Returned. Following her traditional dissidence, she had refused to give the Angels an address, and therefore found herself dumped with relatives she didn't know from Adam. This was why she needed to escape, to check the Frobisher Plot up in Leicester.

Leicester, incidentally, happens to be the origin of one of my greatest idols, Joe Orton of blessed memory (and where is *he* now!?). But why did I need to hear all this guff? I knew we should have left her by the side of the Batheaston road and dashed off. She was dead anyway. But old taboos die hard. Remembering that old Scottish ditty: 'Ye canna shove yer Granny off the bus.' So here she was, curling our ears, ten times gabbier than ever Ben Jonson was.

As an elopement, this did not look promising. But what view can one take of 'the future' when it consists of less than six days?

Here I was, living the impossible dream, reunited with my first and greatest love – pause for violins – on borrowed time (diminuendo), the meter ticking like hammers piercing the skull.

Here's a challenge, for the Last Comedy Act of All Time. Not even Max Wall could have dreamt of this one. Ladies and gentlemen, as I went into the Lost and Faust department . . . Nothing can work. How can there be laughter on the actual edge of the grave? This is far beyond death – this is really serious!

Dawn glimmered as we drove up the M4, joining the M5, into the heart of England. The night had apparently been a short hiatus. Like the Apaches, the Dead rose only by day. The first pale light brought the motorway alive with bubblecars, and the flickering fireflies in the sky became a glut. The fields were once again alive with the Dead, advancing over the green belt like a massed combine harvester. They reminded me of the sheep in a Tex Avery cartoon, who leave not one blade of grass behind them.

'How many people did they estimate in total,' I asked the Dodo, 'from the beginning of homo sap to the present?'

'Seven trillion, or seven million millions, from Australopicanthropus,' he said. 'We did calculations at the Caucus. It drove our mainframe quite spare. You'd be surprised, but there will still be some spaces. Roughly an inch and a half spare for each body. Population compounded, as you know. But stretching your arms will be a thing of the past.'

'We'll be crying out for Judgement, by tomorrow.'

'I wouldn't be in such a hurry.'

'It'll be all right, Jerry.' Alice squeezed my arm. Throughout the journey she had been using it as an anchor. Perhaps to life, though that was too mad to contemplate. What could be going through her mind? And, in those ten years in which her . . . what was left of her was in the ground, where was that mind hibernating, as it must have done, to be recaptured at that moment, of the Rising? The implications were still unfolding: for every mind, every constituent aspect of the personality of each risen Dead must have been floating somewhere in the great unknown . . . or was that what we were all in touch with in our memories? Was anyone marking all this down?

The old saw, Where does the soul go after death. It bothered Plato, didn't it? I can see him now, pursued up the Acropolis by paparazzi, all howling: 'So where did it go, Aplaton?!'

'We'll tell them we're in love,' Alice said, in my ear. 'It worked for David Niven – in – what was that old film . . . ?'

'"*A Matter of Life and Death*."' I recalled. 'But that was quite a different story. He jumped out of his burning Lancaster bomber, without a parachute, but his Angel missed him in the English fog. It was a cock-up in the divine bureaucracy. A black and white heaven, not very appealing. Lots of forms and red tape. It was earth that was in technicolor.'

'I won't let you go without me,' she said.

'Young love,' cooed Ermintrude. 'It was the same for me with Wlad in Paris. He wanted to fuck five times a day but the opium slowed down his performance. He wanted us to make a suicide pact, and leap off the Eiffel Tower in mid-coitus. He was a wild young thing. My father warned me about Poles, but he didn't prepare me for the filthy habits of the English nobs.'

Mine did. I thought of poor Dad with a sudden pang, more of curiosity than anything else at this stage. We were coming up to the Lower Wick service station which seemed deserted, apart from an immense mothership which filled the container truck parking lot. The Dodo suggested we might forage for provisions in the station mall. There was no need for inhibitions, given it was the end of civilization as we knew it. We cautiously disembarked. At closer view, there was a smattering of the Dead wandering about the place, just kibitzing, eyeing the abandoned souvenirs and chocolate-bar dispensers absently. A very elderly dead woman was gazing raptly at a display of teddy bears in the Kiddishoppe. There was a row of Telecom booths which none of the Dead seemed to have any use for. Who knows what century this lot had come from. In the raw, untagged, unspeaking, all of human time appears to collide.

I rummaged in my pants for a card. It had not occurred to me that any of these artefacts, such as money, might have any use now. I had nothing, except some tiny two ecu coins. I dialled the operator, but there was no answer, as expected. I signalled frantically to the Dodo, who, bless his rejigged heart, handed me a chargecard.

'The card code is 67548,' he informed me. I was in luck, the automatic voicelink was working. I picked out my Hammersmith number, but got an engaged tone on the first three digits. Everyone who knew how to use a phone was obviously using one. The Dead calling the living, or vice versa. I tried eight times, and gave up. Then I tried my parents' home number in Islington. The phone rang, and a voice answered.

'Who iss dis?'

It was a rasping, male, Eastern European accent. I instinctively homed in.

'Who is this? Joseph Duvid?'

'Joseph Duvid? Dat's me. Who's speakink?'

'You don't know me. I'm your great-grandson, Gerald Davis. Is my father there, Joseph Davis?'

'Joseph Duvid? Dat's me.'

'No, I mean your grandson, he's also called Joseph, Joseph Davis. Or my mother, Sophie, Sophia?'

'My mudder? She's not here. I tink she must haff gone maybe to Warsaw. Maybe to Prszemysl, dat's vere her people came from.'

'I don't need to speak to your mother, er, Joseph. I need to speak to my mother, your granddaughter-in-law. Sophia and Joseph, they are the people who live in the flat that you've come to. I'm your great-grandson and they're my parents. It's very difficult to get through on the phone and I have to speak to them.'

'My grandson? He's not here. Dey vent out to organize de resistance. Ve are not goink to take zis lyink down. You understand me? Dis is not gut for de vorkink class. I fought de fascists in Cable Street. Osvald Mosley, he vanted to be Gott also. Den ve had Hitler. Ve fought. I vos in Italy. Ve shed our blut for freedom. Ve are not goink to knuckle under to any bosses or any religious autorities. Religion iss de opium off de masses. Dey say ve haff come back from de dead but it iss chust anudder trick off de rulink class. Dey tink dey can get chust dat little bit extra out of us. But I von't giff dem de satisfaction. Ve are goink to fight. Ve are goink to organize. You listen to me, dis iss chust de beginnink.'

'Is Ben Jonson there?' I tried another tack, to get this lunatic out of my ear.

'Ben Jonson? I don't know no Ben Jonson. Dere vos a Marty Johnson in de Bet'nal Green Branch. But he vos in der Independent Labour Party. I didn't belief dose people can be trusted. And I vos right. Vun hundred per cent. Mosley vos in der Independent Labour Party. Do you know dat?'

This could not go on much longer.

'Can you give him a message? No, not Marty Johnson. I have nothing to do with Marty Johnson. To my father, Joseph Davis. And my mother, Sophie? Tell them their son called.'

'From vich cemetery?'

'I'm not calling from a cemetery! I'm alive.'

'Now ve all are! Dey say it's a miracle, but I'm still suspicious.'

'You don't understand. I'm alive, I always have been, like my parents. Listen, just tell them Jerry phoned. Tell them I'm all right and I'll try to phone again but it's difficult. So many lines are engaged—'

'I'll giff you a gut line dat's free,' he said. 'Ready to vear! Dat's de cominik trend. It'll sveep de country. I guarantee it. Gut qvality, easily affordable for de vorkink man und voman. And if some rich man makes some money from it, I don't care! It's a gut tink.' He lowered his voice. 'But don't tell my vife. She'll report it to de central committee.'

I rang off. It was quite hopeless. Alice came up and hung on to my arm. The Dead were ambling about the shopping precinct, some of them carrying out useless items of merchandise, such as suitcase locks and talking books. One upright, gimlet-eyed soul had carried a pile of tuna tins from the Delimart, and was trying to make them bounce against a wall.

'ET phone home?' I asked Alice. Resurrecting an old private joke. But she shook her head. She had already told me she had left her parents a note, and that was it. It seemed that, on my limited observation of the three dead people I had picked out so far – Ben Jonson, Ermintrude and Alice – there was a notable lack of scruples in their interface with the living world. Or with the rest of the Dead, for that matter. Something had got lost on the way. Was it conscience? Or humanity? What did those words mean any more?

132

I had hoped the drive up the motorway would give me time to sort out my thoughts. To calm the blitzkrieg in my brain. Ermintrude had put paid to all that. Not to speak of the dog nestling between us. The Dodo suggested we take a rest in the station cafeteria, before ransacking the place for food and staples.

'Better hurry, before all the tuna is gone.'

He went over to switch on the coffee machine. It was good to be with someone survival-trained. He had been on a course, he told me, where individual commandos were dropped on remote northern islets contaminated by nuclear waste, with a geiger counter and a water divining stick to reach the nearest safe haven. 'It was not only your upper lip that got stiffened,' he reminisced fondly.

We had worked out our strategy in the van. Just before Birmingham, at a place called Stock Green, said the Dodo, there was a secret regional bunker, another 'Caucus', built in case of nuclear war. If the pattern observed in London pertained here too, a reasonable assumption in the circumstances, its official function would by now have been aborted by the flood of Returnees. The Solaris Syndrome. Providing we could find our way in, however, we stood a chance of finding one of the bunkers-within-the-bunker, otherwise known as the Red Queen's Rooms, where we just might be able to ride out the next six days, bypassing the Judgement, to emerge on the seventh day, the Day After, to – what?

'You never know until you try,' said the Dodo.

It certainly sounded a better bet than marching on the Angels with banners drawn and bared proletarian breasts. My poor ancestors, ever determined to be on the losing side.

The aroma of freshly brewed espresso wafted over from the Dodo's brave efforts. By force of habit he brought cups for Ermintrude and Alice too, though neither tried to take a sip. So far, Ben Jonson had been the only dead man I had seen eating, and he could probably scoff for the lot. Another possible result of being buried standing up . . .

Still amazing what you end up taking for granted. My dead resurrected girlfriend beside me. Her dead great-grandmother, leafing through *Vogue*. 'What's all this about the return of "Hot Pants"?' she mused grumpily. The coffee helped a little, but not that much.

A commotion at the entrance to the shopping arcade interrupted my runaway train of thoughts. A whole group of Dead, fresh in their white sheets, came striding up in a military formation. They looked very young, vigorous, and un-English. Darkly handsome, Mediterranean looks.

'*Quid hoc sibi vult?*' One, who was clearly a ringleader, called out, making a beeline for our table. I suppose we stood out in our living mufti.

'I beg your pardon?' I said, espresso in hand. The leader swept his hand round, knocking my cup right across the room.

'*Quid hoc sibi vult?*' he repeated. '*Quo jure damnatis nos? Qui tacet consentit!*'

'*Omnia mutantur, nos et mutamur in illis,*' said the Dodo, looking the man straight in the eye.

'*Roma locuta, causa finita,*' said the man. He motioned to his cohorts, who began kicking over the chairs, throwing ashtrays and sugar dispensers about, leaping behind the counter and trashing the racks of stale donuts and buns. Others grabbed hold of the milling dead browsers and began manhandling them into a corner. One tried to grab hold of Alice, but the Dodo kneed him in the groin. Another seized me round the throat in an armlock. Ermintrude, pulling her knitting needles from her holdall, thrust at the assailants, piercing them in the thighs, arms and torsos.

'What the fuck . . . ?' I managed to huff out before my windpipe cut off. Luckily, help was at hand. A band of Angels, wings flapping, rushed in, as if from nowhere, with pointed metallic rods. At the touch of the rods the attackers went limp, pulled back and then filed out sheepishly. The Angels followed them, mumbling and skittering.

'*Vivit post funera virtus,*' said the Dodo, picking himself off the ground. We rallied together, gasping, though Alice and Ermintrude looked not much the worse for wear.

'What was all that about?' I wheezed at the Dodo.

'Roman soldiers,' he said. 'Probably the Ordovician Legion. They must have been killed here, in one of the wars against the old Brits. Colonial habits die hard.'

'Fascist brutes,' muttered Ermintrude, putting away her needles. They hadn't seemed to have made much impact. Lucky for me I was not on the receiving end. 'They were the same under Mussolini.'

'I think we'd better move on,' said the Dodo. We abandoned our abortive coffee break and proceeded to the Delimart, filling up three trolleys with tinned foods, long-life milk, bottled water, pasta, rice, tin openers – remember all those desert island cartoons?? – matches, candles, paper plates, cups, serviettes. Watching carefully for Angels, or rampaging Roman and possibly other troopers, we rushed our booty back to the van.

18

We parted from Ermintrude at Junction Nine of the M5, where we had to stop due to a broken-down bubblecar which lay across all three lanes like Moby Dick taking a break from Captain Ahab. It was a mini-daughtership, about thirty feet round, and was the first Angelic transport I had ever seen stalled. About five Angels were gathered around it, with their usual bird-like twittering, massaging its hull with what appeared to be giant soap cakes. Alice, the Dodo and I climbed out of the van to stretch our legs and gaze at the by now familiar vista of Returnees ploughing their furrow. When we turned back to the van Ermintrude announced she had convinced the Angels to take her to Leicester.

'I can't leave Frobisher fretting much longer,' she said. 'He's so utterly useless on his own. He can't even fix a light bulb.'

It was frankly a relief, as we watched the repaired daughter-ship lift off with the great-grandmother inside, not quite waving from a window. Her parting words to us were, 'I should have shot Dirty Bertie.'

But the road was clear, apart from the bubblecars and the ubiquitous Dead in the fields. We sped on, the geriatric dog asleep and wheezing in the back. Alice untiring by my side. Though I was becoming less and less sure about what lay at the end of her dazzling gaze. It was not death, but a different kind of life that seemed to glitter in those pupils . . . What kind of thoughts were churning around behind there? What kind of memories beckoned?

'This is the turn-off coming up,' said the Dodo.

It was Junction 6, the outskirts of Worcester. I knew nothing about the town, only the sauce. But we turned away, down the A4538, on to the B road, past Gallows Green. This was a slow process, as the Dead were drifting, naked, in droves, over the road. Like a mass convergence of nudists. Instantly redundant comedy themes stirred in what was left of my brain: a whole new set of road signs, hazard messages illustrated by coffins, or a Bela Lugosi figure, complete with cape. DEAD XING. But we honked at them and they moved aside, enabling the Dodo to locate and turn down an un-marked narrow road across a nondescript, slightly less crowded field.

'Still a lot more shipments to come,' commented the Dodo. But Alice did not seem to respond. No solidarity among the Dead. I had realized that when we left Bath with Ermintrude. Everyone yearning to reduce back to microcosm. The nuclear family, the proton, the quark. The smallest item in the gargantuan mass. I had sensed, in that roomful of strange reunions, how far we had regressed now that our electronic eyes and ears to the world had been shut off. No longer the global village we had been accustomed to. Now all we could glean about this new, alien planet was what we could directly see, hear or touch.

'This is it,' said the Dodo.

An abandoned farmhouse. It was barely a barn, with two storeys and a rough slate roof, two rusty tractors parked outside and a pile of farming equipment, generators, pumps, scattered piping. A couple of Dead people were ensconced on two old rocking chairs in the yard. We bypassed them and the Dodo swung open the unlatched front door of the building.

Inside seemed as abandoned as out. The front door led directly into a huge kitchen, with an old Aga stove, an unplugged and empty fridge, and cupboards containing dusty crockery and dirty utensils. There was a collection of about twenty woks hanging on the wall, and an old Chinese calendar of the various years of the Rat, Dog and Pig. It looked as though nothing had been used in the last three or four years. There was no sign of edibles and comestibles.

Through the kitchen we traipsed into a large barn of a room with bare bricks gazing on a stone floor. Empty shelves around the walls. Five scattered wooden chairs. A rickety table, with a pile of yellowing newspapers. I looked them over. They were a few *Times* and *Daily Telegraphs* from 1993. 'TORIES TROUNCED IN COUNCIL ELECTIONS' was one headline. 'BOSNIAN SERBS SPURN PEACE' was another.

'"Dust to dust, ashes to ashes,"' said the Dodo. '"For in much wisdom is much grief, and he that increaseth knowledge increaseth sorrow."'

'Look at this,' I said, trying to strike a lighter note, as I pointed out an ancient ad to him. 'They're selling a 486 for over a thousand quid! I put mine in a skip two years ago.'

'We can all go on the skip now,' said the Dodo. Alice was wandering around, touching the shelves, marvelling at the dust on her fingers. How do they feel, sense things, after? We had had no time to talk at all, to try to ask or answer the unaskable questions. Everything happens too fast when, literally, there is almost no time left.

The dog nuzzled at what appeared to be a storage cupboard at the end of the room. 'Good dog!' said the Dodo approvingly. He slid open the doors to reveal an empty space apart from a row of dangling coat hangers on a rod. Extracting a clip of plastic keys from his pocket he inserted one (which I noticed was marked 'Tesco Saver Credit') in an almost invisible slot in the back panel. The panel rolled smoothly aside to reveal an antechamber beyond of familiar gun-grey walls.

It was a twin of the lift in the photocopying shop in Soho. Once we stepped inside the door closed behind us. The Dodo picked out a code on a numbered display panel and we all began to descend. Dodo, dog, Alice and I. Curiouser and curiouser.

'We shall make a preliminary recce,' said the Dodo. 'Then we can collect the survival pack from the van. There's a negligible risk they've changed the exit codes. But in for a penny in for a pound.'

I am always being told the caveats too late. But now I was the one hugging Alice. She didn't seem perturbed by this turn of events. I suppose once you've been buried for ten years entombment loses its terrors. Somehow we seemed to be growing more and more distant. I once read about this syndrome affecting returning hostages, who had been kept in cells for years for defunct political reasons. Professional counsellors, it appeared, were required in these instances. Ten million pages of personal services.

The lift stopped, giving out on to a grey, steel-lined tunnel. It curved down and round to the inevitable steel door with AUTHORIZED PERSONNEL ONLY marked on it below the usual skull and crossbones. But here there were no armed guards, or any other sign of life.

'This is the Central Midlands Caucus,' said the Dodo. 'A standby in case we lot under London sustained a fluke nuke. You know, ze bomb zat reaches ze parts ozer bombs cannot reach. It would be mainly military personnel who would run this. Some kinky colonel would be King of the Castle. It was operative on Orange Alert till the Rising. But maybe they all rushed above for their dead-uns. I don't have a code from now on,' he explained. 'It's voiceprint checks, *mano a mano*.'

But the dog was nuzzling at the steel door. 'There's somebody behind this,' said Alice.

'Not smellable,' said the Dodo. 'This door's five feet thick. Reinforced titanium, with shredded wheat and what have you.'

Nevertheless the dog was scrabbling at the thing with redundant claws. Alice said: 'Living people. I can smell them as well.'

'Well, let's see if we can share the odour,' said the Dodo. 'Stand by for voiceprint identification.' He stepped up to a small grille in the wall by the door and said clearly: 'Fruits of the forest.' A whirring, clicking sound ensued, and then the great door began to swing open with a deep hydraulic hiss.

'I'm not sure this is a good idea at all,' I said, but Alice and

Buster had already stepped inside the unlit vestibule beyond.

'Nothing ventured, nothing gained,' said the Dodo, following suit. I shook my head and crossed over the threshold.

Immediately the dog began to bark and lunged forward into the darkness. There was a skittering noise and a flurry of movement, and suddenly we were not alone. Hands were grabbing hold of us from all over and I found myself flat on my back, with two heavy figures sitting on my legs, a third on my chest and a fourth on my face. Crazy voices called out from the gloom:

'Kill the dead! Burn the Lazarenes!'

One does not argue with such high emotions. I felt my legs and arms being bound with thick rope, but my face was freed enough for me to see, in the light of old oil lamps and miners' torches, the Dodo and Alice likewise secured. The dog was leaping about somewhere, accompanied by cries of those mauled by his geriatric gums. Then he rushed off into the darkness.

'Forget the dog! Bring the Lazarenes!'

At least 'bring' was better than 'burn'. Trussed like missionaries in an old Tarzan movie, we were carried bodily down the tunnel. Shadows flitting over the steel walls like an ancient Hammer Film. Reality need not apply. My mouth was free so I shouted out:

'I am not a Lazarene! I am a free man!'

But the natives merely broke out in hymns:

'"Rock of ages, cleft for me . . . Let me hide myself in thee . . ."'

Here was another fine mess the Dodo had gotten me into. I had to say these people were in fine voice, whoever they were. I had visions of us being eaten by the Mormon Tabernacle Choir. It was indicative that in the least favourable moment the shape of a new comedy routine shimmered vaguely. God, who had entered the talent contest, was determined to eclipse all comers . . . assured of the largest audience in history.

'Set them down! Set them down!'

We landed with a bump in a room hung with oil lamps revealing a range of blank monitors and redundant mainframes. A shaggy-haired man in a ragged sweater came up and looked us in the face.

'"I am the Resurrection and the Life!"' he bellowed. 'None other!'

'Right you are, Guv,' I blurted out. This was no time to contradict him.

'Jesus!' he said, 'Jee-sus! He is the alpha and omega! Not the pit-spawn of Beelzebub! Jee-sus! He is the One! Unfortunate creature – it was not He who brought you back from the grave!'

'I've never been in the grave, cross my heart,' I babbled. 'I'm as live as you are. I swear to God!'

'Do not take the Name of the Lord in vain!' He was throwing spittle into my face. The others were gathered about him, men and women, taut and restless and breathing harshly. They were all dressed in casual sweaters, or work overalls and faded dungarees. Some actually carried hoes and pitchforks. You couldn't believe it till you saw it.

'Satan!' he cried out. 'It was Satan, not the Good Lord, who has caused this brazen blasphemy! It is Lucifer who has launched his Rebellion against God, with his pseudo-Angels! If this be God's work, where is Jee-sus? Where is the Lamb of Bethlehem? Who else but Satan dares open the Seven Seals against God's Will and Testament?'

'I don't know,' I said. 'I was always weak on theology. I'm just a poor stand-up comedian. I used to work the Comedy Shop in Charing Cross. You've absolutely got the wrong bodies. We're all alive, we're not part of the Dead.'

'How is it you got down here then, eh, Smarty?' If his face could lean any closer into mine, it would be in back of me. I'm sorry, I stole that from Groucho.

'I can explain this,' came the Dodo's voice, from behind me. 'I have the appropriate authorization and codes. I am, or was, a servant of Her Majesty's Government. M19–DUO, Department of Ultimate Options.'

141

'And who's the girl?' another voice sneered. 'Alice in Wonderland? I suppose you all dropped down the rabbit hole?'

Oof, that was close. 'Leave them alone,' said another voice, female this time. 'I know who two of these people are.'

Lawks-a-mercy, but I knew that timbre. It had shouted at me often enough from the bedroom. 'Turn the TV down, for God's sake, Jerry! Some people have to get up in the morning!' Jee-sus, indeed.

She came up round the bulk of the shaggy-haired monster. A little bedraggled in her farmyard overalls, but still the determined look, the disapproving cock of the head, though she was badly in need of a hairdo.

'Cut them loose, Daddy. They're not dead.'

Nice to be told this by one's most recent ex-girlfriend. My very own Karen, who had left me in Hammersmith, to return to her primeval faith . . .

142

19

I should have known it. I had thought, in my naivety, that one of the advantages of the Resurrection would be that Jehovah's Witnesses would no longer wake you up on Saturday morning. But I should have realized that some religions don't give up that easily, even at the materialization of their beliefs.

It is better to travel hopefully than to arrive. Certainly, that is these people's motto. Reconciled into their reluctant good grace, we sat around the abandoned bunker's conference table, surrounded by blank screens and a redundant map of the world, left in shadow. Alice beside me, my hand clutching hers. Karen's gaze, flickering between us, making it clear she was well aware she had Alice's fate in her grasp. She could have no doubt who Alice was. I had been weak enough to show her those Italian photos, in the early days of 'you show me yours and I'll show you mine'. She showed me snaps of her ex-husband Trevor the Clever, Professor of Polytechnic Priapism, but one dreadful glimpse was enough. I remember she remarked how happy Alice and I looked, with San Pietro in back, as she leant forward with suckling sympathy . . . Not much sympathy now, but a hard-edged gravity, as she sopped up a bowl of gruel with what looked suspiciously like shards of Rakusen's Matzohs.

'We were taken in at first, like everyone else,' Karen's father, who introduced himself as Brother Duff, explained softly, transformed from demon-slayer into affable squire. 'When Karen rejoined us, we were all rejoicing in the imminent Coming of the Lord. We have always believed in the Living Word of the Bible. "And if any man shall take away from the words of the book of this prophecy, God shall take

143

away his part of the book of life." Revelations twenty-two, nineteen. Of course we knew Our Lord cometh. But this did not square with what we saw. We observed things about these "Angels" which should not be spoken about between honest folk. We were perturbed, but we still clung to the Prophecy. We were ready, on the Day, for the Call. But then our sister, Ada, who has already been touched by a special Grace, began to prophesy. She opened our eyes. She told us it was all a lie, a plot by Satan. He had broken loose from his confinement in Hell, and had climbed upon the Beast, Behemoth. Together they were able to call upon the powers of Deceit and Treachery. God was bound by His Divine Mercy to accept the Plan, to force Mankind to the Ultimate Test. To see whether they could differentiate, at the most crucial point, between Good and Evil. And Mankind was failing the Test. All their seed was to be damned. Only the Elect, the latterday Jobs, who realized the celestial Hoax, would be saved. But we had to fight the Forces of Darkness.

'We followed Ada to this bunker. She had been a mainten- ance worker here, back in the eighties. She knew the location and the entrances. We found the security gates open, the personnel within had fled from the terrible sight of their loved ones "returning". We took their place and resealed the exits. We have shut down the power to conserve it. We might have to be down here for many decades. We have our own resources, food, animals. We have our men, our women and our children. We have always intermarried safely. Our mental health is perfectly preserved by our Faith. We need nothing from the external world, or from this fraudulent "salvation". Even if the entire human race perishes like lemmings, we shall survive, as Adam and Eve and their seed. But we have to purge ourselves of Uncleanness. And so the Dead cannot be tolerated here.'

'They can be destroyed,' said a sallow woman beside him. 'They burn like matchsticks. It's terrible.'

'But do they rise again elsewhere?' asked another man,

who looked like a bank manager gone to pot. 'Does it do any good? Perhaps the second time they return in another, more frightful guise?'

'There's no point in speculating about Satan,' said Brother Duff, slamming the table with his palm. 'Satan is Satan and his wiles are legion. The only good dead man is a dead, dead man.'

A murmur of assent went round the table. Alice's hand was clutching mine ever more fiercely at the talk of burning and matchsticks. Karen looking at her impassively. I remember her saying: 'She looks so beautiful, Jerry. It must have been devastating.' So it was, Karenkins, so it was. To stand, facing the wall, with the guts kicked out of you, unable to breathe. There is no way I can let her go again.

But can I drag her with me to hell?

And what if, to re-open a dreadful, but dreadfully logical train of thought, what if these Eighth Day Adventists, or whatever they might call themselves, fundamentally were right? There's nothing divine in this at all. It's all, as we suspected, a trick of some sort, whether by an alien force from Tralfamadore or Old Nick, what's the difference? We may all be going down the tubes for nothing, victims of our own sad, mad dreams . . .

I did not want to think what would happen if these maniacs discovered Alice was dead. But I was at a loss to figure out a way of carrying on this conversation. 'My father has been forming a resistance group as well, in London,' I said, engaging my mouth before my brain. 'He's trying to gather round the old members of his group, the Socialist Workers' League. My great-grandfather, who fought against Oswald Mosley, has joined them. They've classified it as a class struggle.'

The Dodo kicked me under the table. 'We should pool our resources,' he said quickly. 'I'm sure there are many pockets of resistance like this one. People who want to fight the good fight. That's what we came down here to do, to contact the independent nuclei. It's a time to forget old human rivalries and rally together against the enemy. As in the Second World War. The Battle of Britain. The few against the many. I know there are several other centres. Carlisle, Falkirk, Aboyne. And Benbecula, in the Outer Hebrides. That's the fall-back Royal Bunker. But I don't know if the Queen herself is, uh . . .'

'The Monarchy is an instrument of the Devil,' said Brother Duff, 'and the government too. Only God can rule, through the Love of His Son, the Saviour, Jesus Christ. He has called us, through Sister Ada. This is where we must make our last stand. "For perfect love casteth out fear, and he that feareth is not perfect in love." John, Chapter four, eighteen. We stand here because of our love for each other, which is the love of Christ.'

'Amen.' The echo went round the table.

'For behold,' said Brother Duff, 'I saw an Angel come down from Heaven, having the key of the bottomless pit and a great chain in his hand. And he laid hold on the dragon, that old serpent, which is the Devil, and Satan, and bound him a thousand years . . .'

This went on for quite a while. I could feel the palpable fear coursing through Alice, the first genuine emotion I had sensed since we had clinched so impossibly on the threshold of her parents' house. A kind of 'coldth', streaming from her hand into mine. But what can the Dead have to fear? Apart from the boredom, that is, which crept over us, rooting us to the hard boardroom chairs.

'The Lord is Our Shepherd, We Shall Not Want.' 'There is a Green Hill Far Away.' 'John Brown's Body No Longer Lies amoulderin' in the Grave.' And other firm favourites. Eventually they brought us the second course after the soup, battered mess tin plates of baked beans. It would not be a silent night tonight, brothers.

'We can't let you go,' Brother Duff said finally, having emitted a burp which could have awoken the Dead had they

146

not risen already. 'We've sealed ourselves off from the Outside. We will sit down here for two weeks, until Satan's Day has passed. Then we will send out raiding parties. Until then you will remain among us. Brother Fisher will see to your needs and instruction.' The seedy bank manager bobbed his gawky head. 'Bed them in Cubicle Six. There is a separate niche there for the woman.' He rose, and all the congregation rose with him, their bowels and mouths softly rumbling.

Karen brought blankets to our cell, and left us with a sympathetic look. What we needed was a deepcast mining drill. There were two bunks on one side of the room and a single, as advised, in a corner. We were allocated two oil lamps to hook on to the bunks. The remaining wall space was taken up with framed colour photographs of the British landscape in Tory Party dreams. Rolling hills, woodlands and cricket. Enough to warn the hackles of the heart.

It was a very long afternoon. At six-thirty p.m. they brought us more plates of baked beans. A real cock-up in the provisions department. Diligently we cleaned up Alice's plate too, so as not to arouse further suspicions.

'We should sleep on it,' said the Dodo. 'Where there's life, there's hope.'

That left hope five and a half more days. Just about one hundred and thirty-two hours . . .

The Dodo took the single bed, leaving Alice below and me above on the bunks. Her voice tingled up towards me:

'I can remember things now, Jerry. Those horrible moments in the plane, as it began to spiral. All of a sudden they announced there was a problem with the engine and we were going to make an emergency landing. You spend your life dreading those words. There was a woman beside me who simply went white. She didn't cry or anything. It was as if the life had suddenly drained out of her. I held her hand. I didn't feel frightened, just numb. I thought, this is only a movie. But the whole plane was really bucking and shaking. Bags were falling out of the lockers. The oxygen masks dropped out, which was useless because we were going down. And I thought, I promised to phone Jerry as soon as I got back. And I thought, you'd hear about this on the radio, or on television, or you'd just pick up a late *Standard* extra, and see the headline. And I felt, bizarrely, that I was letting everybody down.

'And then it simply stopped. There was nothing in between. That's not quite true. There was a vague sort of rumble. Because when I opened my eyes on that hill I knew something was missing. Some huge chunk of memories. I could remember my childhood first, then my house, then my friends, then you, but I couldn't tell in which order things had happened. The schooldays seemed nearer than the death. I didn't remember the things I've just told you. I just knew I had died and I was back, I thought, in heaven, because it was such a bright day and the hill was so beautiful. There were another hundred and fifty-odd people there who looked vaguely familiar. None of us had any clothes on, but it seemed perfectly natural. There was a clearing on the hill, and a little monument with a plaque which said in Portuguese and English: "In Memory of the Victims of Aer Lisboa Flight 443, 19th October 1989, May They Rest in Peace." And there I was. And then I was sure I was in heaven, because there were these Angels, looking plump and jolly, with their wings and their racks of white robes. They had this common patter in several languages, which I could hear all over the hill: "Good morning. I am your appointed guardian. You who have passed away have now returned. I am appointed to bring you with all possible speed to your nearest loved ones or any other destination of your choice. You do not have to speak. We can read your thoughts. Any information gained will remain strictly confidential. Congratulations on your return." And then when we were in the cars a gentle voice intoned, as if inside my head: "seven days from now there is a final judgement. This cannot be postponed, altered or abjured. It is a balance of divine justice.

148

Relax, and enjoy your pre-eternity. All mysteries will be made clear in due course. God is an equal opportunities deity."'

20

There's the good news, and there's the bad news, and who can tell them apart. After she had spoken, Alice fell asleep, incredibly. One learns something new about the Dead every hour. I gazed at her in the oil lamp gloaming as her breath rose and fell, her breasts moving rhythmically under that flimsy T-shirt. Do they become, simply as that, alive, fully alive again? Only to be cast, like all the rest of us, into the pit? Even Mayflies have a better deal than this.

The Dodo, too, slept soundly. No bliss obliged, or whatever. I suppose it's what they used to call moral fibre. Either that or a complete lack of imagination. Or both. The idea that the living ought to stick together against the Dead seems to have taken some battering. We are reduced to age old enmities. Perhaps this is the whole point. When God, or the Black Hole, made us, something went wrong in the chemicals. That old imbalance in the pineal. The left lobe not connected to the right lobe. Now He's called in all the models, like those ads you see sometimes hidden on the bottom of page thirty-five:

IMPORTANT SAFETY MESSAGE

To all owners of a homo sapiens (Mark III thru X) type brain: Owners of such a type are advised urgently that under certain conditions (in fact most conditions) it is possible for this type to overheat and malfunction during the thinking cycle. Owners are advised that all these models have been recalled to the factory to be replaced with a new malfunction-free type which will be provided in due course.

If you think you have a homo sapiens (Mark III thru X) type brain, don't call us, we'll call you.

Talk about the scrap-heap of history. For the first time in

days I was experiencing a true to whatever erection. An insatiable desire to continue that interrupted sexual renaissance of 1989. How are the Dead in bed? And does it count as necrophilia if they're alive? The opportunity, with a little enterprising endeavour, to pop along to Vienna and look up the Returned Freud, or Jung, or whoever specialized in this knotty problem, was it Krafft-Ebbing, or Krafft-Flowing? Didn't Freud die in London, in Hampstead even? *Noch besser*.

Joseph Junior, advise me now! I must think flaccid thoughts, urgently. Nearer my God to thee. Downward Christian Soldiers! Think of Hanukkah candles and the dead Saturday afternoons of Grandpa William's Ipswich soirées. Think of the *Jewish Chronicle*. Ah, that's better! For hand relief might not pass unmarked . . .

I was becoming more awake by the minute. My boner was returning thick and fast. Why was I being plagued by scruples? But could I wake her, my beloved, from her first good sleep in ten years? On the other hand, hadn't she slept enough?

I climbed off the top bunk, gingerly. 'Alice!' I called softly in her ear. She made a mewing noise and turned over to face the wall. I slid my hand under her blanket. 'Alice!' Then I stopped.

There was a scratching sound at the door. It was a wooden door, which might in theory be amenable to a good solid battering, not to speak of the Dodo's training with locks, but we had heard the guard, Brother Fisher or whoever, moving about during the day. Nor did the Dodo seem in any hurry to escape, given the options outside. But now he jerked awake, that tripwire in his brain picking up an unusual move. I pulled my hand from under Alice's blanket, but he was already poised, ear at the door.

The strange scratching was now accompanied by a muffled animal whine. 'It's the dog,' we both realized in unison. 'Buster!' I called out. The dog responded with a kind of muted howl.

'There can't be a guard there. Unless Buster's eaten him.'

'We'd better act, or they'll catch him,' said the Dodo. 'We can't squander an outside asset. Even if he doesn't have any teeth.' He was kneeling by the lock, juggling it with another part of his magic clutch of keys. 'I hate premature ejection,' he said, 'but man proposes, life disposes.'

I wish he'd stop spewing out these wee homilies. But he had the lock open in a jiffy and there was the beast leaping all over us. This was definitely a deboner. Alice woke up, and joined the fray. Soon we were all choking on dog hair.

'Seize the time,' said the Dodo. 'Let's vamos, muchachos.'

There was an empty chair by the door, but no sign of the Fisher. We plunged away, left, down the corridor, the Dodo leading by the pencil beam of a pocket torch attached to his magic key ring. But the tunnel dipped and we seemed to be descending steeply. The Dodo hesitated at a fork in the shaft.

'I thought you knew these bunkers,' I complained.

'A smattering, dear boy,' he said. 'There are twenty-five thousand miles of the critters, and that's only dating from World War Aye Aye. There were secret boltholes in King Alfred's time.'

'Didn't stop him from crisping the dessert, did it?'

'Secret projects are sweetest,' said the Dodo. 'Empire building. A hidden budget is the key to power. Who pays the Angels' salaries, I wonder? Or is God really beyond economics? Follow the money, that's the golden rule.'

But the tunnel came to an abrupt stop, in a sheer, doorless wall, and we had to retrace our steps to the fork. Out of the darkness an oil lamp glimmered, carried along by an evidently shaky hand.

'Jerry! This way!' A fierce whisper in that familiar voice. Karen's dishevelled head appearing in the pool of light, her face sweaty, her eyes drooping with fatigue. 'There's a backup exit along this path!' She urged us. We followed, like troglodytes in a mouse hole. At least now we were going up. A much sounder policy.

'Dad has called the flock to a special night meeting,' she explained hurriedly. 'I was coming to get you when I heard the dog. They'll notice I'm missing soon enough and come after us. But I don't care. I've had enough of it all.'

'Karen—' I wanted to explain to her about Alice, who was bounding along by my side, but she waved my stammer away. 'Don't, Jerry. I realized it immediately. They're all paranoid as hell. I knew as soon as Aunt Ada came out of her shaking fit we were in for a whole New Dispensation. It must be happening all over the world. True believers who can't take the proof, finally. It's all ego, to be the few who know the Truth. Once it's available to everybody they go crazy. They want to kill the dead. It's insane. Now we're getting to the rough part.' The oil lamp shone on a ladder of rungs, leading up a narrow conduit. 'I'll go first with the lamp,' she said.

'What about Buster?' asked Alice, anxiously. She was becoming more live by the minute. All the old disproportions.

'A gentleman can never abandon a dog,' agreed the Dodo. He shone his pocket torch on our immediate surroundings, lighting, luckily, on an emergency fire hose. I helped him pull it out and we fastened it in a makeshift cradle around the beast's shaggy stomach. The dog gummed my arm but I ignored him.

'Hoist secured,' called the Dodo. We began climbing, Karen first, then Alice, then Jerry, then the Dodo, we last two between us lifting poor Buster. He snuffled and whined but mercifully did not bark, yet. Only the Dodo, appallingly cheerful, gave song capriciously, echoing spookily inside the tube:

'For despi-ite of all he's done, He remai-ins a-han Englishman—'

'For God's sake give us a break, Dodo—'

'We have nothing to fear but fear itself, Gerald.'

'Shut up and climb, you idiots,' countered Karen.

153

It seemed to go on for aeons, taxing even the Dodo's capacity for sang-froid and stiff upper lip. Eventually we emerged and sprawled puffing and panting on to the floor of a gently ascending wider shaft. Karen's light shone on a rough chiselled inscription on the brickwork lining the tunnel:

THE BRUMMY OIKS, 1995.

'It's easier now,' Karen. 'This was our way in. Then we opened the main entrances from inside. Ada remembered the codes. Pity she didn't remember her own brain. But she was always a bit like that – semi idiot-savant.' She led us up what appeared to be an old mining tunnel, following a rusty, broken rail track. The air was musty and thick, far from air conditioning. Buster was overjoyed to be free of his brace, and began barking with relief—

'That's them! That's the Lazarenes!' Shouting and clomping erupted from ahead. A criss-cross stutter of torchlights rushed towards us.

Now I know exactly what Boris Karloff felt like in James Whale's *Frankenstein*. Right down to the iron bolts dragging the feet.

The shaggy shape of Karen's old man loomed.

'Betrayed by my own daughter! Death, where's thy sting?'

Exactly, I would have thought, the point of the whole affair so far. But religious maniacs have no sense of irony. The Dodo pulled us all back, keeping his wits about him, or so I thought, very briefly.

'Stand back!' he called out. 'I'm armed. I'm an authorized member of Her Majesty's Forces, to be allowed to proceed without let or hindrance. You are all trespassing on government property!'

That was ludicrous enough to stop them in their tracks, for a moment.

'Tricks and snares of Satan!' called out Brother Duff. 'Beelzebub, you have ensnared my daughter. Karen, do you choose the Dead over the living?'

'Dad, you've got to listen,' Karen tried pleading. 'Jerry is not dead, and neither are the others. You're eating yourself up with all these suspicions. What's happening up above, it's God's work, not Satan's. Aunt Ada is a certified schizophrenic. You had her committed yourself, back in ninety-four.'

'Karen, you don't know what you're saying,' called her father. 'Come back to us while your soul is still drifting. Jesus loves you, girl, but he can't save the Damned.'

'She's dead as well,' called a mournful female voice from behind Duff. 'My poor Karenkins, they killed you down there. Now there's no way back!'

'For God's sake, Ada!' Karen's voice quavered. 'You can't believe that, Dad!'

'The other girl is definitely dead,' called a male voice, 'I smelt her at table. She could not sing God's words. They are all evil, they must be destroyed.'

Sooner or later we were going to get to that. I knew it. Something snapped in me. I strode forward.

'Get out of our fucking way, you assholes! This has gone far enough!'

'You've gone far enough, Lazarene!' called the male voice. The man stepped out of Duff's shadow into the torchlight. He was carrying a formidable looking shotgun, which was pointed right at my chest. 'Brothers, light a fire for the Lord.'

'Wait a minute, Brother Hoag,' said Karen's father. 'This requires guidance, not rash decisions. There is at least one soul here to be saved.'

'They are all lost,' stated the gunman. 'Brothers and sisters, light the fire.'

Alice had come up to grab my arm but I pushed her back, towards the Dodo. Edging my body between her and the gun. It is a far, far better thing that I do, et cetera . . . But on the other hand . . .

'Which one of you idiots gave Hoag a gun?' Karen asked in her best where-have-you-hidden-my-shoes-this-time thundertone. But her father was hesitating in the cross-lights.

A confused murmur went up amid the shadowy faithful. But at that moment of potential sanity the stupid dog, Buster, chose to make a run àt Brother Duff, whether in hostility or out of a sudden friendly passion I would never know. Because, as Karen's father went down under the onslaught of the senile beast, I stepped forward to haul him off and defuse this new misunderstanding and Brother Hoag shouted:

'Keep off, Lazarene!'

But I didn't realize he meant me.

I stepped forward, and Brother Hoag fired two shotgun rounds straight into my chest from a distance of five or six feet.

I could see the flash of the barrel, and feel the rounds slamming into me like two great sledgehammer blows, and a sharp blink of Alice's terrified face, and a sense of flying through the air, and the whole lot of them receding, rapidly, into the distance, and a loud, shrill scream, which was not mine . . .

But it's true, I don't remember the pain.

PART 3

The Interlife

21

I was lying on the grass on the slope of a gentle hill. Featherlight clouds hung in a blue sky. My hand was lying on a little hump in the green ground. A few small ants were climbing over my thumb. I shook them off.

I raised myself on an elbow. I was buck naked. I was sure it was me, because I recognized the cashew-nut-shaped birthmark on the right thigh. Though the body seemed in better condition than I last remembered. The little pot belly had gone completely. I flexed my arms. There were actual traces of muscles. There appeared to be less hair than there should be. Gone, it seemed, was the intermittent heartburn.

Was there anything else? I vaguely massaged my chest. Two small nipples, in the right location. Taut abdomen, neck bones, hip bone. Toes and fingers moving. The vital organs in place. *Alles in ordnung.*

I was not alone. What appeared to my still unfocused eyes, at first, like a flock of sheep flowing down the hill resolved itself into a loose mass of humans, naked men and women, and children, too, moving slowly across the grass. Below, by a light wire fence and a row of trees — were they sycamores? — were three pure white bubble-shaped vehicles. A flock of twenty or thirty white-robed figures with wings were walking jauntily up the hill towards us, each with a cargo of white folded linen slung over its shoulder like a pile of waiter's towels. The leader of the pack wielded an old-fashioned loudhailer, its call wafting over the breeze:

'Good morning. I am your appointed guardian. You who have passed away have now returned to life everlasting. You still await your final dispensation in the Last Judgement, due now in three earth days. I am appointed to bring you with all possible speed to your nearest loved ones or the destination of your choice. You do not have to speak. You have the right to remain silent.'

But a light touch at my shoulder made me turn away from the speech. A kinder, more familiar face was looking into my own. Twinkling bluish eyes under a short cropped flaming red head, and the feathered wings flopping behind it. My brain suddenly focused, like two parallel lines meeting:

'Hoppy!'

'Bravo, Gerald. You're quick off the mark. It's because you haven't been dead very long. Last in, first out, that's the principle.'

The tiny chink of recollection was widening. Despite the general sense of well-being, the unimpeded flow of the blood round the body, the heightened awareness of something beyond the physical surroundings, there was also a slight anxiety.

'This was not a natural death, was it, Hoppy?'

'Very natural in the Old Order, old chum. Gunshot wounds. Very common. It was the primary cause of fatality in southern Los Angeles, Miami Beach and Odessa from 1997, no ethnic group excluded. Though it was unusual in the north Midlands. Can you get up? How are your legs? Don't pay heed to that windbag, Montefiory. I'll take you where you need to go.'

I struggled to rise, and found myself walking, with Hoppy's support, as he threw a white robe around me, down the green hill towards the bubblecars. I was beginning to receive strange flashes from inside the frozen brain, thawing moments that seemed oddly distant. A name, and a face, shone through:

'I want to go to Alice.'

'No, you cannot nominate another Returnee, at this point. But don't worry, reunifications will be dealt with in due course. I can inform you that she has come to no harm, not that harm can be caused to a Returnee in this Interim, despite

160

some fallacies to the contrary. Your alternative companion, Miss Karen Duff, by permission of her father, the Reverend Brian Duff, has removed both Miss Howard and Mr Armstead from the anti-Lazarene ambit. The incident which led to your death was an unfortunate oversight. The weapon would not have fired had your party been overground. We have had some difficulties with subterranean conflict. So much to do, so short the time. To quote Joe E. Brown: "Nobody's perfect."'

It's a bit late in the day for such an admission. But beggars cannot be choosers. He led me, skirting the larger bubbles, to a smaller, personal model.

'I don't think I've ever been inside one of these,' I said, tentatively.

'*Ma'alesh*,' he said. '*Itfadal, effendi*.'

I climbed in. It seemed larger inside than out; a kind of fluffy white, like a furry egg, with two soft cosy armchairs, into which we both sank. There was no visible steering or controls. I could look out through a large oval window that was not apparent from the exterior. I could not feel the bubble lift, but the ground fell away, and all the little people became even littler. Within a few seconds the feathery clouds were about us.

'In the absence of a legitimate choice,' said my Angel, 'I am transporting you to your next of kin, i.e. your natural father, Joseph Immanuel Davis, and your mother Sophia Benedicta Collodi. Do you oppose this itinerary? Answer in words of one syllable.'

'I didn't know my father was called Immanuel. He never told me that.'

'We all have secrets. I take it the absence of a negative implies a positive?'

'Whatever you say.'

The things you discover too late for action. Something within me knew I should feel more strongly about these choices, about my apparently recent last moments alive. But there was also a tangible inner calm, a holding back, that sense, again, almost an odour, of something else, that lay not in the past, but the future . . . an intangible swirl of snippets of thought, taste, sounds. Plaintive flutes, and the far clash of cymbals.

It's tinnitus, Jerry, I told myself. Ringing in the ears. Not surprising, after a shotgun blast at point blank range. What do you expect?

The flash of terror in Alice's face . . .

'You will get used to it,' Hoppy assured me. 'Disorientation. It's worse the longer the hiatus. Imagine Cro-Magnon man, appearing at Charing Cross station. Or a medieval Japanese emerging into the chaos of Tokyo. Everything has to be taken into account. Holding Areas established. Post-death shelters. What we were working on at Hammersmith was the tip of the iceberg, as you found out when you tried to search the system. Digital data was only a tertiary convenience. You might say that the Dead themselves were the "information banks" to be accessed. But these terms are misleading. Howsoever, we do what we can, with only three days to go before J Day.'

I tried to tear my mind away from the clouds to make some rough calculations on my fingers. There were ten of them, an impossible number.

'Three . . . four . . . five . . .' Murky memories of our descent underground. There had been six days left, then, after a half night, five, or five and a half . . .

I had been dead for between thirty-six and forty-eight hours. What had been happening during that time, to me, to others? Where was the famous 'out-of-body' experience, the detaching of the soul, the flying psyche? Where was the great bright light described by near-death survivors, at the end of the tunnel? The harp and the wings . . . Well, they were spoken for.

'I can't remember anything about being dead,' I told Hoppy.

'There's nothing to remember,' said Hoppy. 'As you have realized, it's a temporary condition, but not analogous to sleep. There can be no dreams. There might be, however, a range of disturbances connected to the Act of Rising. An individual cause must emanate from the Creator. You might call it an "energy" which binds the past into the present. It has nothing to do with the physical remains of the old body, as you have seen. These still remain in the earth. Some Returnees have tried to dig up graveyards to find their corpses. This is not an advisable course of action, as it may cause distress to the living, who are finding it hard enough to adjust.'

You bet your ass. But that is no longer your problem, Gerald Davis. You have been advanced to Stage Two. Like those videogames in which the perils increase the more you succeed with the joystick.

'So what happens now at this Day of Judgement?' I asked Hoppy. 'Do I get bonus points for being dead already? How does it work? Does my case reopen?'

'It has always been open,' said Hoppy. 'I gave you a prognosis based on balance-to-date. I can't foretell the criteria of the Judgement. I am simply a celestial servant, Gerald.'

'But what were you before? Was there a before, Hoppy? Before you got your wings? What's the structure? Where did you come from? Where will you go when it's all over?'

A sudden image re-emerging from earlier fears: an empty earth, *après* the sound and fury, the untold masses traipsed into the 'Judgement Centres', the last dribbles marching through, leaving eerily deserted streets, garbage strewn, the Last Day's newspapers flapping in the wind, the empty houses with their half-eaten breakfasts, the unhoovered crumbs on the carpet, TVs still crackling with blank static, watched only by the family dogs or cats pawing restlessly, waiting for masters who would never come back. The sudden silence after the cacophony of ages. And then, the rustle of wings as the new owners saunter in to stake their claim . . .

'If only you knew, Gerald, if only you knew.' My Angel shook his head sadly. Of course, I had forgotten the evidence of Alice's experience – they read our minds. This, too, we had not suspected at the start. They had kept this ability carefully hidden. And what else have they concealed? How much of the earlier phase of their satrapy was a compound deception? And would I know the truth now? And what good would it do me? Might it be that they only read the minds of the Dead? Did that establish a connection? I tried to read his mind, though since I could hardly read my own it was fairly pointless, but he nudged me out of my reverie and pointed out the fresh view from the window.

'Coming home, Gerald.'

By hi-speed grail . . . down from the clouds were familiar contours: the chimney pots and sprawling loft conversions of London; the Dinky-toy shapes of the Georgian and Victorian centre, the winding snake of the Thames, the tall jagged warts of the City – but hang about, where are all the green patches? That should be Regent's Park, and Hyde Park, and St James's – but they all seem to have been replaced by a teeming mass of what appeared to be black ants spilling out into the streets. And the roof-tops too, wherever there was the semblance of a flat surface, were moving . . .

The roads were seething black rivers. Glutted end to end, clogged side to side. Gorged with tiny shifting dots. Human multitudes. It was like carnival time on a gargantuan scale, a carnival without the floats, a carnival without a single ice cream, without steel bands, a carnival of woe, silently writhing.

Rush hour without the rush. For they were going nowhere, yet . . . City life – man loves to cram in with his fellow man, but neither he, nor she, bargained for this. I looked at Hoppy. He looked at me, with that bloated innocent Stan Laurel smile.

'Why, this is hell,' I said to him.

'No,' he said. 'This is only the vestibule.'

22

And thus we hovered over Islington. A dense post-human mass was choking the borough. My childhood fief of Packington Street as bad as the main roads. There was nowhere to set down the bubblecar. Nor could we land on the roof of my parents' apartment block. I could see the crowds sitting around the water tanks and TV aerials, like hordes of refugees.

'I'll lower you to the front stairway,' Hoppy said. 'It looks relatively clear.' There were only forty or so people on it. He slung a silvery rope ladder down a perfectly round hole which opened in the floor of the Angelic transport.

'*Bonne chance*, matelot,' he said. 'I'll see you on the Day.'

'See ya,' I said, and climbed slowly down. The ladder was as thin as string but taut as steel. I found my footing on the top step, squeezing my way past several elderly Dead ladies who were resting their deceased bones on the stoop. I pressed the bell for 3C. It struck me that of course there might be no electricity. But the intercom answered. I recognized Dad's voice:

'Go away, dead or alive.'

'It's me Dad. Jerry.'

'Jerry! Fucking shit! Come on in. Don't let anybody else through.' The buzzer sounded. I slipped inside. The Dead on the stoop glared at me but remained *in situ*.

Doors opened a crack on the landing. Little eyes peeked through, then the doors slammed shut again. I went up the two flights of stairs.

Dad was on the landing. He was dressed in the patched old red sweater I knew had been ripped in the Poll Tax Battle of 1990. I always called it the red rag to his own bull. He looked tired and frazzled but was I glad to see him! It was odd, I could feel the pumping of my heart. I could also hear the shifting creak of bodies in the flat behind him. Shades of Bath — had the whole clan shifted from Przemysl . . . ?

'Jerry!' Dad put out a fist to punch my shoulder. 'You look so fit, damn it, where've you been? Did you find 'er? Did you find, uh, Alice?'

'It's a long story, Dad.' He took my arm to lead me in the door. Pursing his lips at my white robe. 'Like the gear, Jerry. Blend in with the mass. An excellent disguise, son.'

'Dad, I have to tell you, it's, um, not a disguise.'

My mother hurried up to grab my face between her palms. '*Caro mio!* Where have you been, you stupid boy! We thought we'd lost you for ever! The only time people turn up here now is when they're dead.' She drew me into the kitchen. There was only one body there, but he was enough to fill the room. Ben Jonson, waving a chicken leg.

'God's lid, sir! How now, young gentleman! Beshrew me! Will you join a poor player in a Tesco's Frozen Special? Poulet de Loire, last of the Bejam Storebox, sirrah!'

'Good to see you, Ben. No, thank you.'

I had no trace of an appetite. I had noticed on my flight, the lack of the old gurgle, those deep messages from the tum to the throat. Nothing. I had tried to think of my most mouth-watering favourites: Tandoori Chicken Masala. Lamb Pasanda. Scallop and Prawn with Water-Chestnuts. Lebanese Oriental Stuffed Chicken. Beef Rendang. Mutton Hot Pot Chez Paul. Not a slaver. And not a twinge of regret. I should be worried, but I had enough else to worry me. Sophie was opening the fridge and laying out silver-wrapped morsels and plates.

'It's OK, Mum, Dad. I have to tell you. I don't have to eat. I don't want you to worry. But, I'm dead.'

Dad looked at me with that long-suffering gaze of the socialist who begat a comedian.

'Get serious, Jerry. We don't have much time left. While

you've been away, things 'aven't stood still. We've been able to make some preparations. But tell me, how did you get through that crowd? We 'aven't been able to move about since yesterday noontime. The crowd 'as doubled every four hours.'

'I'm dead, Dad. Didn't you see? A bubblecar just dropped me. My Recording Angel, Hoppy, brought me here. I had an accident up north. I was killed in a nuclear bunker near Birmingham by a follower of Karen Duff's dad. They're a brand new sect now, the Anti-Lazarenes. They want to kill all the Dead.'

'You never 'ad a sense of proportion, Jerry,' my father said. 'It's always the smartass. Well, at least eat some of this. Your mother's kept it. *Fress*, before it goes down this black 'ole.' Ben Jonson laughed jovially. But an old, eagle-eyed gent, dressed in one of Dad's dressing gowns, the one with GRIMETHORPE COLLIERY BAND on the back, came into the kitchen and drew near to me. He had a little grey-white goatee. I recognized him from the pictures as great-grandpa Joseph Duvid, the same who had driven me spare on the phone. He took my head between his two fragile hands and looked into my eyes.

'He's dead,' he said. 'It takes vun to know vun.'

'Welcome to the Graveyard Watch!' cried the playwright. 'Is't not wond'rous? A grand concert of the humours, I'll warrant?' He offered me his chicken leg again, which I once more declined.

'Jerry.' My mother slid forward, almost fainting, grabbing my head from the old man as if it were a football. 'Jerry, it's not true! *Bambino!*'

'Oh God, Jerry,' said Dad. 'What did you go and do that for?'

'It was an accident,' I reiterated. 'The Angels should have disabled all weaponry but they screwed up because it was underground. It seems that God is fallible.'

'We already know that,' said Dad, wearily.

167

'Ve are countink on it!' enthused the old man, drawing up a chair by the kitchen table. He pointed a finger at my father. 'Joseph Junior vill detail ze plan.'

My mother sat down, too, shocked but resigned. It was instructive to see how the rush of miracles had flattened even live emotions. The difference between the living and the dead was blurring ever more towards the crucial roundup. Great-grandpa Joseph Duvid looked as if he'd just emerged from a health farm at which amphetamines had been the main diet. His arms waved about like semaphors as he punched his goatee towards his namesake:

'Tell dem, Joseph. It's a real lulu.'

'We were contacted by your Polish friend, Marek. He 'ad got away from his own, ah, guests and was 'oled up in the Channel Four studios. You know, your headquarters in 'orse-ferry Road. That bloke who runs the Channel, that Terrence man. Real wide boy. But 'e was still on course for a plan to record the whole fucking flapdoodle. Still 'oping to get 'is show back on the air, the poor sod. Anyway, 'e 'ad these tiny personal camcorders. Small as matchboxes. 'E was looking for volunteers to carry 'em secretly to the so-called Last Judge-ment. Candid camera, transmitting back to base. Apparently the engineers 'ad found a way to cut through the Angels' jamming. Got pictures on tubes, very short range. But they're working on extending the range, down in the cellars. Good old-fashioned working-class know-'ow. We've got ten of the buggers, "mini-Engs" they call 'em.'

'Ve vill reveal ze whole troot to ze vorld,' enthused old Joseph. 'It's a whole new vay out dere! Television! Now dat can be real power for de people – to let de people know what's really happenink!'

'We took him down there,' said Sophie, wearily, 'on the first day, when it was not so crowded. He was like a monkey in a banana plantation. Go tell him what we already know.'

It's not what you think. Nothing is any more. We are all at least two hundred years behind the times. Or two hundred thousand . . . I looked at Dad. He looked at me, very tired. A shrug.

'What else can we do, Jerry? We can't just meekly go like lambs to the slaughter.'

'It's all right, Dad. They mean well. You can't hurt them.' I remembered it now, the shotgun blast to the heart. The chunks of flesh, bone, shattered nerves, arteries, crashing out through the backbone. I did have a post-fatal flash of my broken, bleeding body lying there in the wild criss-cross light of the torches.

And then the sunlight on the hill.

Would I see Alice again? I dropped my eyelids and tried to look inside myself, but there was only the usual retinal swirl and floaters. Did I care? What had my life become, after my death? It was clear certain things were very different. The loss of desire for food, for example, without regrets. That was troubling, but in an intellectual way. The lack of fatigue. The lack of desire in the loins. That, given my besiegement by an entire pack of my relatives, was not at this moment proof of anything. But there still was a desire for Alice, there still was an ache. There still was pain.

And I knew that I would need to find her.

'I'll take one of your cameras inside,' I said. 'Whatever you want.'

Joseph Duvid slapped me on the back. 'I knew ve could count on you, boy. Come inside, meet de rest of de cell. Ve have a proper surprise for you.'

That would be nice. Death's so short of surprises. I followed him meekly into the living room. The Davis Revolutionary Front, Second Division: great-grandma Esther, who wielded a plank with the best of them in Cable Street in 1936. Her parents, Nathan and Hilde Goldschlaeger, who had been bubbled in to join their daughter all the way from Kimpulung-Bukovina, that outpost of the Austro-Hungarian Empire, and one set of their parents, Rabbi Schmuel Goldschlaeger and his wife Feigeh, the other set presumably having opted to join other siblings elsewhere. Dad's parents, William V., the chartered accountant, and his wife Edna, curled up on the sofa with an old *Financial Times* and the *Jewish Chronicle* Passover Supplement. None of Sophie's ancestors seemed to have crossed the oceans, but there was another man, who sat sunk in Mum's favourite purple Habitat armchair that she had bought from the previous owners of the flat. And he, with that great thatch of hair and facial addenda, could not be mistaken for anyone but himself even in the dimmest light. His eyes were closed, but his head was swaying, perhaps to the rhythm of his thoughts, his lips moving as if he were reciting some ancient text to himself.

'You recognize him?' said Joseph Duvid, in a hushed, awed voice. 'Ve vent all de vay to Highgate, before de crowds got too tick. It vos my idea. But I haff to say he hasn't been much of a help, so far. Maybe for him, returnink vos too much of a shock.'

I'll bet it was. I sat down, surrounded by these lunatics, in my parents' flat, gazing at the drooping lion's head of Karl Marx.

'Vell,' said Joseph Duvid. 'Does efferyvun vant a nice cup off tea?'

23

The eternal mysteries. Just as the Great Question of life after death is answered, it becomes irrelevant and leads to another question. Why? What is it all for? What's to sustain us, if it is all so mundane?

All the questions that nagged us throughout the run-up: what's behind it all? How did they manage it? Were our own leaders in on the conspiracy? Was the CIA or MI5 involved? What about the Dodo's Caucus and its survival techniques? What about the rich, orbiting the earth in their executive jets to try and escape the common fate? No wonder the Angels didn't bother with all that. No Queen, no Country. Just the masses.

Eventually, we, the Dead, gathered to gossip, after my parents had drooped off to their bedroom, exhausted from another day's imprisonment in their own flat, besieged by the Dead hordes. Was it my imagination, or were the crowds outside growing even thicker, their massed murmuring vibrating the windows like a giant humming, deep inside the earth?

Or was the earth indeed singing? Or perhaps lamenting the imminent loss of its all-too-human parasites? Or celebrating? Was it our funeral dirge? The Dodo had mentioned that old occult fantasy, the Hollow Earth. The idea that flying saucers and alien visitors were coming from inside, not outside. Was this where God was hiding, waiting to come out when the rind was scourged of homo sapiens? I remember reading that Hitler, believing another twist of this theory, that we were living on the inner and not the outer curvature of the earth, sent a team of scientists to Indonesia with an extra-powerful telescope and camera equipment, so they could photograph the British naval fleet at Scapa Flow, Scotland, on the opposite side of the curve.

No weirder than our own plans to transmit videos from hell, or heaven, if we somehow struck it lucky, for the delectation of the jug-eared director of Channel 4, if no one else. But he would not be there, either, if all were to be judged. So we would be broadcasting to the ants, the flies and the mice . . .

I found myself, despite my lack of appetite, sipping Joseph Duvid's fine old Russian tea, which was sweet and thick and stuck to the lining like beefsteak. No one turned it down, and it even seemed to revive Karl Marx, who sat up and grudgingly joined in the conversation. It was true, we had been pygmies and he a giant, but now we were all at one level. Immortal and helpless at the same time. Ben Jonson crouched at my mother's low coffee table, polishing off the last of the foil-wrapped morsels I had spurned. He was still the only Dead person I had so far seen eating, and he made up for the other umpteen-quintillion. But he did not seem to go to the bathroom. I noted this for future reference, in case I was commissioned down below to write an instructional volume on *The Six Days That Shnooked the World*.

I appreciated the Hassidic Jews, with their pragmatic plans for the Post-Messianic Age. The assets transferred to the Holy Land, the synagogues and seminaries and foundations to be reconstituted in Jerusalem. Business as usual. The Afterlife as Life, warts and all. Why go to all the bother then? There must be more to it. What did we feel now about eternal punishment and eternal bliss, now that we were dead and on the threshold?

According to Karl, there were grounds for cautious optimism. There was no reason to abandon dialectics. The new tyranny, which he had observed from our window, only seemed to end the history of exploitation by cancelling out the need for labour. But the so-called 'Judgement' obviously cloaked an attempt to establish new relations of production.

The Return of the Dead logically meant an enormous increase in the proletariat, with obvious implications for the continuation and indeed intensification of the class struggle.

Great-grandpa Joseph Duvid vehemently agreed, overjoyed that Marx had finally spoken, after being in a sulk for two days. Carrying the struggle into the next phase of existence, whatever it may be, said Joseph Duvid, was not an avoidable option. Great-grandma Esther also concurred. My grandfather, William V., rattled the *Financial Times*, then laid it down to say he had never heard such rubbish. 'We're dead, so we're dead,' he said. 'We just have to accept it and wait and see what happens next. If God is really behind all this it won't pay to antagonize him.' Grandma Edna agreed with this opinion. 'You can't change yooman nature,' she said. 'But you're dead, voman, you're no longer yooman,' said Joseph Duvid. Rabbi Goldschlaeger the Elder demurred. He looked a simple, country soul, even in Dad's cast-off sweatshirt with BOLLOCKS TO THE TORIES printed on it. I calculated he must have been practising his rabbi-ship in 1860 or thereabouts. He did not speak English of course, but could follow the flow of emotions, and he spoke up, quietly but firmly, in Yiddish. Joseph Duvid answered heatedly and they duelled on for a while, with Marx glowering but Ben Jonson enthusing:

'Jews' arguments,' he said. 'What lively choler. My compatriot, Wm. Shaksper, wrote a play on't. The pound of flesh. 'Tis an admirable stubbornness. But he switched the ending, to butter the nobs. Always an arse-licker, Wm. For my poor self, I always believed we lived but once. But if we are vouchsafed another chance, God's lid, we should take hold of the tree and shake it for all its red apples!'

The dawn crept in on us suddenly. I became aware that time had foreshortened. Perhaps this is why, as the living, we perceived the Dead as so slow at first. But both Ben and Alice had matched the live tempo. We still, it seemed, nourished ourselves off the living, but found our own pace with our peers. I suppose we had become, of necessity, fatalistic, since

Death had literally lost its sting. Nor did we have much room, if any, to manoeuvre. In the new light I could see the crowd in Packington Street had indeed increased. Now the Dead were crowding on to window sills and, in some cases, standing on each other's shoulders, against the walls. I recalled a short science-fiction story by R. A. Lafferty, in which humanoid people from another dimension begin visiting the earth in such numbers that they are eventually walking on each other five levels deep. At the end they leave, so delighted by the 'open spaces' of earth's cities that they call back, 'Next time we'll bring the kids!'

Where is that author now? If he died, he'd be back to see it all happen, as would everyone else who forecast the future. Jules Verne, H. G. Wells, Olaf Stapledon, Philip K. Dick . . . Would they laugh or would they cry? Totally cut-off now from anywhere but this tiny corner of Islington, one can only imagine the tumult elsewhere, as per the Dodo's last reports: in Mecca, Jerusalem, Beijing, Tokyo, Cairo . . . Imagine the Pharaohs, coming to reclaim their kingdom . . . Tutankhamun, elbowing into the Cairo Museum to snatch back his golden death-mask and jewels . . .

Everyone that ever lived . . . And now they were here, on our poor battered, no longer green and pleasant soil. Waiting, waiting for that last dispensation . . . Zillions of Jerrys, pining for zillions of Alices . . . Not even the Angels could cope with this . . . Bumbling Hoppy, with his hapless attempts at human humour . . . The stern Archangel Gabriel, stonewalling Paxman. How long ago it all seems. But it's only been a matter of weeks, not the aeons it seems now. There's no way back.

But is there a way forward?

It struck me that God had a problem. Looking out at the trapped mass, which had no way to move, it was hardly conceivable, even in this dimension of miracles (a Sheckley quote!) that they could be brought to any temporal Judgement. Hoppy's lists and computer round-ups had indicated some form of 'centres' to be set up for the Day. But my earlier image of people stocking up in the supermarkets to stand in line for heaven or hell with their shopping trolleys was patently absurd. There could be no line. With forty-eight hours to go, the sheer impracticalities of the whole endeavour seemed manifest. The Laffertian world demanded a *deus ex machina*.

But I suppose, if you're *Deus*, you can find one . . . I turned back, perceiving movement in the kitchen. It was Dad, raiding the teapot for the dregs of his grandfather's tea. He was carrying a small book under his arm, which dropped on the floor. I picked it up. It was the King James Bible. He took it from me and slipped it in his dressing gown pocket.

I sat down and poured him a cup, as his hands were trembling. 'You gave your mother a real turn there,' he said softly. 'I know, a joke's a way of killing the fear, but that was out of line.'

'It's not a joke, Dad,' I said. 'If it is, it's on me. I took a blast from a shotgun. But it's still me, Dad. We're all who we were. Dead or alive doesn't matter any more. We're all in the same boat. Even Karl Marx.'

'Don't mention that crazy bastard,' he said. 'We went to a lot of trouble to get 'im 'ere. It was my grandpa's idea; I know I shouldn't 'ave listened. But I was so awed to find the old man waiting for us when we got 'ere from 'ammersmith with Ben. The old 'ero of Cable Street. We took Sophie's car and squeezed up to 'ighgate. Hordes of Returnees. Seemed quite 'opeless. Then we saw 'im dodging away from the Angels like a butterfly trying to run from a net. Drew up beside 'im and said, "Karl Marx, I presume. 'Op in." Seemed such a gas at the time. Then 'e found the books on our bookshelves. Lenin, Trotsky, Deutscher and all. Saw 'is face on E. H. Carr's *History of the Bolshevik Revolution*. Began to speed read. Got all agitated. "Socialism in Russia!" he shouted. "What a ridiculous notion!" Then he read some more and got more and more spare. Couldn't stand what 'istory 'ad done to 'is ideas. I tried to calm 'im down. Then 'e went into 'is sulk. It's a bloody good thing I threw Althusser away in last year's spring clean, I can tell you.'

I looked at him. He suddenly looked sunken and old. One sensed the tiredness of the still living human figure, the sapping of vigour moment by moment, the ticking of time's clock. I thought, this is why Alice had offered so readily to spend eternity with me, not her parents. It was not the romantic love I had so blithely assumed. But I was live then, and ticking, too, was I not?

'It's no good, Jerry,' my father said. 'We can't cope with all this. Hidden cameras, resistance, it's all tosh. This is ultimate power, real and naked. I've been reading the Book, to read 'Is mind. It's all so very cruel, under all that talk of mercy and truth and righteousness. This is the real hell, what we 'ave before us, out in the street. There is no Judgement. It's arbitrary. 'E'll leave us 'ere to stew, or pick off the ones 'e wants, who knows what for. If there is anything that's true in this old book of fantasies, it's no morality that I can recognize. Right from the start, why should 'E punish Adam and Eve for what 'E made them be? Why should knowledge be evil? There's an evil idea, itself. Why favour Abel over Cain? Everywhere I found deliberate malice. So none of this should come as any surprise. If you did die, I'm glad you came back to life, Jerry. But when we go, we should be able to go. What's the point of bringing us back to this? We've all been lied to. Power — it's the pattern 'E set up. But I'm not knuckling under. Forget the cameras. I'll just stay where I am. Just sit with us, Jerry. We'll just sit 'ere together, and wait for them to come inside and get us. The Davis family. A stiff-necked lot. The sin of pride, Jerry, it's the only sin worth sinning. Did you read Nietzsche, up there on the fourth shelf? 'E was a crazy and repellent man, in many respects. But 'e tried to define 'is own world. There's that defiant line in *Thus Spoke Zarathustra*:

'"Come! Let us walk now! The hour 'as come — let us walk into the night!"'

24

O Man! Attend!
What does deep midnight's voice contend?
I slept my sleep.
And now awake at dreaming's end.
The world is deep, deeper than day can comprehend . . .

Alas, poor Nietzsche! I knew him well . . . fellow of infinite jest . . . he kissed a horse in Turin one day, didn't he, and was carted off to the bin. And now he is out there too, in his own crowd somewhere . . . Like all the other songsters. Which packed pub are you swaying in now, friend Dylan, and does Death have dominion, after all?

Do not go gentle into that good night . . .

All the crowds, that cannot stop growing . . .

Back, from Cro-Magnon man, past the stone age . . . Is there anyone left under the ground?

We pulled the curtains down, and stopped peeking into the street. Pacing our musky, housebound prison. On the evening of Day Five the electricity stopped. The last vestige of the modern age, snuffed out. Out there, in their secret engine rooms, the great power machines had finally given up the ghost. TV had lost even the Divine Service Message card after Day One, I was told, and descended, like radio, into mush. How would the summons come?

Time running out. The darkest night of all. Even the Dead are exhausted, and sleep. I know I dropped off for seven hours, because I woke with a start to another dawn, the last dawn. And not a dream. Not a spark. Not a flicker of rapid eye movement of any use whatsoever.

177

Ben Jonson too had gone silent. He had been fiddling with an A4 notepad, pretending to make notes of some play which would never be performed, or a sonnet which would never be sung, or a masque which would never be unmasqued.

O Man, Attend! We huddled in the living room, we living dead, for whatever warmth shared ex-humanity can dole out at the last chance. Dad spending most of his time with Mum, who had retreated to her bedroom, understandably unkeen to spend her last day with in-laws. The food had run out, except for Heinz Giant Corn and the driest of Jacob's Cream Crackers. Those aching for privacy would bolt for the toilet, until called out by the next depressive, I did my stint, sitting on the closed seat – another old joy down the toilet, or not, as the case may be – trying my last mad scheme – attempting telepathic contact. I sent out vibrations from the brain to Alice, to Karen, to the Dodo, even to Buster the dog. I thought, for a brief moment, I had broken through, sensing a throaty bark somewhere nearby, but then I recognized Marx's hacking cough, which seemed to have survived the Rising. The eccentricities of the Dead. Ben Jonson, alone, retained his appetite. Karl Marx retained his aches and pains, the cough, the farting, and the piles which made him shift about, groaning. Or was it despair, even from the great dialectitian? Thesis, antithesis, synthesis. Life, death, and – what? Put that in your inferno and smoke it.

And does one sum up the balance of one's life? The pros, the cons, the ups, the downs. Reconstructing that viable defence, the last rehearsal: it wasn't me, officer. I wasn't there at the time, it's a case of mistaken identity. It was my twin brother, Garry. I have sixteen witnesses who can swear blind that I was performing in Yehupetz. I was drunk, it was a youthful indiscretion, I've learned my lesson since then.

Give me another chance and I'll go straight, m'lud. Would I tell a lie, at these prices?

Or the final cry in Room 101: do it to someone else. Do it to . . . ? How low will one go, at the brink . . . ?

178

It's still a total conundrum: how are they going to get us into the court? If we get six and a half seconds each, how long would it take for every case to be heard? Or is there a judge for every defendant? Your own, personal accuser. The shadow who has been there, just beyond the corner of your eye, forever? Another SF conceit. Is the judge yourself, your alter ego? Don't come the raw prawn with me, Davis, I'm you, so I know the whole damn schmeer. Two hundred eternal sentences to run concurrently. Or consecutively? Eligible for parole in three zillion AD. Take him away, cherubim!

And just as despair sets in, Alice, beautiful and radiant in her nineteen-year-old freshness, preserved from putrefaction by the inertia of death, rushes in, her hand raised. 'Stop! This man is mine! I love him! Spare him or send me down with him!' In *A Matter of Life and Death* the celestial jury demanded evidence from the girl who was willing to take David Niven's place in heaven. They extracted a small tear from her cheek, on a rose petal. The judge recited an ode on Love. But I don't think the dear old codgers, Powell and Pressburger, were directing this saga.

My father was pounding on the toilet door. 'Come out, Jerry! It's happening!'

'I haven't finished!' I called out to him.

'You've nothing to start with, you silly boy! Come on out! It's hogmanay out there! Ring out the old! Ring in the new!'

It sounded as if he had finally flipped completely. I didn't have a watch but I was monitoring the time. It was the middle of –

Yes, it was midnight of Day Six.

'We've got till three a.m.!' I shouted, clinging to old hacked data.

But had they meant Greenwich Mean Time, or Jerusalem standard? Or Baghdad, legendary site of the Garden of Eden? That, of course, would be three hours ahead . . . My dead pedant's brain was close to bursting.

179

But there was no point in fooling myself any more.
Time had run out.
I crept out of the toilet.

PART 4

Deus ex Machina

25

The living room curtains had been thrown open. Light flooded through the box-sash windows: red, orange, purple, green, blue, white flashes flickering on the astonished faces of the Davis clan, Joseph, Sophia, Joseph Duvid, Esther, Hilde, Nathan, Feigeh and Schmuel, William (Vissarionovitch) and Edna, and our adopted waifs, Ben Jonson and Karl Marx.

Outside it was like fireworks night for deaf-mutes. The sky exploded silently in multi-coloured signs. Right ahead of us, in the direction of Canonbury, a vast notice wheeled in spinning letters of red and gold:

> GOOOOD MORNING TERRA! FOR I AM ALPHA
> AND OMEGA, THE BEGINNING AND THE END,
> THE FIRST AND THE LAST!

On either side other slogans erupted:

> REJOICE!
> THE DAY OF THE REVELATION IS COME!

The great sign faded and was replaced by another:

> WATCH THIS SPACE! YOUR PERSONAL GATE TO
> SALVATION IS DUE TO OPEN IN ONE HOUR, AND
> COUNTING!

And indeed a great digital clock in the sky was flipping down its numbers. It had already reached fifty-eight minutes and thirty-five seconds. Thirty-four seconds. Thirty-three . . .

The massed humming growl that had been our background for three days had stopped, replaced by an eerie silence. Then, when the clock reached fifty-eight minutes, the lull was spectacularly ended. A great blare, as loud as a thousand air raid sirens, enveloped the street like a blanket. It was a sound which seemed to come out of the depths of the earth, not an earth any longer grumbling and snoring, but an earth awakened to a sudden aching need . . .

'Now dat's what I call a Last Trump!' said Joseph Duvid approvingly, though his words were like an echo in a storm. The rabbi, Schmuel Goldschlaeger, was rocking beside me, eyes closed, praying, as was his wife, and Edna, the accountant's spouse. The rest of us were too dumbfounded, though I could see my mother's lips move. How she needed the support of that stubborn, world-weary clan of Italian survivors now, all gathered perhaps in Bastardo, that aptly named obscure haven in the Umbrian sun. Sophia, Greek for Wisdom. But even Wisdom can do little for us now.

The siren blare was increasing, beating us down to our knees. I could see the crowd pitching and yawing within that inch and a half they may have had between them – though, Dodo, wasn't that just a global average? We fled into our innermost room, the kitchen, but the siren blasted through the walls, the ceiling, the floor. Cotton wool was useless, plastic earplugs futile and even the industrial earmuffs which I had bought Dad when the council spent six months digging up the sewer outside were absolutely ineffective. The sound went on and on.

We were banging our heads on the table when the blast ceased as suddenly as it had begun. The lights still playing from the window. We looked cautiously out. The sign had changed again:

THE TREE OF LIFE HAS ENDLESS ROOTS!
THE FIRES CAUTERIZE BUT HEAL!
EACH WILL INDIVIDUALLY BE SUMMONED!
FEAR IS ENDED! REACH FOR JOY!

I did not like the smell of this at all. Something was stirring in me. Perhaps the memory of other gateways with soothing slogans inscribed over them. Or would there be a sign for the showers: delousing and deconstruction . . . ?

Do not panic, Gerald! You're dead, you have no choice now. But it's the living I fear for, whose branch is about to be cut down. My father and mother, embracing. The cruelty, the cruelty.

They shall not pass. If we hide in the toilet, the broom cupboard under the stairs, the storage closet, the abortive loft.

The clock showed forty-eight minutes.

A burst of a different kind of noise erupted in the corridor outside the apartment. Dad opened the front door a smidgeon. The residents of all the other flats were running out, waving their hands and screaming. I must confess it had its funny side; even dead, I can still recognize a good act. It was like the Marx Brothers' cabin scene in *A Night at the Opera*: dozens of people spewing out from small one-bedroom flats. Literally hundreds clogging the stairway, rushing in panic down to the main door. Wrenching it open to let in a swarm of people crammed up against it from the outside. A flailing mêlée of arms, legs and heads. Dad closed the door again.

'Madness.'

'We'd better keep dem out,' said Joseph Duvid, galvanized into a familiar course of action, with Mosley's fascist hordes gleaming in his eyes. 'Barricade de door!' Like lunatics trying to stave off lunacy, we dragged the hall wardrobe up against the door, fortifying it with an Ikea storage box and a wedge of kitchen chairs.

Non pasaran! The old man was actually humming Carmela between his teeth. Karl Marx, sweating from the exertion, looked energized by this engagement. Will the accountant, on the other hand, had joined the three other supplicants in the living room. Mum perked up too, went to boil up a new kettle of tea. Dad laid his stash of mini-camcorders out on the kitchen table.

'Right. We'd better get ready. You can see how small these are. They'll go anywhere, taped under a sleeve, your trouser pocket, shirt pocket, under an 'at, even under your sock. You just have to point it in the general direction. Automatic focus and aperture, seventy-hour battery, automatic transmission. Whatever will be, will be.'

Ben Jonson avidly stuffed three of them round his expanded abdomen. Joseph Duvid, Esther, Mum, Dad, Karl Marx and I each took one, and I taped mine over my right ankle. The light from outside was growing, though our house clock showed 12:40 a.m. I looked out. The sky had whitened, as if lit by an artificial, neon-like glow in which the various coloured signs and slogans were dancing about like gleeful foals.

'Like Theodorus Nitz Commercials,' I said. 'Philip K. Dick,' I explained to my puzzled father. 'They fly about, you have to catch and crush them.'

'It's us they want to catch and crush.'

He had, incongruously, put on his demo overalls, with the multiple pockets, a spanner thrust in the breast and a hammer and screwdriver pushed in under a studded belt. He looked dressed for a confrontation with the British National Revival Party in Millwall, rather than with the Lord God of Hosts in Islington. But who was I to complain? Mum donned her overalls too, but stocked up, more pragmatically, with TCP, mosquito lotion, her compact travelling kit of toothbrush, toothpaste, creams, lip lotion, kleenex pads, Q-tips, scissors and thread, assorted bandaids, Paracetemols, travel hairdryer, mini-coffeemate, pocket torch and a selection of homoeopathic powders for use against stomach ailments, ulcers, gallstones, cystitis and mild carcinogens. They found spare overalls, too, for Joseph Duvid and Esther, but I turned down the offer, having changed quite comfortably into a uniform of my own: Comedy Shop sweatshirt and dirty dungs kept in my own old drawer. Ben Jonson shook his head ruefully at our assemblage.

''Tis not exactly a match of colours,' he mused, 'but 'tis enough, 'twill serve. This is the second instant,' he added, 'that I have gone to meet my Maker. I must say I would tarry another four hundred years. Three throws might strike the jackpot.'

'Right,' said Dad, 'we might as well sit down and wait.'

We sat on the living room chairs and sofa, bathed in the window's brilliant white light. The clock outside glowered blackly: seventeen minutes, twenty-six seconds, and counting.

At fifteen minutes, the sirens blasted again. We stayed in place, gritting our teeth, till they were done. Once again, the sign outside had changed:

> PLEASE REMAIN CALM! YOUR PERSONAL GATE
> WILL OPEN AS SOON AS POSSIBLE. FOLLOW
> ALL AUTHORIZED INSTRUCTIONS.

Where might one find unauthorized instructions, at this point? The bile rises, even from the gut of the Dead. What Wilhelm Reich called the 'vegetative centre'. Where it all begins. The umbilical spot. Here were we separated and here will we be reattached? The rehooked cord, reeling us all in, to meet the fisherman at journey's end . . .

Or a beginning? It's astonishing that the most vexed, unanswerable question of human existence will be answered for us in thirteen minutes' time. And counting.

Twelve. Eleven. Ten. Nine . . .

Will I meet Alice there? Will she meet me?

My father and mother hold hands. She begins to hum an old Italian tune. I recognize an aria from Verdi's *Nabucco*. The lament of the exiled Jews in Babylon:

> Fly, thoughts, on wings of gold . . .
> O my country, fair and lost, O remembrance, fatal,
>   sweet . . .

All our coded hopes and faded dreams.

There was a sudden, great, stupendous silence again. So deep that we could hear our own harsh, restive breathing. Then Marx let out an almighty fart. 'Bravo!' responded Joseph Duvid. But his cry waned on the ominous calm. I looked out.

The clock outside had blinked out, on the three minute mark.

But the ticking of our own clocks continued. The old crock on the wall, that Portobello Road folly. The watches on Dad and Mum's wrists . . .

I looked around the silent crowd and then squinted carefully. Something had changed. I called to the clan. 'Come look at this.' They crowded round.

There was no doubt. The crowd was beginning to thin out. The hour was not yet zero, but the process was in hand –

People were beginning to disappear. It was not easy to make out as the mass was still glutinous, but the whole street was clearly visible under the bright white sky. Here and there, one could tell, little spaces were opening up, spontaneously, then filled as the crowd stretched into the gaps. There were too many heads, too many human dots, to see what was happening at first. But people were vanishing. The Returned Dead, Re-returning, to what? Were they being yanked up into the sky, or falling through holes in the ground?

There was no sign of either method. The gathered Dead were beginning to wink out. 'There, I saw one!' shouted Joseph Duvid, pointing straight down. I looked and caught another one. Definitely a figure had been there, standing in the crush one moment, the next, not.

And the signs had faded from the sky.

'I suggest we get away from this window,' muttered grandfather William, as if we would be spared if we stopped seeing. But we were not, for the next instant he looked round with a cry. 'Edna! Where are you?'

My grandmother had gone, leaving the *Jewish Chronicle* Passover Supplement neatly folded on the sofa. William plunged through the flat desperately, looking in the kitchen, the bathroom, the bedroom and spare rooms. 'Edna! Where on earth have you got to?' He yanked open the door of the stairwell cupboard.

Nowhere on earth, poor William. Rabbi Schmuel and Feigeh tried to calm him down, speaking soothing words in Yiddish, but the accountant blundered back across the room.

'Thieves! Kidnappers! Murderers!'

In the street, the disappearances were speeding up. Ben Jonson and Karl Max were looking down, fascinated.

'Astonishing!' said Marx. 'Malthusianism in action!'

'Well, I'll be hanged!' exclaimed the playwright. ''Tis like the audience at Wm.'s fifth acts, poor bugger . . .'

Dad was looking over my shoulder. 'I've heard about the Rapture,' he said, 'but this is ridiculous.'

Humanity was snuffing out like flies. They were neither rising, nor sinking. They were simply there one moment, the next gone without trace. And no visible agency to snatch them from their place. Death, it seemed, still had surprises in store . . .

'Young Gerald!' Joseph Duvid's cry tore me back from my rapt gaze. 'De Rabbi!' he said. 'De Rabbi and his vife! Dey vent togeder! I saw dem go – completely farshvundern!'

All that trouble, heaving that wardrobe against the door. We looked at each other. Nathan and Hilde, too, had gone, but they had sat so quietly in a corner we had not noticed their evaporation. There were only eight of us left. What could we do? Form a chain and stay connected? This was Mum's immediate thought:

'All of us, let's hold hands!'

We did so, clutching at our human straws. Dad, Mum, Jerry, Joseph Duvid, Esther, William, Ben and Karl.

All we are sa-aying, is give peace a chance . . .

This, the greatest comic sketch of them all and no one to clap, cry, or throw fruit. I always knew I was in the wrong business. Now I knew I was in the wrong cosmos too. But it was far too late.

Ben Jonson ruptured the chain first, winking into thin air, vast pot and all, between grandpa William and Karl. Then William, Esther and Joseph Duvid winked out. Dad grabbed hold of Karl's pudgy hand. I knew he had always wanted to do this, to touch the man who had shaken the world. But now it was just the squeeze of two lost wayfarers, about to drift into the great unknown. We clutched each other, we four, like drowning kittens.

'I won't let you go alone, Joe!' shouted Mum.

They vanished together, leaving me standing in the middle of a suddenly denuded living room holding on to a sheepish Karl Marx.

'I don't believe in that bastard up there,' he said, in that thick Germanic accent. 'Do you?'

'No,' I said, and vanished.

26

I found myself in a small, bare cubicle, rather like the inside of a portakabin. But there were no windows or doors. There was a small table and two chairs on either side of it.

I sat on what I deemed to be the client's chair, the one furthest from the wall. No need to antagonize whoever there was to antagonize. This was not the time for smart moves.

I remembered the camera under my sock but made no move to touch it. There was no waste bin in which to discard it. I crossed my legs and uncrossed them, folded my arms and unfolded them. I cleared my throat, and wiped my nose on my shirt tail.

I remembered my first job interview, at seventeen, for the post of deputy-assistant floorboy at Debenham's Superstore, so I could pay for my beans at Enfield Poly. They wanted to know whether I really saw my future in Draperies and Bedlinen. I had to say I did not. But then I discovered hacking, and reset all the prices, so that people bought sofabeds for five pounds. Or at least, they tried. I could have gone into hacking, I suppose, in a big way. But then I discovered jokes, and was lost.

My poor, redundant living. Telling lies, to find truth. Which was which? I pondered this unanswerable conundrum. And then Hoppy walked into the room.

Or rather, he walked through the wall, to sit down carefully on the chair opposite me, neatly working his wings over its back.

I might have known it.

'You might have known it,' he echoed me, speaking in a soft, soothing tone. 'Who could judge you? There has to be some slight acquaintance with the case. And it could not be you, you're too biased.'

His unhuman eyes blinked kindly. I was going to be judged by an Angelic schlemiel. It was only right and proper.

'It is only right and proper,' he echoed. 'But you have known it all along. You have to be judged by your own standards. Otherwise what is the point?'

I remained silent on that one. It struck me that a properly constituted defence attorney would not be amiss in this pickle. After all, this Angel had told me, right at the outset, that I was going down, not up. I recalled Michelangelo's shrink-wrapped Sistine mural – the clean-shaven Christ – who looked, it now struck me, not unlike a more handsome Hoppy, if in much better physical nick – turning his back on the damned, who floated down to the bottom right corner of the painting, where they were beaten by Charon's oar into the infernal mud.

'Do you believe in hell?' the Angel asked me.

I was very wary of these Do you believe questions. Having made what might have been the *faux pas* of eternity in my last reply to Karl Marx, I was not about to make my fate any worse.

'Since you read my mind,' I said, 'you know what I believe and don't believe.' Is this where I make my stand for a lawyer? But what's the point, they're all in hell anyway. Or on the way. Imagine the consequences. A billion attorneys, arguing a trillion lost cases for ever. Just think of the fees.

'That's not necessarily the case,' he said to me. 'Thoughts are often an inchoate, floating mass. There is something that organizes this stew into coherent concepts, guides for speech and action. Call it the will. Call it conscience, or morality. These are linguistics. Wittgenstein wrote: 'Whereof one cannot speak, thereof one must be silent.' But he saw the flaw himself, later. If you need to know in order to speak, you would never speak. You have to make assumptions and judgements. Everything in your life is judgement. I know this

192

because we do a course on these matters. For ourselves, we do not understand the problem. That is why we are unprejudiced.'

'We?'

'We that you call "Angels". We are made this way to suit your culture. Your old, powerful icons. Jung did some good work on this score. His, ah, trial is likely to be one of the longest. Quite a lot to iron out there. But I can now answer your question: no, we are not human, nor Angelic. We were made by the same Maker who made you, but for a more precise purpose. To guide you from that world towards the next. But, like your biblical Moses, we do not enter into the Promised Land.'

'If it's the land earmarked for me it sounds like your gain.'

'So you believe in hell?'

We're back to the trick question.

'What kind of hell?' I asked him.

'You know what kind of hell,' he answered. 'The fire, the ice, the brimstone, the eternal torments, the worm that gnaws the surface of the eye for ever, the overcrowded stench, the endless torture, the pit of total despair.'

'I fear it, but I don't believe in it.'

'An excellent answer, my Gerald. Why should you fear what you don't believe? Wouldn't it be true that only a true believer, a devout Catholic, for instance, could believe in punishment eternal? Only such a one would expect to go there, if only, as a purgatory, to expiate the sins he or she knows they're guilty of? Just as a devout Moslem knows that only lack of faith can merit such a terrible fate? Or a devout Jew knows that failure in life means banishment from God? It's all in the mind, Gerald.'

I began to perk up. Whadya know, a sixties' Angel. Perhaps my luck was in after all.

' "From each according to his ability, to each according to his needs." That's an old moral imperative purloined by your bearded friend. What is his hell? Continuing injustice, the

perfidy of friends, the indifference of the masses, the mis-
application of his dreams. Not the physical discomfort of his
famous carbuncles and piles. Human beings are capable of the
most astonishing courage. Do you not think they might, *in
extremis*, endure the Catholic hell if they considered it unjust
and outrageous? On earth, they might go mad, but madness is
a temporal condition. You cannot go mad in the afterlife. I can
assure you of that.'

'How do you know, if you can't go there?' I was becoming
bold enough to challenge him. The memory of David Niven's
film nagged at me. If I had a choice of lawyers, who would I
take? Socrates? Clarence Darrow? Melvyn Bayley? Certainly
not my best friend, Marek. He would just fuck things up.

Hoppy sighed. 'You're right, Gerald. It's a sad fate, like a bus
driver, who goes everywhere but has to drive back. There's no
point in deceiving you: *we don't know what lies on the other side*.
When what transpires here is completed, I walk out back into
the world which you have left. I know your accusation. But it
is not for us. We don't supplant you. But it's true, the animals
remain. The planet repairs itself after your fairly brief domain.
Then does it start again? Do the primates march once more
towards their mastery of the tool, the resources, the weapons?
I genuinely don't know. Our job is done, we are returned unto
the bosom of our mutual Maker. We sleep, until the next task,
at which, when we are reawakened, we will have no memory
of this. This is our purpose. And no, we don't think to rebel.
That's a purely human myth. Lucifer. It's an old wives' tale.'

So much for Dante Alighieri. But if hell's a myth, what
about heaven?

'Exactly, Gerald. You are beginning to understand.'

'So you just told me lies to scare me.'

'Not to scare you, but to make you think. To cause you to
look into yourself. To bring out your own inner condition.'

'But I've just been panicking, the last five months.'

'Like everyone else. It's understandable. Fear of the unknown. But rebellion and transcendence are enduring human

194

traits. That is why we imposed so many traditional restrictions on your societies when we arrived. Conforming to your respective images of the stern moral overseers. We are inherently pledged to bring out the best in you in the most difficult circumstances. For this you need the jab in the *tuches*.'

It's funny, you don't look Jewish. 'What are you, Hoppy? An android? An artificial being? Created, made, by whom? Who is God? If all morality is relative, why is He doing all this? And how many times has it been done before? And to whom?'

Now there's a bunch of sixty-four thousand dollar questions.

'There is no Who or Why, Gerald,' said Hoppy, dashing my sudden hopes. 'The Maker is the Maker. Who else? We don't remember. What is artificial? How did it start? The quark? The amoeba? The Big Bang, or the Small? We let you worry about these things. We're just happy to complete a job well done. Morality is not relative. It is a constant you have built, with its multiple faces. You are judged by your own criteria.'

Round and round in these circles we go.

'So that's it, Hoppy. You're judge, jury and executioner. I've already condemned or saved myself. No defence, no legal arguments, no last-minute technicalities. What about witnesses? Those who might, nevertheless, put in a good word. The people you've torn me away from: Alice, Dad, Mum, my old lantsmen, Ben Jonson, Marek, even Karl Marx. Has he been left behind, with the animals?'

'Love, Gerald, is that the thing? The old saw. Is hell or heaven other people? I told you honestly, Jerry, I don't know. *I don't know what happens to you when you leave this room.* This is our special burden. The melancholy of the Angels. For if we knew, who can tell, perhaps we might, despite it all, rebel?'

Indeed. So what are the criteria? My own? I don't think I've been that bad. Tot 'em up, a couple of thousand peccadilloes. Causing occasional unhappiness. Driving my parents, girlfriends, Karen especially, spare. Never cleaning the toilet bowl or the bath. Lying for short-term advantage. Telling terrible jokes for money. Falling short of my own standards. Coveting my neighbour's PC. Screwing up Debenham's for one working week. Masturbation. Spilling my seed. All the sort of nonsense you'd mumble to a priest if you were that way inclined. *Ego te absolvo*. Thirty Hail Marys and fifteen Our Fathers, my son. And change your hairdresser, that thing is an affront to civilization. None of this can be serious.

'I think,' I said, looking on the bright side, as Monty Python so wisely advised, 'I should undergo a period of self-criticism and self-repudiation, followed by community service and a deposit of my soul, if necessary, with the relevant celestial court, as a guarantee of my good behaviour. But I could not bear to be alone. I'll do a period in hell, Catholic, Protestant or Hottentot, if I can be reunited with Alice and with my poor old dad and mum. With a little distance between the generations, say a fifty pee bus ride away. It's a fair cop, officer. I'll pay my debt to society.'

'Society no longer exists,' said Hoppy, 'and it is all completely out of my hands.'

He got up, looked at me, with a look of unfathomable compassion, whether for me or for himself I could not tell. What if he truly doesn't know? What if he's just whistling Dixie, and hell, real hell, eternal, total, remorseless, physical pain exists, and is waiting, for the recalcitrant, the wayward, the unbeliever? What if he is the bus driver to Sheol, but will never know? Is this his eternal torment? And, if so, for what sin, committed by the Angels in what aeon, in what dimensionless core?

What if they are the punished, and we the rewarded?

He shrugged, turned, and walked back through the wall.

I sat and waited alone in the cubicle. And waited. A slow terror taking hold. Was this it? Was I condemned for eternity to be in this waiting room, in this barren antechamber, in this cold sweat of job interview anxiety, the cold sadism of total sensory deprivation? Was God trained by the same CIA operatives who advised Somoza and Pinochet?

'This is not justice,' I said.

The chamber winked out, in the blink of an eye.

27

I was back in the tunnel above the nuclear bunker. At least, it seemed to be the same place: the dark, crumbling brick-work; the chiselled inscription I could just make out on the wall: THE BRUMMY OIKS, 1995; the rusty, broken mine-shaft rails. I could hear the drip, drip of water. There was no source of light, but I could see, dimly. There was a corpse on the ground.

I recognized myself despite the open, staring eyes and contorted face, blackened with grime. The body was sprawled in an unnatural position. The top half was bent away from the lower. The mid-section, the chest, had been blown open by the shotgun blast, and was a gaping hole, oozing black, with shattered bones and entrails spilling out. At second sight, it was not the ooze that was moving, but a glutinous mass of maggots, feeding. Others were marching purposefully into the mouth, nostrils and ears.

My dead cry echoed down the tunnel, off the dank cracked walls, back to me. I ran and tripped over the broken rails. I gashed my nose. I could feel the wound and bleeding.

'Hoppy!' I called out. 'For God's sake!'

My bellow boomeranged and there was no answer.

'Alice!' I shouted. 'Dodo! Buster! Karen! Brother Duff! Mother!'

The words just bounced off the walls mockingly. I sensed an utter desolation. There was just me and the corpse. The two options. I ran down the tunnel. The corpse was blocking my way up.

My way down, however, was also obstructed, by piles of discarded mining trucks, strewn about, spilling mounds of coal. I stopped and looked back. The corpse appeared to be slithering on the ground towards me.

I tried to squeeze my way through the trucks, realizing the origin of this predicament with a tiny twinge of hope: it was the womb-death dream. I was in my recurring ur-nightmare in which I am endlessly looking for a way out of just such a sunken tunnel, lost in a labyrinthine maze of shafts and caves in which lurk unfathomable terrors. Black-clad inquisitors with sharpened pincers, professional torturers waiting in dungeons, shackled friends and loved ones, crying out piteously for a help I cannot render.

The corpse was coming closer and closer, and now I could see it was being propelled by the thousands of little creeping maggots who were pulling it along with them. This, I was sure, derived from some forgotten horror movie in some post-midnight Odeon. The whole point of the womb-death dream was that I could, invariably, wake from it. I only had to decide when the danger was too close and shake myself loose. It never failed.

The maggots crawled closer. Now I could see their individual faces. Tiny chitinous masks of my friends, my relatives, colleagues at work, chance acquaintances. All gibbering with tiny, desperate voices, dribbling slime from tiny, razor tipped teeth.

It was definitely not the womb-death dream. I called myself awake, but no response. The cliché failed to come to my aid. There was no Davis carcass lying blotto in some bed, snoring off a Leicester Square binge. The only Davis carcass was the one dragging towards me.

Fucking shit. 'Hoppy!' No answer. I had to get my feet off the ground, slithering and climbing up on the tipped trucks, scrabbling at the tunnel ceiling. With some relief I found a narrow hole, with rusty rungs, apparently leading upwards. 'Thank you, Hoppy, Angel,' I breathed, pulling myself up. Below, the myriad tiny faces of my shrunken friends gabbled at me.

'Je-e-e-rrie-eeeee, do-on't leeeeave uuuussss . . .'

Shaking and heaving, I pulled myself up the ladder. The passage was incredibly narrow, and I had to squeeze and squash my body, tearing my shirt and skin raw. Was it narrower up above? This was it then, entombment. Edgar Allan Poe. Wake up, you fucking stupid bastard!!

It was narrower. I couldn't pass through. I looked up with my radar vision. The shaft turned into a cone. It was a dead end. The only way was down again.

Think, Jerry. Despite the dramatic poverty, the best option is nevertheless the dream. He woke up and a new dawn was dawning outside the window. The reader may chaff, but you'll be safe.

Not a chance. I tried to wield the brain cells. Dead or alive, you use your assets. If it were the dream, and I were to climb down, towards the maggots, I had as good an option to come out at that point as at this. And if it is not the Dream, I had no option.

Down again, rung after rung. My leg soon touched air, and, gingerly, the mining trucks.

The corpse was gone. No rotting Jerry, no jabbering maggots. So far, so good. Perhaps they'd moved on, in search of other pastures. I might not be the only victim lost in this loathsome hole. Or was this my private hell?

Why couldn't my fears be as Sartre's? I'd take his *huis clos* any day. The closer the huier. Just not alone. Just not alone, for God's sake.

The corpse had gone. I retraced my steps back to the point of my appearance. The tunnel sloped gently up in the direction from which, in my death-scene, the Anti-Lazarenes had come. In hell, as it is on earth? I followed the line of busted rails.

The tunnel bent up, and then sideways, but there was no sign of an end. No sign of life, neither, not even maggots, let alone the Dead. Every now and again I stopped and shouted, cupping my hands, as in the movies:

'Alice! Dodo! Karen! Anybody there?'

The tunnel just went on and on. In real life, in the old world, there must be thousands of miles of these shafts, which human beings once dug to drag wealth out of the ground. What a mad, crazy enterprise! Who was the man who sparked the first fire? Who was the lunatic who invented the wheel? What became of the monkey that threw the bone into the air in Kubrick's *2001*? If I got hold of him I'd tell him a thing or two . . . Those primates didn't know when they were well off, scratching their balls and grunting in the wide open African veldt.

Pain had returned. I was aching all over from my scrabbling falls and climb. I could touch blood from a dozen gashes in the skin, and my Comedy Shop sweatshirt was in tatters. Was I alive again? It hardly seemed possible, given what had just transpired. But my memory of past events was much sharper than it had been when I had been dead up above, and my anguish and longing for Alice had returned full blast.

And if it had returned for me, had it been so for her? What passed for her, in her own little cubicle, with whoever, whatever 'bus driver' had brought her to the final personal test? Surely she had all the credit I lacked: a sinless past, a youth to have redeemed? Would she enjoy, with memory and pain restored, a Jerriless heaven? Or would she be campaigning, like Jill Morrell, for my return? And Dad and Mum? But this depended on the Maker's (I can't call it God down here) ideas on post-Trotskyism. From what I've seen so far, he's agin it. But these may be early days . . .

Buoyed up by my escape from my corpse, I trudged on. At least I was not yet feeling hunger or thirst. I could sustain myself with tiny mercies. Trying to re-exercise the brain. If it was, as Hoppy said, all in the mind, I might have in some sense the power to influence events. I thought an opening. I thought a big huge hole at the tunnel's end leading to a grassy verge on the slope of a good English summer hill, with butterflies and a busy, honking motorway to Birmingham in the middle distance . . .

Instead I came to a bend in the shaft which led, after about fifteen feet, to a complete dead end. There had clearly been some kind of cave-in weeks or years before, I couldn't tell, blocking off the way ahead in a mound of timbers and rock.

I sank down in despair and exhaustion, leaning my back against the rock. If this is a test it's not an easy one. Why did I have to start at Level Ninety-Nine? I remembered a quote from Albert Einstein: 'God does not play dice with the universe.' Well, he certainly does with me.

The tunnel was utterly silent. But then, again, a scrabbling noise. I looked about dreading or hoping for some form of life, even some low vermin, a rat would be a boon companion, I'd settle for a dung beetle! Something living, something real.

But it was not. Coming at me out of the darkness, from the path I had traversed, was my corpse again, sliding, slithering, dragged by its horrible galley-crew over the gravel and stones.

'Je-e-rrieeeee . . . Da-a-veeeeeessss . . .' The myriad little chomping mouths.

'It's a traditional horror movie gambit,' I said aloud. 'The last gasp of the creature, before the saving moment, with the axe.'

But I had no axe, nor, what I needed more than anything else then, a flamethrower. There were only the stones, which I began to throw, but these fell on to my carcass with such a dreadful squelch that I hurriedly stopped. The maggots had fanned out along the entire width of the tunnel. There was no way I could squeeze by. There were no mining trucks to climb on. There was no aperture in the roof. There was only the solid rock behind me. I burrowed into it, scrabbling like a terrified rodent, tearing my fingernails and fingers. There was no give in the mound. The maggots dragged the corpse closer and closer. Its eyes were now staring right at me. There was a worm gnawing at each eyeball.

I screamed like a demented soul. It takes one to know one. I wrapped myself round the rock. I embraced it. I pressed myself face down into it.

The rock gave. It took me in like rubber. It sucked me in like the most grateful lover. I sucked the solid stone with my mouth. It pushed through into my palate. It oozed through into my brain. It pushed at my eyes from inside. It swallowed my legs, my arms, my groin. I've heard about gallstones but this was ridiculous. Boulders were passing through my bowels. My penis stretched, taut to bursting.

Then I was through. I stood up, brushing gravel and dust off my shoulders. I was standing on the stairway of what seemed to be a very old hotel or apartment house. It was not a functioning one, because the five or six doors around the stairway were all sealed up with nailed wooden planks, or cement. Along a dusty corridor all the other doors in sight appeared similarly blocked. The walls of the corridor and stairway were covered in layers of peeling paper, on which there was a very faded pattern of dark brown leaves. Dust was everywhere, the floorboards were bare and broken. Loose joists and timbers were stacked up, impeding easy movement. The window by the stairs was barred with a grille which prevented access to the glass, which was totally opaque with grime. There was a lift which looked completely unused and which did not respond to its pressed button. What could have been a floor number was on the lift door: 999.

I looked down into the stairwell and saw nothing but a swirl of dust. The drop appeared bottomless. I didn't dare go into the corridor for fear of the holes in the floor. It was as if no one had lived here for at least five hundred years. Nevertheless I tried my Tarzan call: 'Aliiiiice . . .' answered by the usual echo.

The stairs led up, too, into a dull grey mist, but I preferred to go down. Gingerly I climbed over the fallen timbers and shards of broken crates, chairs and torn cartons, and tested the stairs. They creaked but held. I started down. This too was an old, old story. I had been in this hotel many a night, but not, usually, starting so high. Nevertheless, as Spencer

Tracy said in *20,000 Years in Sing Sing*: 'Lady, I got nothin' but time.' Or was it Spencer Tracy? And did he say that?

I went on down, checking the lift at each flight, scuffing my legs against the junk and flotsam, but managing to keep my balance. On each floor the lift was dead. My feet and legs turned into blubber. My head began to swim. And then, at the seven-hundred and fifty-sixth floor, the lift shaft buzzed when I pressed down the button. Alleluia! I waited by the door.

What if there was someone in the lift? What if, up or down these endless flights, there were other lost souls trying to climb down, or up? Or would it be my corpse again?

I was ready for anything, but, when the lift door slid open, there was no one there. Just an empty, dusty but inviting lift, with only two buttons inside, marked UP and DOWN, and a grimy panel with a very faded and crinkled paper on which was scrawled:

> THIS ELEVATOR WAS LAST INSPECTED BY
> SYDNEY KOWALSKI, CITY SHAFT SURVEYOR,
> JANUARY 12th 1999.

Which was barely four months ago, Terran Time, Anno Domini. Or had I gone, like H. G. Wells' Time Traveller, into the far future? I pressed the button marked DOWN. The lift juddered, but descended, creaking, hissing and squealing like a slaughtered pig.

DOWN. Remembering Alice. My own, and her fictional archetype. 'One side will make you grow taller, and the other side will make you grow shorter . . . One side of what, the other side of what, thought Alice. "Of the mushroom," said the caterpillar, just as if she had asked it aloud . . .' But there was nothing to bite off here . . .

I felt much calmer as the lift reached the bottom. I remembered elements of the dream. Once, when I had come out of the lift shaft, there had been tiny dwarf figures, with scythes, rushing up to slash my ankles. Their faces, I remembered, were of the most consummate evil – non-human, sterile and dead.

But now I am the dead. And there were no little homunculi. Nor maggots, whom I had left high in the sky. The lift door opened on to a wide platform enclosed by an arching roof of patchy, crumbling tiles. Drawn up, on ordinary rails, was an astonishing apparition, which had definitely not come from my dreams. This was something brand new, or rather, very old, it seemed, as it shifted and rolled its huge beady eyes towards the human figures on the platform. They were all dressed in lederhosen and Alpine caps, with bedraggled feathers set in the crown. Grey, steely, robotic creatures were pushing them with collapsing metal tweezers into an open door in the belly of the beast. It was large, about the size of a subway carriage, black and chitinous, with waving claws and antennae, rather like a cross between a beetle and a lobster, with fluid dripping over its back. It was snorting or breathing harshly through two open nostrils in the front, below the eyes, which now fixed on me with a baleful, weary stare.

'Last call! All passengers must board!' The robot machines rushed up towards me. I waved them away, but approached the creature. It loomed above me, huffing and wheezing.

'Are you an asthma sufferer?' I asked it. But it only wheezed more loudly.

'All aboard!' shouted the head robot, waving a bunch of flags. I think I identified the Union Jack, the Stars and Stripes, the Greek, Israeli, Saudi Arabian and Italian insignia.

'When does the next train leave?' I asked the head robot.

'In another six million years,' it answered.

'In that case . . .' I moved reluctantly towards the door, beyond which the other passengers were already seated, stuck in their unfolded newspapers.

'Six strands,' said the robot. A pincer shot out, nipping off a lock of my hair. 'What's the terminal station?' I asked it, still hesitating.

'There is no terminus,' it said in its Dalek voice. I climbed into the creature. Its door slid shut, and it jerked forward on the rails.

28

At first I thought there were no windows, but then a passenger pulled the drapes. There were two rows of facing seats, the width of the carriage, like ancient British Rail stock. Three passengers sat facing me with one beside me, leaning against the window. Their luggage was rattling precariously on the wire racks above their heads: very old battered suitcases with multiple place labels, lumps of stuff in tied-up sheets or pillow slips, a banjo wrapped in brown paper, a stopped grandfather clock tied up in string, and a chicken glowering from a barred cage. The passengers were all dressed in that bizarre Austrian manner, and all reading identical editions of the *Volkischer Neue Zeitung*, which was headlined '*GRAZ SCHATZ STADTS PLATZ.*' The rest was a mass of incomprehensible Gothic.

I looked out of the window. The glass was grimy but I could see the landscape. We were travelling past what appeared to be an immense garbage tip, a mountain range of household debris, mangled vehicle parts and engines, tens of thousands of black plastic bags, mounds of rags, spectacles, gold teeth, hair. Then the scene changed and became neatly stacked piles of thigh bones, calf bones, forearms, ribs, hip bones, finger bones and skulls. These must have been measured in the millions, by the time we had rattled past for half an hour.

'Valley of the dry bones, eh?' I remarked to my fellow passengers. But they just rustled their newspapers and threw me sharp glances, sniffing and clucking their teeth. The man at the window rolled his head wearily. He motioned queryingly at me with his hand. I understood and nodded. We changed places, and I settled by the window. I tried to wipe it a little cleaner with my tattered shirt, but the improvement was marginal.

'Do you take this route often?' I ventured, nevertheless, to open up a conversation. If there was going to be no terminus, I figured, one might as well try to be friendly. But they raised their papers even higher, so that I could not see their eyes.

'This is a new route for me,' I said, anyway. 'I usually take the Piccadilly Line. It's faster and there are less bomb scares.'

The bones finally petered out. We were travelling along a flat vista of rolling wheatfields under a dull grey sky. Clouds twisted and curled as if driven by strong winds but the wheat did not stir.

At least we were out of the grime. My heart continued lifting. I could at least begin to compose my thoughts, to try and make some rational judgements, to take stock of events. I was not in the Catholic hell. One good point. I was most probably not dreaming. One bad point. My corpse was decomposing. One bad point. I was going through a landscape I could not identify in a land, or universe, or plane of being I had no maps of, cut off from everyone I knew or loved. Three bad points. I was trapped in a carriage with four crazy Austrians in lederhosen. This was not panning out too well.

But at least if you're on the move you might get somewhere. I had a strange trust in the train-beetle that was carrying us along. Somehow it had the look of something that knows what it's doing, even if it has no desire to communicate this to the plebs. The wheatfields looked earthian. I planted my face against the window pane and squinted, trying to make out details. But as soon as I did this, enormous billboards slapped into my sight, obscuring the view completely. Some were blank, great empty white spaces, others seemed to be advertising products I could not quite make out in the blur, as the beetle was picking up speed. COLLIBRATE SLOBODOCKS . . .(?) BLODNOK BIFFS . . .(?) AZUKA-BRIFALADS . . .(?) Portraits of cakestands, jukeboxes, palm trees and beaches, with strange, unhuman figures sprawled upon them in multi-coloured briefs. I sank back into my seat. My companions had mutated into animals in stretched underpants and string vests: a hippopotamus, a wolf, a pangolin and a giraffe. The chicken, glaring from its roof-rack cage, had changed into a small red demon, with blue leprous blotches and a forked tail. Its yellow eyes stared at me beneath the sharp small horns.

'Gravadlax,' it cawed. 'Gravadlax.'

I had none to offer. I ignored it. The others were still immersed in their newsprint. The headline had changed and now said: PLIP SIP PIP DRIP. The columns underneath were in Chinese.

I began to have an inkling of the situation. A variably funny stand-up comic dies and is condemned, perhaps, to a universe of indifferent jokes and bad clichés. Hell, or heaven? I could live with this, I felt, but for how long?

I decided to sit it out, sinking back in my jerking seat. This was survivable, so far. I liked train journeys. I enjoyed the thought of an unpredictable trip. I had been sundered from one life. Let me see what this other has in store. I indeed had nothing but time. I relaxed and felt pleasantly drowsy. Even a little peckish. If that demon turned back into a chicken, he'd better watch out.

I dozed off. When I awoke, the lederhosen passengers were back, along with the previous headline. Everything in the carriage was the same, except one item: the chicken had gone from the cage. I noticed a feather on the lap of the man immediately opposite me, but no other signs of either a struggle or luncheon. I looked again out the window, and started.

The landscape had changed dramatically. Grey skies had been replaced by blue. Green lush hills were rolling past, cultivated terraces with groves of cypresses and pines, vineyards, fields of giant sunflowers. I gasped, turning to my companions. But they remained as they had been. I glued myself to the pane. There were houses! Red roofed, peeking through the trees, nestling in the folds of the hills and perched on each summit. I knew this place very well. I had been here. This was not *déjà vu* but reality!

I did not get where I am today without recognizing Tuscany when I see it. I gave a cry of joy, and tore the newspapers out of the hands of the other passengers. But I was left gaping into the blank spaces of blind eyes, gazing at nothing, and mouths opening and closing like goldfish. I covered them up with the newspapers again. I chattered and danced before the window. In the distance, I could see actual towns peeking in and out through the hills.

'Alice!'

I would know that castle on the hill anywhere. Rising like a ship on the crest of a forest, the walls and basilica of Assisi. Umbria!

I was coming home. There was no doubt about it. I had passed through the valley of the shadow of death. And now my cup runneth over. The train was flashing through the stations: Ospedalicchio, Santa Maria di Angeli, Cannara, Spello, Foligno. We were coming up to the station where we would disembark for Bastardo, Mum's maternal home, twenty kilometres up the road. Past Castel San Giovanni, Bruna, Mercatello. I remembered the little station well: Trevi, beneath the vaulting height of the spectacular medieval hill town. I remember walking up to the top with Alice, cursing and puffing every foot of the steep way, toiling on a hot summer's day to some museum which was closed in lunch hours.

Ding ding ding! The train was definitely slowing down. I could taste, and smell, the luscious verdure. The bloom of spring. The pure clear air. I could see the low white buildings of the station house. The little obscure railway signs denoting mileage, maximum speed. The train was slowing. I tried to pull down the grimy pane, but it would not move. I tugged on the rusty handles but the frame was stuck. There was a group

210

of people on the platform, under the big station sign: TREVI. I saw my mother, shouting and waving. I recognized some of the people around her. There was Adolfo and his mother Sophia from Terni, my mother's ma and pa whom I remembered vaguely from when I was a *piccolo bambino*, old Nonna and the ducal grandfather, Antonio, whom I had seen in photographs, and about a dozen other people, some dressed in casual modern summer wear, others in Renaissance togs, feathered caps and wide blouses. There was a dour old man in cardinal's robes, waving a jewelled finger discreetly.

'Mum!'

I could not see Dad. Was he hiding in the crowd? I could not see him. Mother was jumping up and down, blowing me kisses. I hauled like crazy on the window handles, to no avail. The train just slowed to a crawl, by the sign. My mother leaping up and rapping her hand on the outer pane, then the train picked up speed, jerked forward and carried on, passing the platform.

'Mum! Dad! Adolfo! Have you seen Alice!' I screamed my face to a burst purple. But the stupid train just gathered more speed, creaked and rattled out of the station. I banged my fist on the window till I thought the bones would break, to no effect at all.

'Fuck! Shit! Piss! Bastards! Damn you to hell!' I yelled at the train. But it took no notice, jolting on out of Trevi towards Spoleto.

I remembered the name of the next station. Campello. Five kilometres down the road. If the train slowed there too and if I could leave the carriage I could jump out and even run the distance. But there was no way out of the thing. The window was jammed solid, and the door through which I had climbed in was gone, replaced by a seamless black metal panel.

Who was running this line? I would certainly complain, when we got to the end. But then I remembered there was to be no terminus. So, was this it? Trapped in an endless journey with mutating idiots, unreadable newspapers, and a chicken-demon on the loose? Watching paradise go by out of the window?

The sort of cliché which would certainly be par for the course. Hell as the absence of original material. Doomed in a loop. Would they appear again and again? And would they twist the knife deeper, showing me Alice through the unbreachable looking-glass?

Oh my beard and whiskers. Don't panic, Gerald. Try to wake up. No? All right, think. THINK! This was the motto of IBM, wasn't it? They who went bust in the mid-nineties. But all that is gone, gone, gone. One has to make do with what is; the bare bones. The location, the actors, the props.

The luggage! There might be a clue in there. I pulled the cases and bags from the rack. My fellow passengers, as I had thought, made no move to stop me. They were paper demons. But where was the real one?

If I could find him I might be able to make him talk. Information! By hook or by crook. I emptied the bags. Useless objects cascading. Piles and piles of dirty lederhosen. Filthy socks. Dead alarm clocks with no hands. Fur teacups. Plastic cheeseburgers with plastic bluebottle flies attached. I was rifling Claes Oldenburg's stash. Rotten apple cores, a beheaded teddy bear, a number of airline headphones and eyeshades, emptied tubes of toothpaste, a bicycle pump, a broken TV aerial, a rubber pigeon, an Amstrad PC manual, a banjo with no strings, a set of hair curlers, a box of broken dentures, a jugful of Egyptian piastres, several packets of mashed potato mix, a rusty kettle, three copies of the *American Dental Journal* for August 1966, and a hardback copy of *Clay Pipes and Drainage Systems*, 1936. And, finally, one knotted sheet enclosed unravelling layers of other knotted sheets, mostly stained and torn. I took the chicken cage apart, pulling off the bars. There was nothing but shit-caked straw inside.

'Where is he?' I cried out. 'Where's the chicken? Which one

of you ate him? Where's the bones?' But there was nothing but that one faded feather, which could have come from anywhere.

Campello passed, and Spoleto, the exterior darkening all the time. Either night was falling very fast or something much worse. The train was bucking from side to side. In the dying light, I opened the Amstrad manual. It was full of strange inscriptions and diagrams. One page seemed to be a dissection of the chicken. It indicated a solid egg inside. There were arrows and mathematical formulae. I tried the *American Dental Journal*. It, too, had cross-sections of the chicken, from every angle, with complex graphs. But it swiftly became too dark to read. The view outside had blinked out. My own radar-like tunnel vision had gone too, and my companions slowly faded into black. Soon I could see nothing, but only hear the snores, the sniffing, the rustling of the newspapers, the restless bodies and the rattle of the train.

Then something shifted, and I knew that there was someone else in the carriage. I could sense it, a new kind of smell, not unlike rotting fruit, but not the apple cores.

'Hoppy?' I called out hopefully. 'Mum? Dad? Alice?'

I was answered by a low cackle. I felt around me. There was no one there. Not on my seat, not on the seats opposite. My fellow passengers had disappeared.

But there was someone on the roof-rack. I squinted, and made out the pin points of two yellow, malevolent eyes.

'Yes, it's very confusing,' said the demon, its voice like a file scratching on glass. 'You have so few reference points. And most of them are banal and shoddy. Where is the grand spiritual drama of good or evil, damnation or redemption, ecstasy or eternal pain? When death is no longer a fear, what terrible new fears can be imagined? So many writers, poets, painters tried. Dante, Bosch, Brueghel, Larry Niven, Olsen and Johnson. The poverty of the imagination.

'I remember, when I was at demon school, they taught us about the banality of fear. Every living thing fears extinction.

Even plants shriek when they are plucked. But there is always that individual frisson. The torturer in Orwell's dystopia knew he had to fit the torment to the victim. Most tormentors however make do with the market-oriented, generalized modes. In medieval times, men and women went to the stake and burned for their faith. You have to respect that kind of challenge. And then, all the sermons on the pains of hell failed to deter people from apostasy. Who was right and who was wrong, in this sense? Some thought all would be revealed after death. Others purported not to care, accepting oblivion. Most did not dare to ponder, until the very last moment. Now that you're here you can see the Angel was right: it's not too bad. Faced with the challenges you find you can cope. Of course, you can be tormented further. Love, pleasure, satisfaction can be endlessly offered and withheld. Eventually, you would learn to live in the middle, between all extremes. A liberal outcome. That would probably suit you. You would feel responsible for your fate. Or, you could be granted everything you wish. The train will pull in to the next station, in a blaze of sunlight, and there she is: your beloved, who came back to you from the abyss you thought was bottomless. True love has conquered all. Your mother, your father, secure in the Umbrian sunshine, with a lifetime's antipasti and good wine. The sun gleaming on good clean cutlery. The conviviality of an endless afternoon. Woodcarving and ceramic pots. Museum tours, guided by Buonarotti himself, or Giotto. Heaven is more individual than hell.

'Do you wish for a saviour? Or to be able to save yourself? What, do you wonder, is the premiss here? What are the axioms of the afterlife, the underlying principles, the Ten Commandments? Is it God's kingdom, as imagined by man, or is it an alien place with random rules? Nietzsche or Aquinas? Don't make your choice yet. Death, like life, is a learning process. Your womb-death dream: You named it well for yourself. It was the fear of being born. Now that you are in the womb again, you face the primal helplessness. *The world is deep, deeper than day can comprehend*. There were always insights, sparks. Humankind was the trying animal. Now it's left for some other beast to try. Who knows, maybe the chicken? It certainly deserves a break. You always knew it was all temporary. The human span, the world, the galaxies. You watched them explode from afar. But what goes round comes round. Perhaps it came sooner rather than later. You were not prepared. They seldom are. You have a touching faith, sometimes in faith, sometimes in its abrogation. We love you, and we will do our best to guide you through this next stage. But don't expect an easy time of it. Spare the rod and spoil the child. Now 'op it, Davis. Get ready. I'm about to chop the umbilical. It's over the top and here we go, boy. Let's do it. Ready, steady, go.'

He pushed me in the back, with a force quite out of proportion to something so bunched up and small. I fell, shouting, out of the darkness. I heard the clatter of the train. The wheels clanging over the rails. The whoosh of the air. The heavy puffing of the beetle's flared nostrils. It passed, like a clap of thunder.

I picked myself up. The grass was blue. The green sky was flecked with orange clouds. I could smell the recent rain on the gorse. My suitcase had burst open in the fall. I gathered up my few possessions. The bicycle pump, the torso of the teddy bear, the packets of mashed potato mix, the rusty kettle, two shirts, two pairs of socks, spare underpants. And the torn, faded feather. I stuffed them in the case and snapped the locks shut.

Suddenly I remembered the miniature camera taped to my right foot. I rolled down my sock. It was still there, the minuscule object that might, against all odds, transmit across the worlds and dimensions.

I held the tiny thing up to my eye.

The lens was broken.

There was a faint path through the rough field. A low range

215

of violet hills to the horizon. I picked up the suitcase and set off down the path.

Pretty soon it began raining again.

The raindrops were turquoise and plum.

FOOTSUCKER
Geoff Nicholson

'Spare, sharp and weirdly funny. There are no great themes here, just good, warped entertainment'   Tobias Hill, *Observer*

'FOOTSUCKER is filthy dirty and great fun and is one of the most entertaining novels that I've read in a long while. Now then, who's up for a spot of shrimping?'   Tim Johnson, *Paint It Red*

'The undeniably erotic descriptions of how one so inclined can realise his utmost fantasies, and the carefully contrived plot, bring this dark, erotic and witty novel to its wonderfully shocking climax ... you will never look at a pair of shoes in the same way again'
John Oakey, *Time Out Net Books*

'A stiletto-sharp poke round sexuality's deviant margins'
Tina Jackson, *Big Issue*

'If a fetish is a form of worship, then Nicholson's excellent novel is its bible'   Ian Copestake, *Literary Review*

'Blackly comic and erotic'   The Loafer, *Guardian*

'Wicked, near-the-knuckle, original and disturbing'   *Cosmopolitan*

£5.99   0 575 40027 7

*IND*IGO

THE SIRENS OF TITAN
Kurt Vonnegut

Sixteen years before THE HITCH-HIKER'S GUIDE TO THE GALAXY, there was THE SIRENS OF TITAN . . . Who's in charge of creation? What are they doing about it?

When Winston Niles Rumfoord flies his spacecraft into a chrono-synclastic infundibulum he is converted into pure energy and only materializes when his waveforms intercept Earth or some other planet. So he only gets home to Newport, Rhode Island, once every fifty-nine days, and then only for an hour. But it's some consolation that he now knows everything that has ever been and everything that ever will be. He knows, for instance, that his wife will go to Mars to mate with Malachi Constant, the richest man in the world and the man destined to discover the secret of the universe. (Mrs Rumfoord is not as excited by this revelation as she might be.) He knows that on Titan there is a Trafalmadorian alien who has been waiting 20,000 years for a part for his grounded spaceship. There is, however, something that Winston Niles Rumfoord does not know . . .

'A work of great scope and staggering originality . . . It's an experience not to be missed'
Books and Bookmen

'A classic, ripe with wit and eloquence and a cascade of inventiveness. Alpha plus'
Brian Aldiss

£5.99   0 575 40023 4

*IN*D*I*GO

THE PRIMITIVE

Stephen Amidon

'Amidon drags his reader kicking and screaming along a rollercoaster of modern emotions. Read it'   Will Self

David Webster has the perfect life. He has the coolest wife in town. His house is yuppie heaven with all the original features. His job pays the bills with the minimum of effort. Never mind that his quiet Southern city has been ripped apart by dead-eyed Wall Street raiders; never mind that the career he loved has gone, to be replaced by a copy-writing gig for a redneck real-estate developer, the only guy left who's making any money. The façade is still intact.

Until he runs the young woman off the road in her car. Despite the blizzard of warning signals – no baggage, no credit cards, no identity – he feels responsible. She's hurt, and scared – so why not let her rest up for a few days in one of his boss's many empty properties? Besides, he's curious – what's she running away from?

'Will appeal to those who like their thrillers steeped in mystery and who like to take their humour black, with just a little sugar'

Louise Guinness, *Literary Review*

'A fluid, snaky thriller of great momentum . . . Amidon's storytelling skill is considerable'   Stephen Poole, *TLS*

£5.99   0 575 40017 x

*IN*D*I*GO

THE WHITE HOTEL
D. M. Thomas

'A novel of blazing imaginative and intellectual force'

Salman Rushdie

It is a dream of electrifying eroticism and inexplicable violence, recounted by a young woman to her analyst, Sigmund Freud. It is a horrifying yet restrained narrative of the holocaust. It is a searing vision of the wounds of our century, and an attempt to heal them. Interweaving poetry and case history, fantasy and historical truth-telling, THE WHITE HOTEL is a modern classic of enduring emotional power that attempts nothing less than to reconcile the notion of individual destiny with that of historical fate.

'A remarkable and original novel . . . there is no novel to my knowledge which resembles this in technique or ideas. It stands alone'

Graham Greene

'Astonishing . . . A forthright sensuality mixed with a fine historical feeling for the nightmare moments in modern history, a dreamlike fluidity and quickness'   John Updike

£5.99   0 575 40022 6

INDIGO

FLOWERS FOR ALGERNON

Daniel Keyes

'*progris riport 1 martch 3.* Dr Strauss says I should rite down what I think and remembir and evrey thing that happins to me from now on. I dont no why but he says its importint so they will see if they can use me . . . '

This is the story of Charlie, subnormal floor sweeper at Donner's Bakery and the gentle butt of everyone's jokes. This is the story of Charlie, triumphant subject of a daring experiment in the enhancement of human intelligence. And this is the story of Charlie, forced to watch as the light of his miraculous salvation begins to flicker.

Beautifully conceived and intensely moving, winner of the Nebula Award and the basis for the Oscar-winning film *Charly*, FLOWERS FOR ALGERNON is one of twentieth-century fiction's most remarkable narrative achievements.

'A narrative *tour de force*, very moving, beautiful and remorseless in its simple logic . . . one of the universally appealing stories of our time'
Science Fiction: the 100 Best Novels

£5.99   0 575 40020 x

*IN*DIGO

MUCHO MOJO
Joe R. Lansdale

'Red-hot gonzo stuff with all barrels firing point blank as the madness at the heart of America is probed, lanced, eviscerated, boiled and dragged screaming through the Texas badlands by an expert prose shitkicker'　　　　　　　Maxim Jakubowski, *Time Out*

'Lansdale knows the value of leavening the darkest material with humour, grim realism with moral passion . . . There's a touch of Harry Crews in him, a streak of Cormac McCarthy . . . a tale of evil doings that will make you both laugh and wince, and keep on turning the pages'　　　　　　　　　　　　　　　　　*Locus*

'Funny, compulsive thriller about a gay black and his white slacker friend who inherit a house with an unwanted feature – a child's body hidden under the floorboards. Their investigation leads to one of the more enjoyably raffish thrillers of the year'

Stephen Amidon, *Esquire*

'Lansdale has total trust in the straightforward power of a man's voice speaking when that man has a witch's brew of a tale to tell . . . a rare sort of gift it is, and Joe Lansdale has his in bushel baskets'

New York Times

£5.99　　　0 575 40001 3

INDIGO

Out of the blue . . .

*IN*DIGO

the best in modern writing

FICTION

Nick Hornby *High Fidelity*	£5.99	0 575 40018 8
Kurt Vonnegut *The Sirens of Titan*	£5.99	0 575 40023 4
Joan Aiken *Mansfield Revisited*	£5.99	0 575 40024 2
Daniel Keyes *Flowers for Algernon*	£5.99	0 575 40020 x
Joe R. Lansdale *Mucho Mojo*	£5.99	0 575 40001 3
Stephen Amidon *The Primitive*	£5.99	0 575 40017 x
Julian Rathbone *Intimacy*	£5.99	0 575 40019 6
Janet Burroway *Cutting Stone*	£6.99	0 575 40021 8

NON-FICTION

Gary Paulsen *Winterdance*	£5.99	0 575 40008 0
Robert K. Massie *Nicholas and Alexandra*	£7.99	0 575 40006 4
Hank Wangford *Lost Cowboys*	£6.99	0 575 40003 x
Biruté M. F. Galdikas *Reflections of Eden*	£7.99	0 575 40002 1
Stuart Nicholson *Billie Holiday*	£7.99	0 575 40016 1
Giles Whittell *Extreme Continental*	£6.99	0 575 40007 2

*IN*DIGO books are available from all good bookshops or from:

Cassell C.S.
Book Service By Post
PO Box 29, Douglas I-O-M
IM99 1BQ
telephone: 01624 675137, fax: 01624 670923